TC

Edward Eaton (signature)

Rosi's Time

Book II of Rosi's Doors

Edward Eaton

Young Adult Fantasy

Published by
Dragonfly Publishing, Inc.

ROSI'S TIME
Young Adult Fantasy

Hardback Edition
EAN 978-1-936381-26-5
ISBN 1-936381-26-5

Paperback Edition
EAN 978-1-936381-27-2
ISBN 1-936381-27-3

eBook Edition
EAN 978-1-936381-28-9
ISBN 1-936381-28-1

Story Text ©2012 Edward Eaton
Artwork ©2012 Dragonfly Publishing, Inc.
Dragonfly Logo ©2001 Terri L. Branson

Published in the United States of America by
Dragonfly Publishing, Inc.
Website: www.dragonflypubs.com

TABLE OF CONTENTS

Dedication:

The author would like to dedicate this book to his wife, Silviya, and his little man, Christopher.

Sine quibus non.

In addition to the people at Dragonfly Publishing, he would like to thank Brian Triber, for his assistance, encouragement, and enthusiasm.

PART I

New Richmond

CHAPTER 1

WITH a sigh, Rosi looked at her watch. She hoped no one, or no thing, would see the light green glow.

One o'clock. Rosi was not happy. Who would leave a fifteen-year-old girl alone in the middle of the woods in the middle of the night?

Even the little bit of light from her watch practically blinded her. Rosi slid the eye patch on her left eye over to her right and saw the woods leap back into vision. She was not sure if she looked silly or dashing wearing an eye patch, but it was great for her night vision. Uncle Richard had thought it a childish affectation, but one of her favorite shows had suggested that it might be effective, so she had given it a try. Chalk up another one for the educational potential of television.

Her knees were stiff and it was getting positively chilly. She had spent so much time in this cramped hunting blind in the old gnarly tree, that Rosi was not sure if she would ever be able to straighten up. She tried to straighten her legs, but simply was not flexible enough.

For the umpteenth time, she checked her thermos. For the umpteenth time, she discovered that it was still empty of hot chocolate. For the umpteenth time, Rosi told herself that she should not have emptied in the first half hour she was here.

Rosi shook the thermos just to be sure, as she had done each preceding time. She even held it upside down on the off chance a drop might appear.

She must be going crazy. Benjamin Franklin once said insanity is doing something over and over again expecting a different outcome. Of course, some people said it was Einstein, but Rosi had heard it straight from the horse's mouth. Of course, she could not tell anyone that or they would think she was crazy and lock her up.

Irrationally, Rosi dragged her finger along the sandwich bags for crumbs from her ham sandwich, her warm pretzel, her chips, and her lettuce. Nothing. She even licked the plastic pudding container, to no avail. Maybe she should not have eaten her snack with her hot chocolate.

Perhaps Uncle Richard should not have left her alone this time. He had *lamely* explained that the blind was not big enough for the two of them. Rosi was not happy about the lack of help, but, as Uncle Richard pointed out, he had his own work to do.

I'll bet you do, old man, Rosi thought, scowling to herself. She had followed Uncle Richard one night and watched him hobnob with great lords and flirt with their wives. He was probably eating pastries in the pursuit of an Antique Chippendale Secretary, while she was stuck in a large tree at the edge of a steep run with no snack and only a thin jeans jacket to keep her from shivering.

"What if I get eaten?" Rosi had protested when she saw the drawing of what she was supposed to catch. Uncle Richard had simply replied that Guardians were not supposed to interfere with each other.

Rosi felt that she had interfered quite a bit these last few weeks, even if Uncle Richard called it *training*. She *had* saved his life just a month before when they had been ambushed during a minor war. A war, Rosi had to admit, she had started. She did not think it fair that she had to take all of the blame. That woman should have been able to keep hold of her own jewelry. How was Rosi supposed to know that the woman was Mumtaz Mahal and that her jewelry was the Koh-i-Noor?

Uncle Richard kept telling her that she should know. Rosi was supposed to be reading fat history books every day, but, with work and friends, she did not do as much as she should. *As much as she should*, Rosi realized, meant *any at all*. Besides, Andy could tell her most of what she was supposed to read.

Before Rosi had left The Castle this evening, Uncle Richard had made her go over their plan several times in great detail. She knew it by heart. Her uncle had assured her that she would be fine when he walked her to the door and handed her the keys to the old motorcycle. It was the same motorcycle she had wrecked a few months earlier, but it now looked brand new. It might well be, she reminded herself.

Fine? What does Uncle Richard know? Rosi had almost gotten lost on the way. She had driven to the old riverbed and reconnoitered the area. It had been quiet, though it would not be later. Everything had been in place. Once she had hidden the motorcycle, left the old riverbed, and headed into the woods, she had gotten turned around.

She had walked through the plan forwards and backwards for a week, but on game night, as it were, she could not get her bearings straight. Eventually, she had found the right tree by walking into it. Or falling into it, rather. Quite literally, she tripped over a root and fell headlong into the tree.

When Rosi reached the blind, she discovered that she had forgotten to pack her cell phone. She knew she would be busy, but she would have some time before the sun went down to finish her game. She had been at this game for weeks and was about to be promoted King of Pirates. Rosi was sure Uncle Richard had something to do with the phone not being in her bag.

Then the food that she had packed for snacks had disappeared so quickly.

So there was not much to do but sit here and shiver and hope this thing showed up so Rosi could deal with it. Or maybe it would not show up, and she would not have to deal with it. Let Louis XV catch it himself.

Waiting became really tedious after the sun went down about eight o'clock. Things got worse after about ten-thirty, when Rosi could hear music playing somewhere in the distance. She could not tell what music it was, but she could tell that it was music. The party had started.

Rosi would have to trust Uncle Richard that their family had been somehow entrusted with protecting time from interfering with other times. Rather than protecting anyone or anything from some sort of time space continuum hiccup or violation or corruption or whatever it was so far, a concept which Uncle Richard had said was grossly exaggerated in movies and video games, they seemed to spend most of their time schmoozing with the landed aristocracy and absconding with their furniture and nick knacks.

Uncle Richard was, appropriately, an antiques dealer. One afternoon, Rosi was sure she had caught Uncle Richard on a major screw up. Antiques were supposed to be old. Uncle Richard's customers must take issue with paying top prices for brand new merchandise. Uncle Richard had, of course, an answer to that. "I do not bring it straight here," he had answered. "I have it taken to a storage facility, a warehouse if you please, where it will wait until the customer is ready to buy."

This did not sound very honest to Rosi.

Everything seemed fairly haphazard. This evening for example, why did she have to wait from early evening until whenever it was that the thing decided to show? She looked at the picture under the light of her watch.

Ankalagon saurognathus.

Ugly looking beasty. This plan had better work. This thing, with its ridged back and fangs did not look like it would take more than about three seconds to devour Rosi.

Rosi figured that if they were supposed to be in control of Time, then they should at least be able to figure out what time the Ankalagon showed up.

Uncle Richard had explained, for the umpteenth time, that Time was much more relative than that. Rosi had countered by explaining that nine-thirty was nine-thirty, in New Richmond and every place else. Uncle Richard had riposted by pointing out that when it was nine-thirty in New Richmond it was eight-thirty in Chicago. Time as a unit of measurement was an invention of man. When man created his sciences, he defined time so the math worked. Time as most people know it was simply a rhythm. To the ancients, Time was the rhythm of falling grains of sand. To modern man, it was the rhythm of oscillating cesium atoms. The difference was, Uncle Richard had explained, specious and immaterial.

Time as numbers on a clock was arbitrary. There was no real reason why the day was divided into twenty-four hours or twelve hours. Metric time would be more efficient, except that it would most likely never catch on.

Time zones were even worse. Lines were arbitrarily drawn on a globe. Politics got involved. It made no sense that Detroit, for example, was in the same time zone as New York when it was so much closer to Chicago.

Clocks created a facade of temporal uniformity. One could look at a watch and see nine-thirty. It was only nine-thirty if everyone else's watches said nine-thirty too. Furthermore, nine-thirty in Boston was earlier than nine-thirty in New York in relationship to the Sun. One might be able to come up with an argument that nine-thirty in the morning was somehow fundamentally different from two-thirty in the afternoon. It was hard to do the same when it was nine-twenty versus nine-forty.

Atomic clocks created more uniformity. So did radio and television. The numbers, though, were still made up. The idea that Time was tied to electrons, grains of sand, or the evening news was given value because it made people feel more comfortable. The relative precisions of a grandfather clock, a Timex, a Rolex, or the Master Clock at the U. S. Naval Observatory all failed to take one truth into account: sometimes time flew and sometimes it stood stock still.

The tears in the fabric of time that Guardians had to deal with were not tied to specific minutes and seconds, as those made no real sense cosmologically, but rather to some extended event that then affected some other extended event that historians said came later.

Uncle Richard admitted freely that he was making something of a guess with regards to the events of this particular evening. An Ankalagon saurognathus was in Gevaudan, in southern central France, for over a year, starting in June 1764, hunting and terrorizing the local population. In September 1765, it stopped for several months. Then it started it terrorizing again. Contemporaries simply thought there were two or more animals involved. One dangerous predator either had been killed or had somehow gone away. Another one had taken its place. Uncle Richard argued that there was a better explanation. He had discovered a tear that corresponded to Gevaudan in the autumn of 1765. The most likely time for the animal to cross over would be this evening.

Why did it have to be this evening? Rosi had been planning on going to a party at the old riverbed. Dan was supposed to be there, and she had not seen him for weeks. But she did not want her uncle to think she wanted to avoid her duties to go to a party, especially since she did not particularly like the girl who was throwing the party.

Lois Vernon, the birthday girl, was the daughter of the owner of one of New Richmond's most popular boutiques. All the girls made friends with her because she could get them first crack at the trendy shoes and bags. The guys made friends with her on the off chance they might meet her stepmother, a rather notorious former Russian supermodel. Rosi had no objection to the shoes or the bags. She did object to the girl being perhaps the loudest, most obnoxious, most spoiled person she had ever met.

Lois Vernon did not like Townies very much, but she had to invite Andy to the party, because Angie never went anywhere if Andy was not invited. Angie was always invited because it never hurt to butter up the daughter of the sheriff.

Rosi was invited because she was a Carol. Carols were invited everywhere, every time. They were also expected not to show up and not to cause trouble if they did. Over the last several months Rosi had not only shown up in New Richmond, but had made several social faux pas. Getting arrested for drunk driving. Crashing a vehicle in the middle of Dock Street. Getting washed overboard from a boat she had stolen. Catching the eye of the captain of the high school tennis team. And being a Carol. These all demonstrated to anyone paying attention, that Rosi was not only likely to cause trouble but also likely to garner more attention than a lot of girls who had been around longer.

A girl like Lois Vernon, whose personality could be described in two simple words: *rich* and *loud*, would certainly have a problem with an upstart like Rosi whom everyone in town, even relative newcomers, considered a foreigner.

The only reason Rosi would have gone to Lois' party would

have been to see Dan. Uncle Richard was certainly aware of that. Rosi was aware that the Ankalagon saurognathus probably crossed over, or was going to cross over, because it heard and smelled the party. If Rosi went to the party, she would still probably have to confront the Beast of Gevaudan, as Uncle Richard and everyone on the Internet called it or Jevy, as Rosi called it. She simply had to name it. She certainly could not spend the week talking, or worse, thinking about capturing an *Ankalagon saurognathus*. *Beast* was almost as bad.

"It is one of history's greatest predators," Uncle Richard had scoffed. "It is not a Smurf."

Whatever name it was called, it was certainly strong enough to create a great deal of damage, smart enough to find the way to the old riverbed, and bold enough to try. Rosi would wait for it. She would track it. She would arrange for it not to hurt her friends. She would follow the plan, capture the animal, and return it to France in time for it to continue its rampage there.

Uncle Richard did tell her that Dan's car had broken down earlier that day in Boston and that he would not be able to come to New Richmond this particular weekend. If seeing Mr. Meadows were more important, Uncle Richard would take her to the train station.

"What would happen then?" Rosi never liked the way Uncle Richard gave her alternatives.

"You would come back when you liked, live here, finish high school, and, I presume, start college. When you reached the age of eighteen, you would become the beneficiary of your father's trust fund, and you would move out. I would deal with the situation tonight. Tomorrow, I would start looking for your replacement," Uncle Richard had explained.

"So, basically, you are saying that if I want to keep my position, I have to do everything you say."

Uncle Richard had laughed. "Not at all, young lady. You have a great deal of say. I also understand how important your social life is. However, I will not accept as an excuse a birthday party for a young woman you have gone to great lengths to inform me that you do not like."

Rosi had given in. "If I get eaten, you'll feel really bad."

"I promise to do so." Uncle Richard had finished his coffee and left, on his way no doubt, to arrange for a car to break down in Boston.

Silver lining, Rosi thought as she stared into the gloom of the forest. No Dan meant no Kirk. Dan was supposed to bring his creepy brother with him to the party. After everyone had decided that Kirk had tried to save some drowning sailors a few weeks ago on the Fourth of July, they had made him something of a town hero. Within days, he and Lois were an item. Angie had told her that Lois had already gone to Nantucket twice to visit the bullying creep.

Rosi scowled. No one had invited her!

So now she sat in a hunter's blind in the woods, waiting for some beast that may or may not come by.

* * *

ROSI'S head snapped back and her eyes snapped open. She felt a momentary thrill of fear race through her body. She took a deep breath and shook her head. She must have dozed off for a seconds. It was still just after one o'clock.

The place was unusually quiet. She could hear the faint noise from the party, but she could not hear anything else. There were none of the strange night noises she was beginning to associate with living out in the country.

She slipped her night vision monoscope over her uncovered eye and switched it on. Everything was suddenly bright. It was surprising enough that the first thing she did was to take it off and blink a few times. She held in a chuckle. Each time she had tried this on over the last few days she'd had the same reaction.

She put the monoscope on again. Changing the setting to infrared, she looked at the ground. Almost immediately she saw that something large had approached the tree, circled it, and then moved off in the direction of the riverbed. There was no way for Rosi to tell what had made the tracks. As far as she could tell, it was larger than a bunny rabbit and smaller than a T-Rex. It could have been a moose or a bear.

Would a moose or a bear have caused the other forest critters to go so completely to ground? Would a wolf? Were there wolves around here?

Where Rosi had grown up, animals were what you walked on leashes, saw in zoos, or went on dates with. They only ate you in the movies.

Rosi turned the monoscope off and flipped it up on her forehead. She then moved the eye patch from one eye to the other. Now she had her own night vision back. She had no depth perception, she discovered after it took her three tries to grab the rope. She was reminded of this a few seconds later when she misjudged the distance to the ground and landed with a resounding thump in an embarrassing pile. As far as Rosi was concerned, it did not matter that no one was around to see it.

Rosi patted her pockets and checked her belt. Everything that she was supposed to have was there. She even had her insurance, a five round .50-caliber revolver hanging under her left shoulder. Uncle Richard had made a point of letting her know that only the first four rounds were for the Ankalagon. Rosi shivered at the thought.

Tightening the straps of her now fairly light, snack free backpack, she moved in the direction of the riverbed as quietly as she could.

The breeze was coming towards her. This was a good thing. She had seen enough movies to know that. The wind direction would be bad for the partiers, whose scents were blowing straight for the Ankalagon.

Jevy was a smart hunter. It was not going straight for the kill, but was investigating along the way. Rosi could see this by its tracks.

After half a mile, Rosi could see it through the infrared. It was a blob of red that darted from place to place. After another quarter of a mile, she could see it through the night monocular. It was larger than the drawing suggested. Even at a few hundred yards, it looked monstrous.

She saw it stop and raise its nose. The Ankalagon must have caught the diversionary scent.

The night before, Uncle Richard and Rosi had placed scents at various places in an arc around where the party was going to be. The spots were gradually further and further from the focal point of Lois Vernon's party.

If the scents were placed too far away from the party beach, the Ankalagon might ignore them. If they were too close, then the young people might notice them and change the location of the party. It was imperative that the party location not change. The beach that the party would be on focused the group. If there were enough kids there, the Ankalagon might choose not to attack. Or it might delay just long enough for Rosi to shoot it. If the partiers were in another position, they might panic and run. If the group spread out too far, many of them would be easy prey.

"Or Jevy might not pick up the scent and would stay in France," Rosi had suggested.

Uncle Richard had sighed. "You do realize that a cute name will not make the Ankalagon any less dangerous."

"No," Rosi had said. "I know nothing of the sort. Perhaps it is dangerous because it was given such a scary name. Do you really think King Kong would have been so destructive had his name been Fluffy?"

"King Kong was a fictional character."

"Exactly!" Rosi had made her point.

The diversions were working. Jevy was being led, gradually, further from the partying kids, who laughed and danced and whooped in the firelight.

Setting the monocular to 'telescope', she spied on the kids for a moment. They seemed to be having fun. Rosi did not really know any of them very well. Angie and Andy were not in sight, though they were probably there, as there was a small group of Townies present. Rosi had been to enough parties to know that couples tended to drift away from the fire. She did not particularly like the parties she had been to because she always felt like the outsider she was.

Rosi grinned bitterly. These kids dancing around the fire or making out in the rocks had no idea how close they were to being tonight's dinner and tomorrow's fertilizer.

She looked again for Jevy. By now Rosi could see her without any help. If those kids bothered to look beyond the keg, they would probably see Jevy trotting along a low rise just a stone's throw away.

As long as Jevy stayed on her current scent, Rosi would have the time to make it ahead of her and set off the fireworks.

Perhaps she had been distracted earlier in the evening, or perhaps the drizzle Rosi had felt in the blind had been rain here, but the ground was a lot wetter than she remembered. She slipped several times. Once, she barely avoided taking a header into a deep looking ravine that had a narrow but rapid stream in it. She had clearly gotten a bit off the path she had marked out last weekend. She did not realize how far off the path she had gotten until she saw the shadow of the large beast bound across the riverbed about twenty feet in front of her.

"Jesus!" she said, probably too loudly.

Rosi spun to move away too quickly and half slipped, half fell down a small slope and landed quite loudly in a thick layer of mud. By the time she had turned over onto her back and started to sit up, Jevy was there, standing just feet in front of her.

CHAPTER 2

PERHAPS Uncle Richard had been right. *Jevy* was not really a good name for the monster that towered over Rosi. *Cerberus* sounded about right. Not *Jevy* and certainly not *Fluffy*. Rosi made a silent oath to apologize to Uncle Richard when she got home later. If she got home later.

God, the thing was huge! It looked to be about eight feet tall and twice as long.

The moon was not bright enough for Rosi to tell what color the thing was, but she could see its eyes. There was no white in them, just deep soulless black holes. Under them, a long nose that shot little jets of steam into the brisk air. Further down were the bright white fangs that dripped saliva. One of them was chipped and the other one had a large black cavity on it, Rosi noticed.

Rosi was looking at something evil, and did not like it.

It sniffed her.

She wanted to cry. She wanted to scream. She wanted to run. The impulse to flee was strong, but Rosi knew that she would not make it more than a few feet before the monster caught her. She stayed as still as she could. She figured that the mud she had fallen in was masking her scent and keeping the monster from ripping her apart.

Great, Rosi thought. *I'm probably too bony for a paleocenic predator, anyway. See, Uncle Richard. I did do my homework. Fat lot of good that will do me now.*

It growled and looked away.

Rosi heard what it had heard. Some of the kids were nearby giggling softly.

Go away! Rosi willed. *Run while you can!*

The monster growled again, louder. Apparently, it had not decided what Rosi was, but wanted to make sure that nothing else came and interrupted its deliberations. Just to make sure it was not disturbed it barked.

Cerberus was pressing up against Rosi but had turned its face away to threaten possible intruders. This gave Rosi a chance to take a gulp of air. She decided that she might be able to reach the remote in her jacket pocket. It was not much of a chance, but it was the only one she had at the moment. She began to inch her left hand up. At the same time, she slowly slid her right hand towards the holster on her hip.

Instead of hearing the sounds of partiers fleeing in a panic, she heard the kids calling out to each other. They had heard something and were either stupid, or drunk, enough to want to investigate.

Idiots! Run!

Cerberus heard the kids as well. It sniffed at the air. Rosi could hear it licking its maw with a sickening slopping sound. The noises from the kids were coming from several directions. The beast circled around Rosi, growling in every direction. It nudged her over into the mud.

Rosi used the fall to move her hand a little more. Her frozen and wet fingers fumbled with the button on the front pocket of her jacket. It sounded like everyone at the party was gathering nearby. Rosi could hear Lois complaining that everyone was ignoring *her* party to look for some dumb animal.

Cerberus barked several more times, which only encouraged the drunken teenagers, who were noisily cheering each other on as they searched. It began kicking clods of mud onto Rosi.

Oh, God, she thought. *It's burying me.*

Finally, Rosi was able to undo the pocket button and fish the remote out. She switched the remote on and swore to herself as it powered up with a tinny whistle. Why did everything electronic have to make so much damn noise? It was only a very faint electronic whine, but to prehistoric ears, it must have been as noticeable as a scream.

Rosi turned her head at the same moment the Ankalagon did. They were looking into each other's eyes.

Rosi froze. With her thumb, she pressed the *GO* button.

Nothing happened.

The beast snarled.

"What's that over there?"

"What?"

"Over there by Bart's Hill."

"Some sort of dog."

Rosi did the only possible thing she could do under the circumstances. As the Ankalagon bared its teeth and moved closer to Rosi's face, she butted her forehead against its nose as hard as she could.

She doubted the monster was hurt, but it certainly was surprised, which gave her about two seconds of respite before the Beast roared, opened its jaws wide, and came at her again with its razor sharp teeth.

*   *   *

THE soft thumps got the Beast's attention. Rosi tried to follow its gaze and saw the small group of kids not too far off.

This better work.

"What's that?" Someone asked.

"Do you see the size of—"

Suddenly the sky erupted in light and color. The nearby kids shrieked in surprise, and started laughing. The Beast staggered back and looked up at the flashing fireworks.

The partiers *oohed* and *aahed*.

The Beast barked and growled at the explosions, but it continued to back away.

Rosi glanced back at the kids. They could probably have seen her if they bothered to look, but they were distracted by the fireworks.

Rosi grabbed a few rocks and clods of dirt from the ground and threw them as hard as she could at the Ankalagon. "Go on, get out of here," she hissed.

Behind her, there was applause as the area burst into a rainbow of light.

The beast continued to back away. The rocks Rosi threw had little effect, but they made her feel better.

The flashing of the light made it difficult for Rosi to see as she started moving off, so she picked a general direction and hoped she would not bump into Cerberus or wander into the fireworks. Finally, she was able to put some distance between herself and the fireworks. She looked around. To her despair, she saw that the beast had run up Bart's Hill. A quick look showed her that some of the fireworks had gone off in the wrong order. Instead of driving Cerberus to the south, they had driven it up the steep hill.

Rosi ran towards Bart's Hill but stopped when she reached the bottom of the steep slope.

The Ankalagon stood at the top of the high hill, really more of a spire, and howled. At that moment, as if on cue, the fireworks intensified. They lost the rather stunning pattern they'd had a few moments ago. The shots and explosions were chaotic now. It sounded almost as if there were guns being fired.

Rosi was terrified. Everyone else around the beach must have been as well. She could hear people screaming. It sounded like a lot of people. It sounded like too many people. She could see them in the gloom, shadows running back and forth. She could see them in the flashes of light that went by too quickly to allow her to recognize anyone she knew. Rosi knew she could not worry about them. She had to focus on the beast that was now high above her.

Climbing to the top of the hill was not an option. Even if she could get there while Cerberus was still there, Rosi was not sure what she could do about it.

"You!" someone said behind her.

Rosi spun and, in a flash of light, saw Kirk standing about twenty feet away. "Get out of here, Kirk!" she yelled.

"You," he sputtered. "You are responsible for this."

"I can fix this," she called out, no longer able to see him through the smoke. "Run."

He yelled something, but his voice was drowned out by an explosion.

She could not deal with Kirk right now. Uncle Richard would know what to do. A stray rocket shot past Rosi's face so fast that she could not see it. She could only feel the searing heat as it whipped by. Rosi stumbled and fell into the cold marshy water.

The noise was unreal. A lot of the screams no longer sounded human. Perhaps, Rosi thought, that was because she could barely hear anything. She shook her head to clear it and looked up. In just a few seconds, the situation went from bad to worse. There was someone on the hilltop with the beast. Someone who looked vaguely familiar.

The beast howled and leapt from the top of the hill. It flew through the air straight at Rosi. She could see its fangs grow bigger as it came closer. With a shriek, Rosi threw herself down to the wet ground and curled up in as small of a ball as she could. She waited for the beast to tear her to shreds. She could only pray it was fast and that she would feel nothing.

* * *

SHE then realized that she was spending too much time praying. The thing should have landed and chewed her up by now.

What had happened to all of the fireworks? Stage one, however mismanaged it had been, seemed to have run its course. The ground was covered by a layer of smoke, but the gentle breeze would soon blow that away. It was also unusually silent. There was no beast of any sort in sight. Rosi felt like laughing in relief. She felt like laughing hysterically, but knew she was not done for the night.

A few of the partiers called out to one another. Within seconds, they were giggling, laughing, already telling tall tales filled with exaggeration and outright lies.

Rosi glanced around. The beast must have moved on. She could only hope it went in the right direction. *Time for stage two*, she told herself. She toggled the switch on the remote. After another brief delay, she heard the satisfying pops and swooshes.

The sky erupted in light once again. Rosi looked up. High above, hovering in the sky, were the words "Happy Birthday, Lois! You Rock!" surrounded by flashing roses and smiley faces that shifted through the colors of the rainbow.

Rosi turned and ran. Even if the Ankalagon went in the right direction, Rosi would only have a small window of opportunity.

Uncle Richard must have programmed a third stage to an automatic delay, because several minutes later, Rosi heard another series of explosions. She was out of sight of the beach by now, but could see the sky light up. It was a good thing that she looked back. There, only a hundred feet or so back, was the beast. It was loping in Rosi's direction.

Rosi threw herself against the slope of the hill and pulled herself as close to some scrubby bushes as she could. The beast however did not even break its stride. It galloped by, its teeth bare, flecks of saliva flying in every direction. It was going exactly in the right direction, Rosi realized. It must have picked up the scent. With a sigh, Rosi wiped the spittle from her face and followed. It *was* her job.

Soon, she caught up to Cerberus. It had stopped. Rosi held her breath and listened. She could hear the beast gnawing and slobbering over the lamb she had tied up earlier that evening. She hoped the kill had been quick.

She held back a sob. She knew food came from animals, but simply preferred not to think about it. To Rosi, meat was something you found in the freezer, or better yet, already cooked on the plate. Food was certainly not something you scratched behind the ears.

For some reason, Uncle Richard had insisted that the bait be alive. Rosi had not really understood, but figured that he was not suggesting it to be mean.

Rosi had, however, fed the little lamb several strong sedatives when she left it earlier.

Recognizing a landmark, Rosi felt around for a few moments and found the rope she had left there. It was tied to a tree about fifty feet above at the top of the old riverbank. As quietly as she could, Rosi pulled herself to the top and rolled up the rope behind her, storing it and her pack in a saddlebag on the motorcycle. From the other saddlebag, she pulled out the large, sealed baggy. It was awkward to carry, filled as it was with a liquid Rosi did not want to think about. She hoped this thing was alpha enough to not want any competition.

Rosi went over to the lip of the bank, grabbed onto a tree branch, and leaned over. She could make out the form of the thing munching away below.

"Hey," she called. The Beast went still. "Remember me?"

She dropped the bag and heard it go splat somewhere below. She had aimed right at The Beast and hoped that it had hit. After only a few moments, she heard it roar and saw the dark shape begin scrambling up the steep bank.

Rosi did not wait. She ran for the bike, started it, and took off. The Ankalagon would certainly not have any difficulty following the bike's lights. Rosi had ridden around this part of the woods quite a few times over the last week, but was not about to try going without the lights on. She was not that stupid.

Then it struck her that she was tangling with a 900 pound dog. She clearly was that stupid.

Rosi was also learning that the thing ran a lot faster than she and Uncle Richard had surmised. She had spent some time on the Internet and figured that the beast's speed would top out with bursts of about thirty miles an hour. Rosi did not bother looking at the speedometer. She could tell that she was going over thirty. She could also tell from the rearview mirror that Cerberus was not falling behind.

Rosi was sure that on a straightaway, she could leave The Beast in the dust. Unfortunately, the old road she was following had few straight-aways. It was windy, narrow, and filled with ruts and more of a path than a road.

It was also beginning to rain.

Whatever else this beast might be, it was not stupid. It was clever enough to be a little wary of its new prey. It probably would not take it too long to figure out that she was not much of a danger.

At one point Rosi noticed the Beast to her left. It was trying to run her off the path. She could practically feel its breath on her arm when she entered a straightaway. She was able to put on some speed and pull ahead of it.

The burst of speed took her past where she was supposed to turn off the old river road and lead the Ankalagon towards The

Castle, Uncle Richard, and the trap. Rosi saw the old scarf she
had tied to the tree as a marker as she sped by.

"Great," Rosi muttered to herself. She really did not know a
lot about the geography of the area and was not sure how to get
back on track.

The thing loping after her showed little sign of tiring.

Fortunately, she had plenty of gas. Unfortunately, Rosi could
see lights ahead.

She was about to enter New Richmond, leading a ravenous
and enraged hellhound.

* * *

ROSI did not bother slowing down when she saw the white
wooden fence appear ahead of her.

She did not bother slowing down when she ran over the
kiddy toys, at least one bicycle, and an inflatable wading pool.

She did not slow down, though she did lower her head, when
she ran through the sheets that were hang drying next to the
house. At least one of the sheets came along with her. Hastily,
Rosi pulled it down far enough so that she could see.

Rosi did slow down a bit when she hit the street, but only
because she had to turn to avoid ramming into the minivan on
the other side.

Well, she slowed down more than a bit. Rosi almost did a
complete three-sixty on the wet pavement.

Out of the corner of her eye, she saw the Ankalagon leaping
at her. Rosi twisted her hand and felt the tires catch the wet
asphalt just in time. She heard the Beast's teeth clamp together
and felt a strong tug on the sheet.

Rosi heard The Beast crash into the minivan, shattering its
windows. *Probably just made the thing angry*, she thought, building up
as much speed as she could before the next turn.

It took her a while of winding through the tranquil
neighborhood, followed by an increasingly angry monster that
kept crashing into and running on top of cars, before Rosi was
able to figure out where she was. Or rather, she was able to figure
out that she was near the high school. At least there would not be

anyone there.

She gathered up speed once she was on the parking lot. She really put some distance between her and her pursuer on the football field. Beyond the far goal post there was a pleasant wooded park that sloped down from the field. Rosi had been there several times and knew it fairly well.

She balled up the sheet and, at about the twenty yard line, threw it as high in the air as she could. That might give her an extra second.

Rosi caught air when she left the football field and started down to the park. After a moment, when she hoped she would be out of sight for a second, she rolled off the bike to one side and scrambled behind some shrubs. The bike bounced on for some distance.

Just as Rosi turned, there was a long flash of lightning that illuminated the whole area. She could see the Ankalagon bounding over the lip of the slope as it chased the still moving bike. It had somehow caught the sheet, which now trailed behind it like a white shadow.

Then the light went out and the thunder clapped. The beast landed on the wrecked bike, tearing at it with its teeth.

Rosi tore off her jacket and rolled it up. She threw it at the beast. It then pounced on the jacket, shaking it and tossing it into the air.

Rosi pulled the .50 caliber from its holster and flicked off the safety.

My God, this is heavy, Rosi thought. Perhaps she should have tried this at home first. This was not a pistol. It was a cannon!

The Ankalagon was about thirty feet away. Rosi took careful aim at its head and pulled the trigger. The roar of the shot deafened her. The flash blinded her. The kick almost knocked her down.

She heard a yell that sounded almost human. *I hope there is no one here*, she thought. She shook her head and focused in front of her. The Beast was now about twenty feet away and closing.

She raised the gun again and pulled the trigger again. Something hit her from the side and knocked her over.

Rosi hit the ground heavily, rolled onto one knee, and faced the Ankalagon, which was now only a few feet away. It snarled and bared its teeth.

Rosi put a bullet in its head.

* * *

ROSI knew this one hit.

Something hit her again, or rather, something ran into her, knocking her over. Rosi landed badly, jarring her right arm.

Rosi was a bit more careful getting up this time, because she saw the beast on the ground. Apparently she had been knocked down by the man who was kneeling by the animal, crying, his head buried in its coat.

"Excuse me, sir," Rosi said. "Excuse me!" She tapped his shoulder.

He spun and pointed a pistol at her. The man stood up, keeping a not so steady bead on Rosi. He rattled off a string of words Rosi did not understand. She barely heard them over the ringing in her ears.

Wiping water from her eyes with the back of her wrist, she shook her head. "I can't hear you!" she said. Rosi realized that she could not hear herself either.

His eyes looked around frantically. He was waving the pistol and screaming. Rosi had trouble seeing it clearly, but it looked to be one of those old flintlock things. Probably too wet to fire.

"I can't hear you," Rosi yelled. This was louder, but the words echoed in her ears.

He did not seem to understand. After a few moments, Rosi recognized a few words. At least she heard enough to figure out what language he was speaking.

Rosi pointed at her ear and shook her head. *"Je ne peux pas ecouter."* That was about the extent of the French she remembered from one semester about two years ago. Given the way the man was looking at her, it was probably more than she remembered.

Rosi tapped her ear. *"Ne marche pas."* They aren't working. *"Excusez-moi. Je ne parle pas français."*

The man smirked and said something Rosi interpreted to

mean: "No, you obviously don't."

"*Parlez vous anglais*," Rosi tried.

The man stopped shaking. He stood up straighter and his aim became steadier. "*Vous êtes anglaise?*" he said loudly.

Rosi could hear that. Her hearing was getting better. She sighed. The truth would probably be confusing. "*Oui*," she said.

He sneered. He looked her up and down and leered. He spoke rapidly for a few moments.

Rosi knew quite a few of those words. She had not learned them in class, though, but from Philippe, a foreign exchange student from Paris who had spent far too much time last fall teaching the girls French and not enough time learning English and was sent home just before Thanksgiving.

The man placed the end of the barrel against her cheek.

With an effort, for her arm was throbbing, Rosi raised her weapon and pointed it at his forehead. "Mine's bigger."

The man understood that much. He laughed nervously and raised the barrel, offering Rosi the butt of the pistol.

Taking it in her left hand, she pointed it into the air and, to make a point, pulled the trigger.

Apparently, the man had thought the powder too wet as well, for he threw himself to the ground as quickly as Rosi did when the gun fired with a loud pop.

Rosi was sure she would never hear out of that ear again.

Rosi tossed the spent pistol back to the Frenchman. "Get up," she said, motioning him up. "Up, up, up."

He stood up.

Rosi thought for a moment. "*Qu'est-ce que tu t'appeles?*" What is your name?

The man sniffed and crossed his arms.

"Jesus," Rosi sighed. "*Que'est-ce que vous vous appelez?*"

"Jean Chastel," the man responded.

Rosi shoved the revolver back into its holster and looked around the small park. Sitting down on a rock, she decided that if this rather round and remarkably ugly Frenchman had not been around, the Beast would probably be having Rosi for a midnight snack. She motioned for him to sit. "*Merci, beaucoup*," she said.

Jean scowled and sat. "*Salope*," he muttered.

Rosi pulled the revolver back out and pointed it at his nose. "I know what that means. *Je comprends.*"

Jean said something that sounded vaguely apologetic and completely terrified.

"Just cough up some of the wine," she said, hoping to shut him up. She gestured with the barrel at a half full flagon hanging on his belt. "*Du vin!*"

Jean slipped the sack off and lifted it to his mouth.

"*Non!*" Rosi snapped. "Me first. You've had enough. Me. *Moi.*"

Finally, Jean scowled even more deeply and tossed the flagon at Rosi and lunged at her.

Rosi was waiting for such a move. What was the point in spending so much time watching movies if she did not learn something from them? With her left hand, she batted the wine sack to one side. With her right, she whipped the heavy barrel of the revolver across the man's face as he lunged at her.

He went down calling out some of French's more colorful swears.

She did not understand much of what he said, but Rosi did get: "Ow, my teeth" and "*Mon Dieu.*" She had a fairly good idea of what he planned to do with her face when he had the chance and a shovel. It was not pleasant.

Keeping the gun pointed at the grumbling man, Rosi pulled the stopper out with her teeth and took a swig. The wine was heavy and somewhat sour, but it warmed her up. "You're supposed to have killed this thing?" Rosi grumbled at him. She took out a small flashlight and, after slapping it a few times, was able to turn it on.

Jean did not look any better in the light. He did cross himself when he saw her moving the flashlight around.

"Probably think I'm a witch, don't you?" Rosi said. "Well, you ain't seen nothing yet."

She checked out the beast. One of her shots had hit it in the rear leg. Probably her first shot. It looked like one shot creased its ear. The third shot removed about half of its head.

She found the remains of her jacket a dozen or so feet away. The jacket was ruined, but there was still a pair of pliers in the pocket. Holding her breath, Rosi took the pliers and stuck them into the bullet hole in the leg. She dug around for what seemed like a long time before finally finding the bullet. She pulled it out and shoved it into her pants pocket with the pliers.

Jean looked at her as if she was crazy.

Rosi took another swig of the wine, which washed some of the bile back down her throat.

Jean held out his hand.

"Okay, Frenchie." Rosi scowled at him. She tossed him the flagon. "Just save some for me. We have a long walk."

Uncle Richard was not going to be happy when she showed up not with the animal, but with the man who was supposed to shoot it in three months.

"Come on," Rosi hissed at Jean. "Come on! *Allons-y!*"

* * *

THE most direct route was directly through town. People might overlook that Rosi was walking alone through the town at two thirty in the morning in the middle of the rain. They might even overlook that she was somewhat beat up. They probably would not overlook that she was armed. They certainly would not overlook that she was kidnapping a 17th century French farmer with whom she was sharing an increasingly emptier wine skin. She did let him drink most of it. It was not that chilly. Besides, Uncle Richard might look the other way if Rosi had a drink or two at a party with her friends, but he certainly did not want her drinking regularly or with strangers. His biggest issue would probably be with the low quality of the man's wine.

So, accompanied by a lot of *gauches* and *doites*, Rosi guided Jean the long way around town. It was almost three thirty when Rosi and Jean reached the rendezvous point. The wine flagon was empty, and Rosi was getting chilly again.

Rosi jumped and Jean threw himself to the ground when someone turned on a car's headlights pointed right at the two of them.

"Hello, Uncle Richard," Rosi called out.

"Who is your companion?" came the cool voice of her uncle from behind the lights.

"Jean Chastel," Rosi said. The Frenchman bristled when he heard his name spoken.

"The very one?"

"Yes, sir." Rosi filled Uncle Richard in on the evening's events as quickly as she could.

Uncle Richard then turned and spoke quickly with Jean, who seemed surprised and relieved to hear French spoken. Jean also seemed suddenly respectful. Even Rosi's tin ear could tell that Uncle Richard spoke with a much more sophisticated accent that the poor farmer did.

"He thinks you are a witch," Uncle Richard explained.

"I got that much."

"He also says that you will be damned for eternity and will suffer the torments of Hell. Oh, you are also a heretic."

"A heretic?" Rosi had never heard that one before.

"He thinks you are English," Uncle Richard explained. "He has also asked to buy you. He is offering two pigs. It is a generous offer."

"Thanks, but no thanks," Rosi said, hoping that the Frenchman would hear her sarcasm and contempt. "*Non. Merci*," she added with a smirk.

"He did not make the offer to you," Uncle Richard said. "He made it to me. Did you know that I am rather partial to ham?"

"Very funny," Rosi said sarcastically.

"You have also made quite a mess of things tonight. No." Uncle Richard held up a hand. "Do not interrupt. You were distracted all evening. You made amateur mistakes. I need to deal with this man and go and clear the park area of your problem before the police investigate. You do realize that he is a madman."

"Then send him back to France," Rosi said. "They won't notice it there."

Uncle Richard gave her a look that stifled her laugh. "Tell me," he said. "What he did when you fired the second shot."

"He was trying to get me out of—"

"He was trying to stop you from shooting the animal," Uncle Richard said.

"Nonsense," Rosi blurted out.

"From what you told me, he was kneeling with the animal after you killed it. Then he pulled a gun on you. Did not that tell you something?"

Rosi had no idea what Uncle Richard was talking about.

"The Ankalagon," Uncle Richard went on. "Was his pet. He found it as a pup and raised it. He is terrified that I might know the truth, so he is not saying much other than that you should be burned at the stake, but the story is fairly clear. He set the beast on his neighbors to create a panic, a climate of fear so people would move. He was planning on buying as much property as he could borrow the money for. When he finally would have killed the animal, he would be rewarded, perhaps even ennobled, paid off his debts, and been the richest man in the region."

"And he would have gotten away with it if it hadn't been for this meddling kid and that dog too." Rosi had waited a long time to say this.

"He will get away with it." Uncle Richard turned to Jean and spoke. Rosi could follow enough to know that he was explaining to the man that he should tell everyone he had killed the Beast and how pleased the King would be.

Jean visibly brightened and even smiled. He stood up taller.

Rosi wanted to shoot him.

Uncle Richard apparently sensed this, for he had Rosi hand him the gun and the holster, which he put in the trunk of the car. When he came back, he had a bottle of Champagne and some cups. He poured a full cup for Jean and a little for himself and Rosi. "*Salut*," he said, raising the cup.

"*Salut!*" cheered Rosi and Jean. Both of them tossed back their drinks and held out their cups for more.

Uncle Richard filled up Jean's cup, but ignored Rosi's.

Jean drank his second cup as quickly as the first and held it out for more.

Uncle Richard took the cup from his hand and shook his

head. Before the outraged comment could come from Jean's mouth, he staggered slightly and fell over.

"You drugged the Champagne?" Rosi laughed. "That's why you didn't give me more."

"I put the sedative in his cup," Uncle Richard said. "I did not give you more because you should not be drinking it at all. You are still only fifteen."

"I'm almost sixteen and it's cold and wet here."

"Put him in the car," Uncle Richard ordered.

Rosi looked at the fallen man. "How am I supposed to carry him? He's bigger than me."

"Lift with your legs," her uncle suggested.

After much effort Rosi deposited Jean in the back seat.

Uncle Richard got into the car. "I will deal with the Ankalagon. Unless, that is, you know how to operate a fork lift."

"No, sir."

"Go home and go to bed. I will also take care of your motorcycle."

It was almost a mile to The Castle. "Can't you give me—" Rosi had to chase after the car and pound on the hood again to get him to stop. "Can you give me a coat? A hat? Umbrella."

"You are alive," Uncle Richard said through his opened window. "That is a good thing. Quite a few apprentice guardians did not survive their first solo missions. You stopped an animal that could have caused a great deal of damage. You stopped it with a minimum of complication beyond a few broken windows and perhaps some frightened children who will think they were having nightmares anyway. You apprehended Jean Chastel and brought him to me without anyone else seeing him, and with him seeing as little as possible of this time and place. People have done worse."

"And you, sir?" Rosi asked. "How did you do?"

Uncle Richard appeared to consider his answer. "When I was finished, I learned that the South had won the Civil War. My cousin was furious. It took him days to figure out how to keep Lee from marching through Maryland in 1862. Those were my cigars Special Order 191 was wrapped in. I forged the document.

You have done fine."

The car moved off and stopped again, about ten feet away. Rosi ran to the open window.

Uncle Richard handed out the Champagne bottle. "Please dispose of the bottle when you get home." He drove off.

Not bad, Uncle Richard, Rosi smiled. She held the bottle over her cup and poured. Nothing came out. He had given her an empty bottle.

Rosi sighed. Her clothes were soaked and probably ruined. Her shoes were definitely going into the trashcan. She had almost been killed. She had come very close to shooting Chastel several times during the trek to Uncle Richard if only to shut the man up.

On the other had, she had a belly full of cheap wine, and at The Castle there would be a hot shower, a snack, and clean sheets. Tomorrow was a Sunday. No work. No training. Lunch with Angie and Andy.

It could be worse.

CHAPTER 3

ROSI hardly expected to be given a ticker tape parade when she went into town. No one was supposed to be aware that she had saved the town from being a buffet for a prehistoric predator. She certainly did not expect people to turn away from her. At least one person simply refused to speak to her. A little girl, the granddaughter of one of the fishmongers, burst into tears when Rosi went up to play with her.

"What's wrong with her?" Rosi asked Nellie when she walked by the small shop. She was working for Nellie as part of her punishment for stealing the launch and sneaking out to Widows' Island on the Fourth.

Nellie thought for a moment. "Them as is little tend to cry a lot. I wouldn't give it much stock." She went back to her work. She seemed to be avoiding Rosi's gaze.

This made Rosi feel uncomfortable. She thought she had developed a friendly relationship with her boss. At least Nellie stopped making the fig sign whenever Rosi came in, to ward off the evil eye. This morning, however, Nellie seemed to be finding things to do to avoid looking at Rosi.

Since Rosi did not have to work with Nellie today, she decided not to push it. She gave Nellie a quick 'ciao' and walked off, followed by a grumbled and grudging farewell.

Rosi did check her reflection in a window a few stalls down just to make sure that she had not grown a third eye.

She had not.

"What do you have to say for yourself?" someone demanded.

Rosi was surprised to find herself facing Lois. "What?"

Lois stepped in. "What do you have to say for yourself?"

Of course. Rosi almost laughed. "Happy birthday. I, uh, I am sorry I wasn't able to make it last night. I heard it was great. Uh. Something came up at home. You know. My uncle's getting, y'know. I came into town to…."

Lost in thought, she glanced back.

How had she walked this far along Dock Street? Rosi usually would have turned off by now. She rarely went past *The Cavalier*. She did not like stores where the customers had a dress code.

"I'm sure you spoke with *your* friend Angie today and she told you all about it," Lois sneered.

"*My* friend? If she's not your friend, why did you invite her?"

"Where is it?" Lois suddenly demanded.

Rosi looked at the other girl. The question made no sense.

"Where is it?" Lois repeated. "My present."

Oh. "It's at home." That did not sound right. "Why would I buy you a present?"

"You were invited to my party. You owe me a present."

"I did not go to your party," Rosi said.

"But you bought me a present anyway. You just told me." Lois had a point. "So where is it?"

"I didn't expect to see you, so, I didn't bring it." *Note to self: buy something cheap but gaudy for Lois.* "I kind of figured you wouldn't be awake yet. You know. All the excitement. Party. All that. You know. It's too bad Kirk couldn't make it, but the fireworks and all must have been pretty neat."

"Odd thing is that *my* boyfriend did make it. I guess Danny had something better to do on the island," Lois stabbed. "Lots of pretty girls there this time of year," she twisted.

Rosi shrugged. "Angie didn't tell me the guest list," she said flatly.

"Of course she didn't. She was not there. She didn't tell you anything about it." Lois laughed triumphantly. "So, how did you know about the fireworks? Don't even bother to lie to me. I know what you are."

Oh, God! "What are you talking about?"

"I saw you last night. I saw you right when the fireworks started. On the hill." Lois leaned in. "I know what you are, and now everyone else does as well."

What has Lois done now? What did I do, for that matter?

"I saw you on the hill," Lois' voice was getting shrill. "I saw you change."

"What?"

"Don't even bother to deny it. I saw you. It explains everything. You and your family have been werewolves for generations. You've been feeding on the local population for years. I saw you. I saw the huge hound you became. So did other people last night after you came to town to hunt."

It struck Rosi that she really wanted to be going in the other direction to get to the restaurant, but she was not about to walk away and let this nut job win this round. So she did the only thing she could think of.

She barked. Then she growled. "You're right, Lois. I'm a werewolf. And I'm hungry."

Lois reached into her bag. "I'll show you!" She shoved something in Rosi's face. "The power of Christ compels you!"

"Lois," Rosi said, shaking her head. "You're a moron."

"Back away."

"That's a cross. I'm a werewolf, not a vampire."

"I saw a movie where the vampire turned into a werewolf. They're the same thing. Back off, or I'll dust you."

"You. Are. A. Moron." Rosi started to walk passed Lois, when the girl shoved the cross against Rosi's head.

Rosi grabbed Lois' arm and twisted it behind her back. Then she shoved her against the display window and held her there.

A small crowd had gathered and was enjoying the scuffle. Someone even meowed.

"Go home, Lois," Rosi said. "Leave me be." She let the girl go and began to walk away.

What Lois did at that moment might have worked had Rosi not heard someone gasp. She spun around in time to see Lois about to brain her with the cross.

Rosi leaped back, tripped, and fell onto the sidewalk.

Lois stepped in again and raised the large metal cross over her head.

Someone grabbed Lois and dragged her off. It was one of the employees at the boutique. The Boutique was Vernon's of Paris, though everyone in town knew that Jerry Vernon came from a working class family in Edinburgh.

Rosi decided to leave while Lois was focused on her father's employee. Lois was clearly out of control. As Rosi turned the corner, Lois was beginning a litany of dire threats to the salesgirl, the least of which was getting her fired and put out on the street.

So, I'm a werewolf, Rosi thought. *That explains a lot.*

* * *

ACTUALLY, come to think of it, Rosi thought the werewolf idea might be a bit more acceptable to many people than the truth. She herself might find it easier to swallow. All a werewolf had to do was eat. Her job was much harder.

One of the harder parts was that New Richmond existed in any number of different periods of history at the same time. She could walk down the street and say hello to three or four different people who were living four or five hundred years apart.

Even worse, the number of time periods and their temporal locations were not consistent.

Most people simply would not notice anything. Seeing all of these layers was one of the 'gifts' that many members of the Carol family inherited. Other people had the gift as well. Most of them simply did not recognize it, mentally rejected that which was impossible, decided they were seeing ghosts, or were institutionalized as crazy.

Once the layers were pointed out to Rosi, she began to learn how to see them and recognize them and their relative importance.

Rosi was also learning to find the tears, the doorways, or portals that allowed for people, or Ankalagons, to cross from one period to another. She sensed them through touch. The doorways felt colder to her. Uncle Richard saw colors in the air. Others heard them or smelled them. There seemed to be any number of ways different people could sense them.

Once Rosi found a doorway, she could see it. It was rather hard to describe. Perhaps this was because Rosi had yet to try and describe it to anyone. Perhaps it was also because Rosi could only see them in her peripheral vision. The tears seemed to her to look like a mix of flashing lights, haze, shadow, and shimmering wavy air. They were difficult to find, hard to see, and surprisingly easy to fall into, though Uncle Richard told her that was because her subconscious wanted her to go through *accidentally*. Very few people actually ever did go through, unless they somehow knew that the doorways were there. Rosi did not have such problems.

A few days earlier Rosi had been carrying her breakfast plates to the kitchen. This was a chore she had done dozens of times. This time, however, she turned to say something to Uncle Richard and, instead of the kitchen, she ended up in the desert.

A man on a camel rode up to Rosi and took her to a caravan, which took her to a town and put her on the auction block. Fortunately, Uncle Richard bought her.

"Why didn't you just show up and save me right when I appeared here," Rosi had complained. "Why make me go through a week of being pinched and prodded and having my teeth checked."

"I hope none of the men—" Uncle Richard had looked like he was about to go back and string someone up.

"I'm talking about the women. The men were great. Very polite, considering they were going to sell me as a harem girl. I thought they were all a bit scared of me."

"That is certainly a reaction that you will get from men in the future as well."

"Because of my part in the family and all that?"

"No."

Uncle Richard had explained that a doorway rarely led to a specific instant. Rather, the doorways led to events, periods of time which for some reason appeared to be somehow contained and finite. "For example," Uncle Richard tried. "If you go through one of the doorways, you might end up at some point during the French Revolution. You could not guarantee that you would show up before or after Louis XVII was executed."

New Richmond was one place in the world where the doorways were clustered. Uncle Richard would not talk much about the other places or even say how many of them there were. He did say that each place had some sort of process for controlling and containing access to the different periods.

Rosi got the feeling that Uncle Richard was *not* telling her that Guardians from other places had *not* always been as ethical in their approach to their job as her family was.

There were several types of doorways, Rosi had learned. Some were dormant or extinct. Rosi could not tell which was which, but Uncle Richard said that the difference was as significant as the difference in volcanoes. "An extinct volcano will never erupt again," he explained. "A dormant volcano has not erupted for a while and we hope it will not erupt today."

There were doorways that were active. There were also those that were *occurring*, which meant that the periods were interacting at that very moment.

The doors around The Castle and the estate were seals. The Castle was built where it was because the spot had the highest concentration of doorways.

"But the doors seal the tears," Rosi had asked. "Problem solved?"

"Not necessarily," Uncle Richard had said. "It is simply a door. It can be opened and closed. The tears can grow. No one has ever figured out all of the laws that govern them. There is debate as to whether there is any set of rules that can be applied. I think there is. I think that there are patterns that suggest reason behind it all. I will admit that I am in a minority."

Uncle Richard had yet to teach her how to bind a physical door to an intangible tear in the time space continuum, but he assured her that it was possible. "We have been doing it for thousands of years," he had told her.

The Carols, as well as ancestors of many of the local families, had shown up in 1649. They had married into the local tribe and The Carol had become the Guardian.

The tribe, called the Fula-Puli, had been dying out when the English refugees arrived. It had almost died out a few hundred years before. Then, it had mixed with several boatloads of Viking explorers. The new breed had used its power to push the other Norsemen out of Vinland. New Richmond, Uncle Richard pointed out, is better served through isolation.

There had been several times over the last three thousand years that Europeans had somehow arrived in the area and married into the tribe. Again, this was something Uncle Richard did not go into in any great detail about. "You will find out when you need to," he told her once.

Much of Rosi's time over the last three weeks had been spent hunting around the estate for unsealed doorways. It was kind of like a scavenger hunt. Uncle Richard would give her clues, and she would have to come back with a location and a time period.

"Why aren't they sealed?" Rosi had asked one day. It struck her as a no brainer.

Uncle Richard had uncharacteristically simply shrugged his shoulders. "It is not an easy thing to do," he said. "No one ever bothered to shut them. Apparently, those doorways, or more appropriately, those periods, would have no effect should someone interact with them. There would be no confusion."

Confusion was the word used to suggest that one period was interfering with another.

Why *confusion*?

"Well," Uncle Richard had explained one day during lunch. "You know that Richard Nixon resigned as president in 1974." Rosi nodded, not sure if she did. "Imagine if you went online today and learned that Nixon has been reelected twice more as president."

"I'd be surprised that I got a connection," Rosi had laughed.

"Do not be impertinent. Answer the question put before you."

"I don't know. I suppose if I knew it had happened and if the history books said something else, I'd be a bit confused."

"That is why we use the word," he said, a bit too smugly, Rosi thought. "One thing *we* can do is retain the memories of *our* history. Once you learn history, by doing the readings I assign, you will have an idea of when things get confusing."

"What if something adjusts history in a way which is so insignificant that we can't tell, but perhaps it will be significant in a hundred years?"

"Let the future deal with its past. You deal with yours."

* * *

"WEREWOLVES?" Angie almost fell out of her seat laughing.

Rosi covered her face with a napkin to keep the root beet from coming out of her nose. The two of them sat at Zablonski's, their regular burger place. The restaurant was located in an old house that once belonged to a Revolutionary War hero and one of New Hampshire's first congressmen. The family still owned it, though their name had long since changed through marriage to Enright. Gus Enright, the owner, still lived in the upper floors. He was quite old, blind, and deaf, but was regularly wheeled down into the main dining room where he would sit and tell stories of his family and of New Richmond. Rosi had yet to be there when that happened, but had been told by Andy to be prepared for a call from him the next time it happened. Old Man Enright knew more perhaps than even Old Nellie, Andy told her.

Angie caught her breath. "That will keep everyone talking for a few weeks. Don't worry. Soon it will simply go into the local lore of the Carol Family. Next month you'll be zombies. A few years ago the Carols were supposed to be a man/crab hybrid. So, anyway, about last night, there are rumors of some sort of ghost dog romping through the streets by the high school. Did you her about that?"

Rosi wiped her eyes. "Why didn't you go to the party?" It was a lame way to change the subject.

"Andy was feeling a bit tired," Angie said. "I thought you'd gone."

"No Dan, no reason to go."

"I tried to call you several times."

Rosi smiled and shrugged.

Angie lowered her voice and leaned in a bit. "If we are supposed to cover for you, it would be a lot easier if we knew what was going on. Look, Andy's going to figure it out one of these days."

"Perhaps he will. Perhaps then he can explain it all to me." Rosi picked up the menu and began reading it, even though their order was already in. The staff at the restaurant knew what Rosi wanted, so did not bother to ask her. She liked intuitive restaurants. She just wanted to sit down and get her food.

Angie picked up a menu as well. "Kirk," she said under her breath.

Rosi was surprised. BAs, or Boston Aristocrats as the locals referred to them, rarely came to this side of the Commons, preferring newer, trendier establishments.

Out of the corner of her eye, Rosi could tell Kirk had come up to the table and was hovering. Finally, she was annoyed enough that she slammed down the menu and looked up at him. "What?"

Kirk grabbed a chair and pulled it up to the booth.

"Feel free not to join us," Rosi said. Angie made warning noises. Kirk was flanked by two of the lost boys, who hovered a few feet back.

Kirk sat down anyway. "You're a werewolf," he smiled.

"So they say."

"Since you're a girl, that would make you a were—"

"Don't even think it." Rosi started to rise.

Kirk giggled. "I've been thinking it for months. What gets me is that last night wasn't a full moon."

"Kirk, your girlfriend's a—ouch!" Angie had kicked her under the table.

"That's all right." Kirk reached for a fry from the plate the waitress put on the table. Rosi snatched it away in time. "You can say it, Lois is a moron. But you were there last night. So was something else."

"Quite a few drunk teenagers," Rosi suggested.

"There was something else there," Kirk said.

"What was it? Pray tell."

"I don't know what you are, Rosi Carol." Kirk giggled again. "But I'm going find out. I'm going make it my business to find out."

The sound of Kirk's laugh made Rosi cringe. "How?" Rosi enquired, stifling a laugh.

"You're going tell me."

"I am?"

"Oh, yes. You will tell me. I will know. There's a secret to your family. It's why you're rich and everyone fears you. I'll have that secret. I'll have the power. I'll have the wealth." He leaned in and whispered. "I'll have the girl." Kirk leaned in and put his face close to Rosi's face and sniffed deeply.

Rosi pushed him away and stood up. Kirk lost his balance and he and his chair toppled backwards. "Get away from me, you creep."

Kirk shot to his feet faster than Rosi thought he could. He giggled and grinned as he and his two friends stepped in.

Angie was on her feet trying to get between the two. "Come on, Rosi. We can go over to Andy's."

"I haven't had my lunch yet," Rosi said, not looking at her.

"We should go." Angie insisted.

"You made a big mistake, Rosi Carol." Kirk snapped his fingers, and one of the boys grabbed Angie by the arm and pulled her to one side. Kirk and the other boy stepped in closer.

Rosi was feeling pressed into the booth. In another moment she would lose her balance. She glanced around to see if any of the wait staff or managers was there. The place was about half full. No one was moving or making a noise.

"All right, Kirk," she began. "You want a piece of me? You and me. Outside. One on one. That's fair. Remember? Dan said that. Fair."

"I bet you would like that."

"I'd like to wipe that smirk off your face."

"One on one with me, after all the one on one between you and my brother I heard about."

"You don't know what you're talking about," Rosi spat.

"I know enough. I can smell it."

"Jerk!"

"I know all about you and your useless father and your tramp of a mother—"

Rosi did not realize that she had slapped Kirk until the sound stopped ringing in her ears.

Kirk straightened up. Keeping his gaze locked on Rosi's, he nodded to his friend, who picked up the chair and held it while

Kirk sat. The friend then grabbed Rosi by the arm.

Rosi tried to pull her arm away, but the boy's grip was too strong. She felt herself pushed onto her seat. She noticed that Angie had been forced to sit as well.

Kirk giggled. He reached over and ate a handful of Rosi's fries. Then he pulled out a cigarette and lit it. "When my boys and I are done, your precious Danny won't be able to get within a mile of you without throwing up." He blew a puff in Rosi's face.

"Hey," came another voice. "Hey, kid. There's no smoking in here. Take it outside."

Rosi recognized it as the manager, a nice middle aged man who was Old Man Enright's son-in-law.

"What's that?" Kirk sneered.

"If you want to smoke, sit on the patio."

"Bite me, old man."

"Then leave the premises."

Kirk turned around and flicked the cigarette at the man's face. The man flinched. Kirk stood up, pushed the man over, and kicked him.

Rosi tried to break away, but could not.

"Hey, Angie," she finally yelled. "Isn't that your father?"

That broke the spell.

The boy holding Rosi's arms let her go and moved off.

Rosi grabbed an empty serving tray and whacked the boy holding Angie with it several times until he fled.

Giggling and flushed, Kirk, keeping his eyes on Rosi, led his friends to the door. "I'll find out, Rosi Carol. Or someone else will. I remember Widows' Island."

"You were stoned," Rosi shot back. Kirk was not supposed to be able to remember it.

"What are all the doors for, Rosi?" Kirk giggled. "Where do they all lead?" Before Rosi could respond, he turned and hopped out of the restaurant.

Rosi sat down. The situation had made her short of breath.

"You okay?" asked Angie. "You look paler than I feel."

Rosi laughed. She felt drained, but otherwise fine.

The manager came up to Rosi to thank her. Most of the

others in the restaurant had turned back to their meals. It was almost as if they had forgotten what happened.

Angie had not. "One day, you're going to have it out with Kirk."

Rosi shrugged. She was angry and shaken, but she did not want to dwell on it. Their food came, so they focused on eating instead. What with the training and her work, she did not have that much time off and preferred to spend it not thinking about Kirk.

* * *

ANGIE, Andy, and Rosi had each been punished for stealing Andy's uncle's launch and taking it to Widows' Island.

Angie and Andy, who had been boyfriend and girlfriend since preschool, had been forbidden to see or talk with each other for a week. That had been, Angie insisted, the longest week in her life.

Andy spent much of the summer working with his father, who was a fisherman, so he worked almost every day. Sometimes he worked in a small cramped office and tried to make sense of the paperwork. At least once a week, he went out with the others on their fishing boat. This summer was the first time he had ever gone out for a trip that lasted more than one day. Andy's father had decided that Andy was letting the women in his life push him around too much and that some time spent in the company of men would be good for him. Yesterday afternoon, he had just returned from four days at sea. It had been his longest trip yet.

Angie's punishment was cleaning detail at her father's jail. She got to scrape up months of dust. Of course, cleaning the jailhouse only took about a week, but Sheriff Kaufman decided that cleaning it also meant painting, grouting, leveling, scraping, planting, and landscaping. She was even expected to do some light plumbing.

"You might as well learn how now," Rosi had pointed out. "Andy will never figure it out. He'll be too busy as a college professor."

Angie regularly altered her plans for Andy's future. Recently, she had read that college professors received great benefits, so that was what he would be. "Insurance is very important," she said. "Especially since I plan on having about five kids."

Rosi's job was to work as Nellie's assistant at her stall. Each morning Rosi would wake up early, eat breakfast, and make her way to Nellie's stall. There she would spend the day carrying things and cleaning up fish guts. Each evening, she would go home and throw her clothes away. Someone always took them out of the trash and laundered them, usually by the time Rosi was done with her shower. Rosi would eat. Then she would start her training for the day.

After about a week of working for Nellie, the smell of fish no longer made Rosi retch, though she still could not bring herself to eat it. After about two weeks of working with Nellie, she knew more gossip about New Richmond than was probably good for her. She could not help but snicker when she saw Dr. Samuels and his roly-poly wife go by. And she figured she knew a few secrets about the BAs, especially former Ambassador Hennessy, that could topple the odd bank. By the end of the month, she even had grown to enjoy working with Nellie. She never actually saw Andy's uncle, who spent all of his time in their apartment above the warehouse and would only bellow down orders for food or liquor to Nellie every two or three hours. In fact, she had enjoyed her time so much that Rosi had offered to come by a couple of days a week to help out after her sentence was over at the end of the next week.

"I canna pay you much, lass," Nellie said, regretfully.

"Pshaw. Don't pay me anything. All I'd do otherwise is sit around up at The Castle and play video games. I should pay you."

"I could give you pick of catch," Nellie offered, knowing full well that Rosi could not stomach seafood.

"If that is the case, I'm afraid I'd have to be paid," Rosi laughed.

Rosi's unwillingness to eat seafood was one area where she and Nellie would never see eye to eye. Nellie thought it the silly affectation of a child and dutifully prepared fish or scrod or other delicacies, even sea cucumbers once, for lunch everyday. Rosi would dutifully thank her boss and simply not eat. Of course, this meant Rosi would spend much of the day hungry. From time to time, there would be enough of a lull that she would have time to run over to another stall and buy something edible, but this was fairly rare.

She asked Uncle Richard once if someone could prepare lunch for her to take. He had pointed out that lunch was part of the deal with Nellie and it was not the job of his staff to prepare "redundant meals" for a "recalcitrant child." However, following that conversation, the breakfasts and dinners she regularly found in the dining room became marginally larger.

Of course, missing a meal from time to time was no great disaster. Rosi had to watch her weight. Dan would be coming back soon.

Another area of contention between Rosi and Nellie was that Rosi would not tell her much about The Castle. Indeed, Nellie seemed to know more about it than she did, Rosi had tried pointing out. Furthermore, after working ten hours a day six days a week and then training with Uncle Richard, Rosi was hardly inclined to explore much.

"I'll tell you more when I have time," she promised, keeping two fingers crossed in case she had to break this promise.

As it was, Rosi's time was pretty much filled with work and training. She did find some time for her friends. Occasionally, her email worked long enough to contact the real world. Every few days, she was able to read Dan's emails and send back some sort of silly answer that made her feel stupid and dull the moment she clicked *Send*.

This particular day, Rosi was not working. So she had promised to help Angie clean the Sheriff's squad car. After that was done, she expected to hang out with her friends for the rest of the day. However, Andy was under the weather, and Angie was planning on spending the day nursing him. So Rosi walked Angie to Andy's and gave a wave to the patient. He would be in worse shape after a day of Angie's ministrations, Rosi thought.

"Stay away from Kirk," Angie warned. "He used to be simply a jerk. He's gotten weird lately. He could be dangerous."

"I wasn't planning on looking for him," Rosi said.

"It might be best to make sure you avoid him. I know I won't be able to talk you out of the Meadows' barbecue, but—"

"What barbecue?" Rosi burst in.

"The annual barbecue at Dan's house."

"They do this every year?"

"That's why they call it *annual*," Angie pointed out.

Rosi laughed sarcastically. "Thanks. Why didn't someone tell me about it?"

"Because you've only been here a couple of months. Dad only got his invitation yesterday. I hadn't really—"

"You're going," Rosi said.

"We never go," Angie said.

"You have to go with me." Rosi pleaded and cajoled until Angie finally agreed.

The first thing Rosi did when she got home was to check the mail. There was no invitation. There was nothing.

The rest of the day was spent anticipating the worst possible explanations. Most of her options ended up with Dan either cruelly dumping her or dying in a horrible car crash. Rosi dialed Dan's number at least ten times on her phone, but never pressed send. She reread every email he had sent. There were not many. With few exceptions, they all began with Dan apologizing for not writing much, he was terrible with emails, etc. Then he would describe his days, which seemed to be spent mostly playing tennis or SCUBA diving or snorkeling. Usually the apology was longer than the rest of the email. There were no clues that he was not going to dump her in any of them.

At dinner, she snapped at Uncle Richard. He insisted that she explain what was wrong. When she told him, he laughed.

"How can you laugh?" she exploded.

"Because, young lady. It is Sunday. There is no mail on Sundays."

CHAPTER 4

WORSE than not having any mail on Sunday was not having any mail on Monday either. Of course, Rosi rarely got mail.

The last mail Rosi had received was a questionnaire from the lawyer who had sent her here. Or rather, it was from his law firm. He was far too busy and important now to bother with her. She had filled it out at once, saying many nasty things. However, she tore it up and threw it away the next day. She might not like him, but he was doing his job. He had already sent Uncle Richard several long reports on Rosi's holdings. Rosi did not know much about finance, but she knew enough to realize that as long as *Ivy League*, her pet name for the lawyer as his real name was one of those long New England monstrosities with hyphens and numbers in it, avoided taking too much initiative with her money, she would be quite comfortable. Her father *had* known what he was doing. His methods may have been slightly unethical, but the Securities and Exchange Commission had yet to say that *literally* going to the future was insider trading. Rosi would not make money this way, but she was definitely not going to give it back. Was that wrong?

That night, Rosi could not sleep. When she did doze, it seemed to her as if she could hear doors opening and closing, footsteps, and, sometimes, a child laughing. When she got out of bed in the morning, she got the feeling that some things in her room had been moved around in the night.

On Tuesday, she waited by the mailbox until the mailman came.Rosi tried to look casual. She sat on a blanket and pretended to read. Fortunately, almost no one ever drove past The Castle, and certainly no one she knew ever came out here without telling her first. When the mailman finally came, there were only bills. She almost handed them back.

Rosi was sure she had done something wrong. She was in

agony. Did Dan hate her? Was there someone else? Was she too fat?

"Don't even go there," Angie said to her that afternoon by the pool. "Most girls would love to have your body."

"Don't worry," Rosi said. "I'm not gonna go all Ana on you." She slid another slice of pizza onto her plate as if to prove her point.

"Mail takes time," Andy said. "I didn't get my invitation yet."

Angie laughed. "You never have and you never will. If you go, you'll be my guest."

"Tomorrow, next week, whenever," Andy went on. "The Meadows' barbecue is always the last Saturday in August. Mr. Meadows fires up the grill and opens the bar at three every year. When they're out of propane and booze, they send everyone home."

"What's your point?" Rosi asked.

"Just go," he said.

Rosi was flabbergasted. She had a pretty good idea how fragile her social position was. Showing up unannounced could....

Andy seemed to know what she was thinking. "I've never been," he went on. "But it isn't the kind of event where your ID is scrutinized and you're announced. C'mon, it's a cook out in New Richmond not at the White House."

That night, Rosi worried herself until well after midnight, when she finally dragged herself to bed, falling asleep in her clothes, very intentionally not thinking about Dan. Instead of dreaming of Dan, she dreamt of fires and explosions. Her subconscious mind filled with flashes and screams, bright colors, fear, triumph, death.

Rosi awakened with a start and sat up in bed. The roaring sounds seemed to echo in the still air and the flashes seemed to linger, burnt on her retinas. She could almost swear that she smelled a hint of sulfur hanging just out of nostril range.

On Wednesday, Rosi rushed into town when Angie told her that she had seen Mrs. Meadows at a shop. Dan had to be back now, she told herself. She carefully arranged to be at the right places at the right times. She spent two hours at the pizzeria and ate a whole pizza. She had four sundaes at the ice cream shop and drank three cups of coffee at the Cavalier. She drove to the country club several times on the off chance he might be there.

At about four, Rosi decided that he was most likely trying to call her, so she dragged Angie out to The Castle where they sat by the phone until almost eight when Angie decided she simply had to go home.

That night, Rosi dropped off fairly late as well. She woke up in the middle of the night. The first thing that struck her was that the lights were off. Had she not fallen asleep while reading? She felt around and found the book where it had slipped down under the covers. She had just decided to see if the light bulb had burned out when she was overwhelmed by a feeling of not being alone.

Something was in the room with her and it seemed to be right next to her. There was a blackness so much blacker than the rest of the darkness that surrounded it that it practically shone. Rosi stared at it and it stared back at her. She could even smell it, but she was not sure what the aroma was. She leaned forward, and it leaned forward and seemed to sniff at her.

Rosi screamed and dove under her blankets, wrapping them around her, pulling in all the loose ends, making for herself an impregnable womb of blankets and sheets and stuffed bears and pillows, allowing just enough of a hole to breathe through, though she could not believe she actually breathed much. When she did breathe, she made sure she breathed through her mouth as slowly and silently as humanly possible so whatever it was would not hear her and would go away.

Finally, she thought she heard the distant reflection of something moving away from her, up the stairs and out. Murmurs drifted down for the barest moment. Then there was only silence.

Rosi did not move again until she was sure the sun was up, her clock radio was singing its hymn to morning, and she had heard her first sounds of the outside through the open windows. Once she was positive that the sun was up, she finally did sleep for a few hours, only to be awakened when Angie called.

When she discovered that there was no mail for her again, she drafted several emails to Dan lambasting him, begging him, flirting with him. Angie clucked obediently over the phone and talked her out of sending them. Several times, Andy spoke up so Rosi could hear him from Angie's, encouraging her simply to show up at the party.

Then Rosi remembered that she was waiting for a phone call and could not afford for Dan to get a busy signal. After she hung up on Angie, she remembered call waiting, but was too embarrassed to call her friend back. At least not until she was done with her next email.

Rosi did not eat that day and she stayed up late that night watching war movies. Several times, it seemed to her as if she heard noises outside her rooms, but when she turned down the sound, the noises stopped. *They might simply be echoes from the movie,* she thought.

* * *

"ARE you planning on playing baseball today?" Uncle Richard asked.

Rosi blinked her eyes and sat up. She must have fallen asleep on the couch. The sun was up. A quick glance at the various clocks in the room told her that it was eight o'clock, six twenty three, and three thirty five.

She stretched, letting her joints crackle and snap. Rosi took a big sip of flat root beer and swished it around her mouth to clear up the morning breath. There was no sink nearby, so she spat it back into the glass. Then she ran her fingers through her hair and shook it out.

Uncle Richard coughed discretely. "If you need some time to perform your toiletries, I would be more than happy to wait for you upstairs. No? It is an exceptionally nice day outside. You should get up and come upstairs. It is lunchtime. I strongly suggest that you eat today." He started up the stairs. "If you are going to play baseball, I suggest you do so with a bat that has not been autographed by Mr. James Creighton."

Rosi noticed that there was a baseball bat lying on the couch next to her. She must have gone to sleep holding it. Then she remembered that she had carried the bat when she checked the rooms at one point the night before. She had slept with it. "You're probably right," she said, walking over to put it in a rack of bats, all of which had been recently autographed by some of baseball's greats.

"Uncle Richard," Rosi said. "You've never come in here to wake me up before. Was there something else?"

He seemed to think for a moment. "Of course," he said, almost smiling. "I do not suppose that you would have any interest in attending the Meadows' annual barbecue next weekend would you." He took out a letter and waved it in front of him. "I received an invitation this morning—"

Before he could finish, Rosi was across the room and had torn the letter from his hand. She quickly read the rather formal invitation to Richard Carol and family, then came to the short handwritten note from Dan.

"R," it began. This was a good sign, Rosi decided. "Sorry I won't be around this week. We are all going camping. Yawn! See you at the party! D."

Rosi was so happy she kissed Uncle Richard, and then pulled back quickly, embarrassed.

"It seems as if you do want to go to the barbecue," Uncle Richard sniffed. "I will send a short note to Mrs. Meadows accepting on your behalf. I generally do not attend local social gatherings, for obvious reasons. I do not, however, see any reason that you should not go and enjoy yourself."

Rosi was no longer listening to him. She had already rushed to her closet and started pulling clothes out. She was also on the phone to Angie.

She only had a week until the party.

* * *

THE next day, Angie and Andy came out and watched Rosi try to choose the dress she would wear.

Rosi had a lot of clothes and tried most of them on. She ran the gamut from schoolmarm to streetwalker, country bumpkin to Monte Carlo sophisticate. Finally, Angie and Andy convinced her that a simple sundress and sandals would be perfect, knowing she would change her mind many times between now and the evening in question.

Rosi also spent much of the next week trying to figure out what to buy Dan for his birthday present. She had no idea what Dan would want. She went into every store in town and finally settled on buying him a book about tennis heroes. It was not much, but would show him that she cared about his interests. Rosi decided that such a gift was too impersonal and took the book back. Then she bought the book again, because she could not think of anything else.

She and her father had always given each other books. Then again, her father had been in publishing and loved books. Rosi returned the book and thought about buying him a nice jacket, but realized that she should not be buying him clothes. Clothes were too maternal. So she went back for the book, which the salesman had decided not to unwrap in anticipation that Rosi would come back for it.

"I'll have mom pick you up and we can go together," Angie offered on Friday.

"No!" Rosi almost shouted. "Sorry. I think I should show up alone. You know, so he only sees me."

"Okay. So we'll see you about three?"

"Four," Rosi said. "Best to be a little late. Maybe even five or five thirty. If I'm there too early, it'll look like I'm desperate."

Rosi slept well the following nights. Nothing seemed to bother her. As the party approached, she worried about it, but there were no funny noises in the dark of night.

The night before the party, Rosi awakened in the dark. It smelled a little like smoke. She immediately rushed around the rooms checking for a fire. There was none. Then she remembered that she had used the grill the evening before. That would certainly explain the smell.

She laughed at herself. This whole business with time was making her paranoid. Uncle Richard had given her the week off.

She had a lot to read, but he was going to be *elsewhen* on a buying trip and was not sure if he would be back in time for the barbecue, so he had left Rosi to her own devices. A few evenings of not wearing uncomfortable clothes was doing wonders for her. She did, however, take the time to learn the Minuet, like Uncle Richard had asked just before he left wearing a toga.

* * *

THE last Saturday in August was a beautiful day. The sun came up and chased away a light misty chill. By noon, the temperature was in the mid eighties and stayed there. A soft breeze from the sea kept the day from getting too hot or mucky. Rosi woke up and stood out on her battlements to listen to the birds and the rustling leaves. She watched a little television, talked to Angie on the phone, and took a long hot bath.

"You look nice," Uncle Richard said to her just after four, as Rosi was dragging the scooter through the stable doors.

"Thank you," she blushed. "The Meadows' barbecue. So you made it back in time."

"Apparently," he said.

"Didn't stop the Renaissance by any chance? Did Michelangelo still paint the Sistine Chapel?"

"Yes, of course." Not amused, he walked over to her and began looking at her carefully.

"I'm not wearing any make-up Uncle Richard" Rosi said. She had tried a couple of times over the summer to put on a little rouge or eye shadow. Whenever she did, Uncle Richard somehow appeared out of nowhere and made her wash it off. It was terribly unfair. All of the girls in the city had worn make-up. At least, the girls the boys liked did. Rosi had been careful not to try today, because she had timed everything perfectly and did not want to ruin her schedule by taking the time to scrub her face to Uncle Richard's satisfaction. She liked the old man, but he certainly had some funny ideas about young people.

"So you are not," he sniffed approvingly. "Are you positive you wish to go out today?"

"Of course I am." *What a question* Rosi thought.

"Could you not find another day to see your friends?"

"No! The barbecue is today!" He knew this. Rosi knew he knew this.

"It might get chilly," Uncle Richard went on. "It might be best to stay home."

"I have a sweater in my bag." She showed him.

"You have not been well."

What is he trying to do, destroy my life? "I'm fine!" Rosi practically screamed.

"Do not use that tone of voice on me, young lady. I am merely concerned about your well being." Uncle Richard was beginning to look a bit miffed.

"You're not my father! I talk like I want to."

"I could ground you again."

"You'd have to lock the doors and throw away the keys. I'm going!" Rosi started the scooter and peeled out, whipping around the corner of the stables and almost hitting a tree. She stopped once she was out of sight of the buildings and wiped away the tears blurring her vision. She had been going too fast anyway, but Uncle Richard could be so frustrating.

She checked her eyes in the mirror nervously. They were a little red, but they would get better by the time she got to the party. Rosi slipped on her sunglasses and started off slowly, knowing exactly how long it would take her to get to the Meadows' house. She had driven there every evening since she got the invitation. She had even experimented with different constant speeds, finally deciding on one of the slower speeds, because she did not want to get there too soon, and wanted to be as safe as possible and wearing the helmet was not going to happen this time because wind blown hair would be sexy and alluring. Helmet hair was not an option.

Rosi cut around behind the warehouses to avoid being seen by Nellie or Young Captain Sam. They would certainly tell Uncle Richard that she had not worn her helmet. Worse, they might let him in on the secret that her dress was significantly shorter now than it had been at The Castle and that she was also wearing heels. It was a quiet drive. There was no one about.

Then she drove past the entrance to the Country Club and into the residential complex of the BAs.

Should I let him hold my hand right away? Would it be just fingers or a full hand hold with palms touching? Her palms were sweaty, and she could not wipe them because her dress was white. *Maybe if I rub them together and flap them in the breeze. Maybe that will work. It is better than nothing.*

They would be around other people at first. How could she get him to suggest that they go someplace alone? Or should she? Rosi did not want to seem too eager. Dan had made it clear how he felt the night before he left for vacation, but this would be the first time they were together in public.

No, Rosi would let him make the first moves. That would be best. Yes. They had not seen each other in almost two months, so it would be best to go a bit slow.

* * *

THE Meadows' house was near the club. It was not the closest to the clubhouse, but it was on the golf course and it had an unobstructed view of the ocean. From the house, you could look completely down the coast and see the haze that indicated Boston. It was not much in the daytime, but it was probably a pretty view when it got darker.

The house was fairly large. Daniel Sr. was a very important man. He was not the most prominent of the BA parents, so his house was not the largest, nor the closest to the clubhouse, nor did it have its own path to the beach. However, he was fairly important and rich, so he had a house that was easily three or four times the size of Angie's. There was a gate at the foot of the drive and a sizeable front lawn that led to a small guesthouse and a tennis court. There was a large backyard, complete with garden, pool house, swimming pool, patio, and built in gas grill. Dan's parents had three cars: a Mercedes, an Alpha Romeo, and a minivan that was used to run errands and usually driven by the housekeeper or the handyman, neither of whom lived in. The cars rested under a carport, not in a garage.

Rosi had done her reconnaissance very thoroughly.

Most of the guests had driven. Their cars crowded the driveway and were parked up and down the street. Some of the guests had probably parked almost as far from the Meadows' as they would have walked otherwise. Had they walked, however, they would not be seen driving their flashy cars. If they were unfortunate enough not to be able to park nearby and be seen in the process, then they would be able to tell stories about how hard it was to park.

There were a few late arrivers just reaching the gate when Rosi drove up. Beeping her horn, she squeezed through them, zigzagged through the cars, and parked her scooter near the garbage cans behind the carport. She shook off the dust and stray bugs and went around to the back of the house.

The backyard was filled with people chatting, eating, and drinking. Rosi looked around, hoping to see Dan, or catch sight of Angie and Andy.

Angie and Andy were the easiest to find. They were the only two townie kids there, so they were off to one side. When Rosi went over to join them, the people in the vicinity seemed to edge a bit further away.

The adults are just as odd as the kids, Rosi thought.

"You didn't say anything to Mrs. Meadows," Angie said when Rosi walked up to her.

"Who?"

"Dan's mother, silly," Angie laughed. "You stood right next to her while you were looking for us. She was talking to you."

"She's on her way over here," Andy piped in.

"You must be that girl that Kirk saved," Mrs. Meadows said. "How utterly charming of you to come to see him. Kirk! Your friends are here."

Kirk, who had been somewhere nearby, came over and scowled at Rosi and the others.

Rosi smiled at Mrs. Meadows and held out her hand. "Rosi Carol," she said. "I'm a friend of Dan's."

"Nonsense, dear. Kirk! You must come here with your little friend. I want a picture of the two of you together."

"That's quite all right," Rosi said.

Kirk simply scowled even more.

Angie and Andy laughed behind their hands.

Mrs. Meadows pulled Kirk over to Rosi and began posing them together. "Dan!" she cried. She seemed to have a breathless way of saying everything. "Where's my camera?"

"Right here, Jane." Dan appeared and handed the camera to his mother.

It took Rosi a second to remember that Mrs. Meadows was Dan's stepmother. However, she was not really worrying about that right now. Dan was here.

Someone was calling to Mrs. Meadows fairly urgently. "Dan, you keep these adorable children together here. I'll be right back." Mrs. Meadows wafted off.

Rosi was horrified. Dan's mother had just referred to her as a child. Uncle Richard had done the same a few weeks ago.

It began to get chilly.

"What's wrong, Rosi?" Angie asked.

It was getting very cold.

Dan stepped in. "Are you okay?"

Rosi felt as if she were going to fall over.

"Andy, get a chair," Dan said, taking charge. "I'll get you a jacket. I'll just be a sec."

Don't go, Rosi pleaded silently. She was so dizzy.

Kirk was sniffing the air.

Angie grabbed Rosi's arm. "You're freezing!"

"Get her something to drink," Kirk suggested absently.

Angie stepped away.

Kirk giggled softly.

"Not now, Kirk." Rosi was feeling sick to her stomach. She glanced around, but could not see any obvious doorways. She could smell smoke. She could almost see something, someone, just beyond the now everyone else was in.

"What do you see, Rosi?"

"I don't see anything."

"Don't lie to me, Rosi Carol. Tell me what you see!" He was spitting his words through his teeth, obviously trying not to be too loud. He was also clearly very excited.

"Leave me alone." Rosi tried to walk away, but only succeeded in sitting on the ground.

Kirk squatted next to her. He grabbed her arm.

The temperature dropped again and Rosi exhaled steam. Then Rosi saw it. There was smoke. There was fire. New Richmond was burning. The people were screaming and running and dying. There were explosions that seemed to be getting closer.

"Jesus!" Kirk said. He could see it as well. "What is it?" he asked.

When is it? Rosi wondered, standing up.

Just then, as Rosi could see Dan coming back with a jacket and Andy dragging a chair from the poolside, something landed on the lawn and began rolling towards her and Kirk. It was a metal ball and had a fuse on it. *A cannon ball?* "Get down!" she yelled.

She gave Kirk a violent push and, just as the cannon ball exploded, dove behind a table of hors devours, knocking it over and sending food scattering everywhere.

"What is going on here?" Jane Meadows rushed over. "Why did you, Kirk?"

"I dunno, Mom," Kirk said. "She just attacked me is all."

Rosi sat by the overturned table amid the finger food as the fires and screams faded.

Kirk smirked. Dan, Angie, and Andy stood and looked at her. They appeared concerned but did not dare approach her. The various parents and adults began to gather around.

"Is she trying to ruin everything?" Mrs. Meadows wailed. "Is she on drugs?"

"You'd better keep your distance," one woman said. "She could have a gun."

Everyone moved back a step.

"Call the police!" someone yelled.

No one went to the phone, though the crowd surrounding Rosi grew.

Rosi smiled, and then started to giggle. The giggle turned into a laugh. She could feel that someone was moving her. She wanted to say something. She wanted to get up and join the party. She wanted to see Angie and Andy and Dan. She wanted to scream and cry and dance and yell.

Mrs. Meadows was about to dump a wine bucket of ice on Rosi when Uncle Richard appeared as if from nowhere. By now, Angie had gone to Rosi and was helping her up.

Mrs. Meadows was yelling at Uncle Richard, demanding that he pay for any damages that Rosi did. She was practically hysterical.

Rosi looked around and noticed that Dan was nowhere to be seen. He must hate her for ruining the party. She wished she could tell him what had happened. She wished that Kirk would say something. Everyone would think him crazy, but at least she would not be the only crazy person there.

Mrs. Meadows was shrieking by now, calling Rosi things that she did not even want to know the meanings of.

Finally, Uncle Richard turned away from Mrs. Meadows and came to Rosi.

"Are you all right?" he asked. "Are you all right?" he repeated when she did not answer.

"Something bad happened here," she said quietly. Only Uncle Richard and, maybe, Angie could have heard her.

"Nothing happened here other than you lost your balance wearing shoes you did not leave home with." Uncle Richard turned to Angie. "Please take her to the street. Your father will take the two of you home. I will be by later."

He turned back to Mrs. Meadows and silenced her by raising his hand.

Rosi could not hear what he was saying.

CHAPTER 5

IT was only about six when Angie and Rosi got to The Castle. The sun was warm and there was a light breeze out on Rosi's battlement.

Rosi was crushed. She was sure Dan would hate her and that Dan's mother would forbid them from seeing each other.

They tried to watch some movies, but Angie did not like war movies, and just about everything else had a romance in it and made Rosi want to cry. So, Angie did her best to entertain her friend, by telling her gossip about high school life in New Richmond.

Finally, Rosi began to feel a little better. She could not tell Angie what had happened. All she could say was that she had felt cold and then had fallen over. It made her feel silly.

Angie clearly did not believe her. "You'll tell me when you're ready," she said with a sigh.

Angie did do a good job of distracting Rosi. Soon, they were giggling and laughing and screaming the way fifteen year old girls are supposed to. They cranked some tunes, grilled some burgers, lounged in the Jacuzzi, and talked about boys.

Rosi kept looking at the telephone, as if looking at it would somehow make it ring.

"Does he even have your number?" Angie asked later that evening. The two were lying on her bed eating popcorn and telling ghost stories in the dark.

Rosi sighed. "You know, I don't think he does."

"Then he probably won't be calling for some time," Angie yawned. She always got tired when the lights were off.

Rosi herself was nodding. Realizing Angie had fallen asleep, Rosi pulled up a thin blanket and draped it over the two of them. A few minutes later, she turned the television off and closed her eyes.

The two girls fell slept on the couch, side by side and hand in hand.

After a while, the quiet darkness was disturbed by a growing wind. Still asleep, Rosi pulled a blanket over the two of them. She was having a nightmare.

Rosi saw a storm. In flashes of lightning she saw figures that ran about the room, bringing in boxes, positioning themselves about the battlements. The men began firing their muskets at some far away foe. One man's shoulder exploded and he bled to death in muted anguish. The lightning made strobe like flashes, making the man's final throes look somewhat like an old nickelodeon reel, and his screams of agony sounded something akin to one of Uncle Richard's '78s with the volume turned down low.

The men continued firing and dying.

Rosi curled up closer to Angie as the temperature dropped lower and lower. The hellish snapshots flared up then blacked out.

More men rushed in. Sailing ships were filling the harbor, pouring forth spears of flame and claps of thunder into the night sky.

"Rosi."

"Mmm?" Rosi was barely awake.

"Do you have a warmer blanket?"

"Just a second."

"It's too cold and I'm having the strangest dream." Angie said.

"Me, too."

The two girls, still half asleep, sat up unsteadily. As one, they turned and looked around the room.

The sounds and sights came flooding in. Muskets fired. Cannons boomed. Men screamed.

The two girls clutched each other and watched as the town below burned with fires that were raging out of control.

One of the men, an older man, grabbed a younger man. "Go and warn Major Hanley," he bellowed over the noise. "Tell him to watch to his artillery and pull it out of range of those 50s. Beg

his pardon and ask if he would be so kind as to regroup his
cavalry by the lighthouse to form a flying unit."

"Yes, sir!" the younger man yelled back. He turned and ran
up the stairs.

Everyone ducked as an explosion shook the tower.

The two girls screamed and hugged each other.

The older man rose and brushed himself off. "Charlie!"

"Sir!" A very young boy carrying a bucket of water paused
just to throw the water onto one man's burning shirt then turned
to his superior.

"You must—" the older man began. Then the two were
forced to duck as a cloud of rock dust blasted through the room.
"You must," he continued as he helped the boy up. "Find Mr.
Phillips. My compliments to him and beg that he look to his
flanks. You have that, Charlie?"

No one would ever know what little Charlie's answer would
have been. The older man stood there looking at the stump that
was once his hand and the lower half of Charlie's torso. Charlie's
torso collapsed to one side, while the older man slid to the other.

The metal ball that had so ravaged the two bounced off the
other wall, dropped to the floor, and slowly rolled, its fuse still
burning, under Rosi's bed.

All the men in the room and on the parapet froze and stared
at the now not so empty void under the bed. Screaming, they
dove for cover.

Rosi and Angie did not have time to react. The force of the
explosion lifted them up and tossed them across the room with a
loud tearing sound.

Rosi landed, rolled, and ended up on her feet. Angie,
however, bumped her head against a stair. Rosi helped her to sit
up and hastily shoved an old t-shirt against her bleeding forehead.

"Is this some sort of joke?" Angie called out, barely audibly.

Rosi shook her head.

"Is this the dream you were having?"

Rosi nodded.

"How can we be having the same dream?" Angie pressed
hard down on her head and grimaced in pain.

"I don't know!" Rosi called back. Angie would be fine for a moment, and Rosi had to see what was going on.

Rosi rushed out onto the rampart and was stunned by what she saw. The port was filled with ships. Some were fighting each other, circling around in a wave born dogfight. The defenders' ships were clearly the smaller ones. Lightly armed fishing boats sent to sting the great fighting vessels. Desperate charges of would be Davids. Rosi watched as one British ship simply sailed over one of the smaller ships. She could even hear the crunch as it crushed the smaller one like a gnat. Some ships were firing cannons at the shore. Other ships were making their way to the land's edge to disembark rank after rank of red coated soldiers.

On the land it was chaos. There were skirmishes, battles, and charges. Much of the town was an inferno.

Rosi ran to the other side of the tower. Small pieces of lead and shrapnel whipped through the air about her. Her mind was trying to register what she saw there when Rosi felt herself being pulled away.

A young man with a scar on his right cheek was screaming right into her face. "Are you mad? Are you trying to die? Get out of here!"

He threw her into the room, right by Angie, who had started to step out after her friend.

The young man turned to Angie. "You, too, boy!" He lunged at her, his arm going right through her. "What the?" He stared at his hand sticking out from Angie's back. "Sweet Jesus."

At that moment, there was another great explosion that shook the tower. A large clump of stone hurtled through the air. Rosi watched aghast as it passed harmlessly through Angie and struck the young man in the chest, sending him backwards in a spray of bright red.

Seeing that her friend was fine, Rosi started to rush over to the fallen lad. She was stopped by Angie, who grabbed her and dragged her to the other side of the room.

"What are you doing?" Angie cried over the noise and cannons and screams.

"He was trying to help us!"

Rosi started forward again, but Angie kept a hold on her hand and jerked her back to the wall. Rosi stumbled, reaching out to catch herself by grabbing the handle of the odd door that was placed pointlessly on her back wall.

The door sprang open.

All of a sudden, time seemed to stand still. Rosi and Angie looked at each other, not sure what was going on.

Then came the noise.

Angie would later describe it sounding like a giant straw being sucked on in a giant empty glass. Rosi would have to agree.

The men began to drift slowly to the door. It was not a wandering kind of drift, but rather they slid through space. They were soon followed by the musket balls and the shot that hung still in the air. They all slid towards the door, and began slipping through it, winking out of sight with no warning. The slide became faster as the door sucked in the ships and the inferno and the soldiers and the bright morning sun. The scene rushed by the two scared girls. Then the door ripped out of Rosi's hand and slammed shut with a resounding thud that seemed to echo across the harbor.

Rosi and Angie sat there for a minute, unable to let each other go. Finally, they started breathing again. Then they began to cry.

Refusing to be alone, they crawled together over to the phone. Angie picked up the receiver and dialed a number. "Andy. It's me. Angie!" Her voice was shaking so much she barely recognized herself. "You'd better come out here. What? What?" She turned to Rosi. "Alone?"

"Yes," Rosi sobbed.

"Alone."

Angie did not bother hanging up the phone. She just let it fall from her hand and bounce once or twice on the floor, coming to a rest under the desk.

Neither of them needed to say what to do next. Rosi reached out with her foot and snagged a blanket, pulling it to her. Together, they crawled up the stairs and out to the front of the house.

That was where, about forty-five minutes later, Andy rode up on his bike and found them. They had wrapped the blanket around them so tightly they resembled Siamese mummies. Their teeth were chattering, even though the temperature was still securely over eighty, and tears were running out of their eyes and noses. It took them another ten minutes before they could speak to Andy.

That was fine with Andy, for it took him almost as long to catch his breath, even with the help of his inhaler.

Finally, the girls were able to speak. They were shaking and confused, so Andy practically had to interrogate them to find out what had happened.

Andy was fascinated. "I've heard of this before," he said.

"What is it?" the girls both wanted to know.

"The phenomenon doesn't have a scientific name. But it seems that there are occasions that people can actually see past incidents."

"We didn't just see it," Rosi protested. "We felt it."

"Not a lot is known about the phenomenon. As I said, it doesn't even have a name."

Angie broke in. "You're babbling. Tell us what we saw."

Andy thought for a minute. "You know that the British lost Boston in March, 1776. That meant that the only major base of operations in the north would have been Quebec. Not a lot of people back then knew too much about New Richmond. There is even some evidence to suggest that its Charter was actually different and it wasn't part of New Hampshire, but I've never seen any primary documents to support that. I'd have to see the Royal Archives or get to the British Museum to see those, and that isn't likely. It's a question of money, really. I'm sure I could make a strong enough case to gain access to most of the papers concerning—"

"Andy!" both girls screamed.

Andy returned to reality. "Oh. Well. In 1780, a British Admiral, Nathan Cromwell, a relative actually of THE Cromwell, formulated a plan to seize New Richmond. With a port of this size, he could control the sea access to most of the area. He could block the Maine Territories from Massachusetts. It was pretty clear to most English politicians that England would have to cede most of the colonies, but if New Hampshire were secure, all of the land that is now Vermont, New Hampshire, and Maine would have remained under the British sphere of influence. The face of American, and North American, politics and diplomacy would be vastly different. The Northern states would almost certainly have rejoined England in the 1810s. They almost did anyway. England would have been able to seize most, if not all, of the Louisiana Purchase territories after the war of 1812. That would have meant that the bulk of the U.S. would have been Southern states. There would still be slavery!"

"Relax, Andy." Angie was getting a little concerned as her boyfriend's face started turning red and his eyes glazed over.

"Oh, yes. What you saw. Maybe you both dreamed it."

"Nonsense!" came from both of them.

"Okay. Then you saw something. But what you described couldn't have been Cromwell's attack. Everyone knows that most of his fleet foundered on the reefs. His land forces were left unsupported and were wiped out. Cromwell died a bitter man in Barbados about twenty years later, still vowing revenge against the town and your ancestors, Rosi."

"My ancestors?" Rosi asked.

"Yes. This attack was very personal to him. That's the only thing I can think of that could possibly be what you saw. There were certainly expeditions to the area from Boston in the late seventeenth and early eighteenth centuries. Against fellow settlers or against the Indian tribes. Indeed, King William sent a fleet of four ships to the area for some reason in 1689, but all that is known about it is that it came. Nothing else. None of those incidents was large enough to possibly have been your vision."

Angie shook her finger at her boyfriend. "Don't you for one second doubt that we saw what we told you."

"I believe you. I believe you. Before I say anything with any certainly, I'll have to see your room, Rosi."

"God, I knew you were going to say that." Rosi did not want to go back there, but she understood why he would feel the need.

"Do you want to wait until morning? Until light?"

"Yes," Rosi said. "But we can't sit out here all night. Let's just get in and get it over with."

Andy took Angie's hand. Angie took Rosi's. The three of them edged in through the front door. Angie was proud that her man had taken the lead. Andy generally was not an active boy, but his desire for learning had driven all fear from him.

Doors swung open and slammed shut around them as they made their way to Rosi's room. The house seemed to moan and contract and expand with every step the three took. They could hear scurrying footsteps ahead of them, and then behind them, and then ahead again.

It crossed Rosi's mind that perhaps she should have tried to find Uncle Richard. Had he been around, he certainly would have shown himself by now. Not much happened in The Castle that Uncle Richard did not know about. Besides, there was something about the vision that she had seen that felt to her as if it was not Uncle Richard's concern. Exactly why it wasn't, Rosi could not discern. Uncle Richard was the Guardian. There had been something she had seen just before the boy had pulled her away from the edge of the battlement, something not quite right. There was something she was supposed to have seen. There was some reason she was supposed to have seen it.

Uncle Richard had once talked about an inexplicable force that drove the Guardians. There was nothing random about the times they visited and the events they adjusted. Uncle Richard was sure that there was a mathematical number, a constant, that guided the tears, the confusions, and the Guardians. There were numbers and patterns that appeared regularly in nature. Why not in time? When Uncle Richard was not fleecing the ancients of their wares, he was holed away, God and Uncle Richard only knew where, trying to figure out the pattern and put a number to it.

And why had Angie not forgotten? Rosi herself forgot any number of events before she began to figure out what was going on. She really did not know how many she had forgotten. She had simply forgotten them. Perhaps, if Angie had not forgotten it was because the event was not done, or rather, it was not with them yet.

Finally, the three reached the stairs and they stumbled down them as quickly as they could.

In front of The Castle, the night had been calm and the moon full and bright. By Rosi's tower, the night was dark, moonless and punctuated by commas of lightning.

"Fascinating," Andy thought. He let Angie's hand go and went over to the window to look out. To one side of the door out to the battlements, it seemed as if there was a storm going on that had yet to slide over to the other side of the tower. "Turn some lights on," he called out.

Rosi kept hold of Angie's hand and the two of them crept carefully along the wall, Rosi's other hand sliding up and down against the wall hoping to hit the light switch.

It hit the switch and someone else's hand at the same moment.

The lights came on.

* * *

SHOCKED, Rosi spun, saw four people in the room, and screamed. The four other people screamed, as did Angie and Andy.

Then they all stopped.

It was Kirk and Lois and two of Kirk's silent friends. The four of them were lurking along Rosi's wall.

"What the hell are you doing here?" Rosi asked.

Kirk was emboldened by his friends. "You've got secrets here, Rosi Carol."

"They're my secrets, jerk." Rosi was too tired to get into a fight, but she was really angry to see this kid in her room. "Andy! Call the sheriff."

"The phone's not working, Rosi," Kirk sneered and giggled at the same time.

Lois held up the frayed end of a phone cord.

"He's right, Rosi," said Andy. "It's not working."

Rosi didn't take her eyes off the intruders. She and Angie

were on one side of the room. Andy was on the other. The four weirdoes were between them. Rosi was still wrapped in the old blanket. She took it off, spun it tightly and flicked it out whip like, hoping to force the four away. Kirk flinched back slightly, but refused to back down. Lois hid behind Kirk, clinging to him.

"How did you get here?" Rosi demanded. "How did you get inside my house and my room?"

"I followed my nose," he laughed crinkling up his face tightly. "Tell me what we were seeing this afternoon. Don't pretend you don't know what I'm talking about. There's a secret that would give us such great power. We saw part of it at the barbecue."

"You're mad," Rosi retorted.

"Like a fox!" Kirk giggled rubbing his hands together gleefully. "This house is like a maze. Hard to find this room. Hard to find. But I did. I did. The treasure's mine. It belongs to me. Me! You stole it from me. You and your sacred ancestors think you're so special. What have you kept hidden from me? What do you owe me?" Kirk was drooling and specks of saliva flew from his mouth.

"I owe you naught," Rosi shot back.

"How long has your kind ruled this place?" Kirk snarled. "How long have you held this town back? How long have you held these people back? You've kept them, but can you keep them ever from the real world? This town is a farce. We are living in another time. There must be a reason other than your own obscene pleasure."

"And what obscene pleasure do you get stalking me in my bedroom? Why are you and your friends here? My secrets are mine. I would not share them with filth like you."

"Be careful," Kirk sang. "Names with never break my bones but this will cut you!" He pulled out a big knife.

"Jesus, Kirk!" Angie shrieked. She stepped forward, but Rosi grabbed her.

"This isn't your fight," Rosi told her friend.

Lois laughed. "Cut you! Cut you! Cut you!" She danced over to Andy. "Do you like me?"

"You're repulsive!" Andy shot back.

"You are so lying," she laughed. "He's so lying!"

"You making a move on my woman?" Kirk's eyes widened. "I'll take you after I'm done with this little witch."

"Leave him alone, Lois." Angie started for Andy, but one of the silent boys shoved her roughly to the floor.

Kirk waved his knife at Rosi, who backed away until she ran into the wall. "I'll take care of him when I am done with you," Kirk leered. "By the time I'm done with you, you'll tell me everything."

"There's nothing to tell you," Rosi said, trying to think of some way out of this. Something had seriously gone wrong with this boy. She much preferred the old Kirk, bully and creep as he was, to this. "Uncle Richard!" Rosi yelled as loud as she could. "Uncle Richard!" Rosi saw a flash of fear in Kirk's eyes. It left as quickly as it appeared.

"He's not here," Kirk crowed. He stepped in and raised his knife.

"I know where he is, Kirk!" Rosi said. "I know how to get to him. That's where the power is. Great power, to thrill the soul. Do you want that Kirk? Can you handle it?" She stepped towards him. "I can take you there. We can deal with these things, these beasts later. Andy? Wouldn't understand it if the power kicked him in the face. Angie? Useless. Can't see beyond this dump and that chump. Lois? A cow. You can see it. I can tell you can. You know the power is here."

"Yes, I do." Kirk simpered. "It is all around this building. Throughout the town. It's always there, just beyond touch. Just beyond smell. Such power, ill used by you—"

"Ill used by fools like my uncle. I see such potential, but I cannot touch him. That is a curse I must bear as a Carol."

"But I," Kirk said. "I am not of your blood. I can. I can! I can strike him down."

"Can you do that for me?" Rosi purred, slipping her hand in his.

"I would do anything for you."

"I would be ever so grateful," she whispered in his ear.

"Just show me where."

"Here!" Rosi threw herself and Kirk at the odd door. As soon as she touched the door, it swung open.

Rosi dove past the two silent boys and grabbed Angie and pulled her away from them.

"What the—" Kirk froze. He watched.

Kirk watched dumbly as his hand stretched out and drifted through the opening. His shoulder followed. In a blur of color, Kirk and the two silent friends were sucked through the door, which then slammed shut.

Lois, who had been standing on the other side of the room, started screaming. Rosi stepped for her. Lois turned and ran from the room.

"Oh crap," said Andy.

"You okay, sweetie?" Angie asked, not able to take her eyes from the door.

"Does peeing yourself count as an injury?" he asked, trying to laugh.

"No," said Angie.

"Welcome to the club," added Rosi. "Keep my hand, Angie. Let's go over to Andy."

Carefully, they stepped away from the wall and inched their way across the floor. They were in the middle of the floor, when the door swung open again.

Angie dropped to the floor and grabbed hold of Rosi's legs to keep from sliding forward. Screaming, she slid anyway, knocking Rosi over. Rosi reached out and tried to grab Andy, but he was just out of reach. Andy, upon seeing the door open, had wrapped both arms around the leg of the desk and refused to budge.

"Andy!" Rosi screamed. "Grab hold!"

The two girls nudged forward just a bit. Angie's legs were beginning to be pulled into the suction.

"Andy! Just reach out! Just reach out one hand! Andy!"

Andy finally opened his eyes and watched as his friends' bodies elongated and disappeared into the gaping maw of the doorway.

"Andy!" Rosi screamed.

They were moving further away. In a second, it would be too

late.

"Andy!"

Andy closed his eyes and prayed for strength. With a yell and with all of his strength, he wrapped his legs around the desk leg and dove for Rosi.

He missed her by a hair. The edge of her blanket brushed against his hand as it, too, followed the girls inside.

The door snapped shut again, leaving Andy alone, sobbing, and lying on the floor.

* * *

DAN approached the front door of The Castle and was surprised to find it open. He stepped in and was about to call out when he saw Lois running towards him. She was obviously terrified. She was in a panic and seemed about to cry.

"What's wrong, Lois?" Dan asked.

Lois simply screamed and ran away from him, moving deeper into the house.

Dan was in pretty good shape and should have caught her easily. It seemed, however, that every time Lois ducked through a door, she got further and further away from him. Finally he lost sight of her. He could tell that Lois had gone somewhere upstairs, but he could find no way to follow her.

There was one last, bloodcurdling shriek from Lois, which was followed by an even more unnerving silence.

Suddenly he heard more girls screaming. This sound he could follow, and eventually he came to what must have been Rosi's room. Dan had quickly looked around the room, grabbed a field hockey stick from the wall, and ran down the stairs screaming bloody murder hoping to startle whoever might be there. All he found was Andy, curled up on the floor, fumbling with his inhaler.

The room looked as if it had been in the middle of a tornado and it smelled like smoke and burnt matches, even though there was no sign of fire.

Making sure there was no one outside, Dan left the door to the ramparts ajar to let in some fresh air. He grabbed some wet towels and started to help Andy clean himself up a bit. It gave Dan time to think, and Andy time to relax enough to, Dan hoped, tell him what was going on.

PART II

Zilla's Farm

CHAPTER 6

EVENTUALLY, Rosi and Angie stopped screaming long enough to catch their breaths. Although she did not open her eyes, Rosi could tell that they were outside. The air felt like outside air. The singing birds sounded like outside singing. Rosi held on tightly to Angie, keeping her face buried in her friend's shoulder.

Angie clung back. "Rosi?"

"Yes, Angie?"

"Have you opened your eyes yet?"

"No." Rosi was not sure if she wanted to. It was not supposed to work this way. "Maybe Kirk is someplace around here." That would not be good. They would have to be careful. Slowly, carefully, Rosi opened her eyes. They were lying on the ground in the woods. "It's okay," Rosi said.

Angie opened her eyes to see a bright morning. It was bright enough she had to close her eyes again and then open them slowly. "How the—"

"What?"

"How? Where?"

Carefully, they unwrapped their arms from each other and stood. They were, indeed, in the middle of the woods. Spinning around and arcing their necks revealed no sign of anything other than more trees.

"Don't move," Angie whispered suddenly, grabbing Rosi's arms and holding her still.

"What is it?"

"We're being watched." Angie told her.

"Is it Kirk?" In the back of her mind, Rosi had a fleeting image of things far worse to be watching her than an annoying teenager, however vicious he might be.

"No." Angie sounded spooked.

Rosi's stomach dropped. Carefully, and oh so slowly, she turned her head. There, nestled behind a shrub, a face peered out at them.

Rosi tried to peer into the dark eyes to see if they told her anything. And then she got it. She let out a loud, piercing giggle. "Angie, you dork," she laughed.

The face disappeared and they could hear rustling.

"What?"

"It's a deer. Look!" Rosi pointed and the two girls watched a stag bound away through the trees and disappear over a rise.

"Well, how was I supposed to know?"

"The antlers kind of gave it away, and the 800 pound body with four legs and a tail."

They both laughed at Angie's unfounded fright.

"I don't think that a deer weights 800 pounds," Angie said.

"I don't know. I've never seen one before." Rosi had no idea what deer weighed. "I grew up in New York City after all! Jeez! Haven't *you* ever seen a deer before?"

"In movies." Angie answered. "So what do we do?"

Rosi thought for a moment. "Do you think we're anywhere near The Castle?" It would be a lot easier to figure out where they were than when.

Rosi remembered what Uncle Richard had said about people's minds reacting in different ways. She also remembered that he had explained that most people who experienced other whens experienced them very briefly. Prolonged exposure made it more difficult for the mind to rationalize and convert to remember-able events, and harder for Guardians to cover up.

"There are only so many islands in the South Pacific," Uncle Richard had once quipped in a rare show of humor. Rosi hoped he had been joking.

If she could get Angie back to The Castle and to their time fast enough, it was possible that Angie would then remember the whole thing as some sort of shared dream or a fugue state.

Rosi also needed to talk with Uncle Richard. She understood stepping through the doorways on purpose. She understood walking through a tear by accident. This time, something had reached out and brought her here. If the visions from last night, in her time it would have been earlier this evening, were connected, then she was being stalked. Whatever was going on certainly was not random. The first thing to do, though, was to get Angie out of the way.

"I'm not sure we're on Earth," Angie said, letting go of Rosi, but not moving away from her. "We just got sucked through a brick wall and it forgot to email me our itinerary."

Angie had a point, Rosi thought. "But, we saw a deer," she said. "We must be on Earth. I've never heard of alien deer, have you?"

"No."

"Well there you are." Rosi looked around. Of course, the question in her mind was: *Did a tear in the fabric of time and space have to be confined to one specific planet?* She had brought up the subject one morning a week earlier and Uncle Richard had changed the subject. "And I've never heard of an alien Maple tree," she said, pointing at the closest tree to them. "Logic," she added, just in case Angie had not followed her line of reasoning.

"Well, Rosi," Angie said after a minute. "We could stand here and discuss where we are, or we could go someplace and ask someone."

"Good idea. Let's move on."

They stood there staring at their toes.

"Rosi?"

"Yes, Angie?"

"Do you have any idea where we should go?"

"That's a very good question." Rosi thought for a moment. "No," she decided, finally. "If we are near New Richmond, we could go there."

"Ah. And where is that?"

Rosi considered her options. "No idea. But," she continued suddenly. "If we are near New Richmond, the ocean is bound to be close as well. If we find the ocean then we'll know more than we know now."

Angie nodded in agreement.

They considered their hands for a minute.

"Angie?"

"Yes, Rosi?"

"Do you have any idea how to tell what direction the ocean is in?" Rosi knew there had to be some quaint local trick to telling direction or figuring out which way was north. In movies, small town people always had some sort of innate connection with nature.

"You know, I should know that. I did grow up on it." Angie said. "Wait!" Rosi started to say something, but Angie held up her hand to silence her.

Rosi covered her mouth and held her breath.

Angie bent over and slowly began turning in a circle. Her left arm began to rise. One finger pointed to the sky. Then her nose turned upwards and pulled her face and head along with it. Angie spread her arms, her nose pointing high, and sniffed deeply.

"That way," she said, pointing. Angie started walking.

Rosi ran to catch up. "You mean you can smell the ocean?"

"Of course I can. Can't you?"

"I don't know. And you can smell the direction."

"No," Angie scoffed at the idea. "I can hear it. It isn't very far away.

Rosi put her hand to Angie's shoulder and stopped her. She listened for a second. She could clearly hear waves. She felt silly.

"And the sun rises in the East," Angie went on. "A rising sun, combined with the sound of the surf, gives me a pretty clear idea that the ocean is that way. "Besides," she started walking again. "That was a Pine tree."

"Oh." Rosi trotted to catch up to her friend. "It was an honest mistake."

"It's like mistaking a dog for a Volvo. What do they teach you down there in the big city?"

After a few minutes, they stopped and Angie dug pieces of twig from her feet. "Did you notice something?" she asked. "It's cold."

Angie was right, Rosi thought. It was cold. It felt nothing like summer, but more like late fall, or maybe early spring. Did they feel different? The air was briskly chilled, and occasionally there were small patches of frost on rocks and the sides of trees.

At first, the girls had been too confused to notice the cold. Now as they slowly trudged through the woods, the cold was beginning to hit home. Neither of the girls was wearing shoes. Angie only had on the t-shirt and gym shorts she had borrowed from Rosi the night before. Rosi's wardrobe was different only by the addition of the thin blanket she had been holding and absent mindedly slipped around her shoulders.

Rosi noticed that her breath was coming out in a light steam. She handed the blanket to Angie. "I've been wearing it the last ten minutes," Rosi pointed out, when Angie protested. "We'll trade off."

Angie pulled her hair and tied it back with a scrunchy that was on her wrist. Rosi did not have one, so she wove a loose braid and hoped it would keep her hair out of her face.

"We must look a sight," Angie noted.

The two laughed awkwardly. There was something not quite right about the atmosphere, but they could not place it.

As the sound of the waves got louder, they expected the woods to end, but the trees showed no sign of thinning out. Finally, the forest ended abruptly. There was a short distance, about fifty yards, to where the girls figured the water would start.

"Why can't we see the waves?" Angie questioned.

"Must be just over that set of dunes."

And they were, the girls discovered, at the bottom of a very long drop. They reached the edge of the sheer cliff so unexpectedly that Angie had to grab Rosi to keep her from going over. They looked up and down the coast, but could see no sign of civilization.

"That's odd," Rosi commented. "You should be able to see a city from here." There was no haze. It was an amazingly clear day. The sky was cloudless and the rich blue seemed to go on forever. The wind was a little chilly. Rosi mused that had she had been properly dressed she would have thought it a glorious day.

"We might not be near New Richmond," Angie decided. "We might not be near any kind of city." She sat down and patted the ground next to her.

Rosi sat down and they both pulled their legs up under their t-shirts and hooked the hems under their feet. They were stretching the shirts, but it was better than being cold. Angie wrapped the blanket around both of them and they blew on their hands for warmth.

The cliff stretched on to either side as far as they could see. Down below, there was a thin stretch of beach, but no way down could be seen.

It felt like they had been hiking through the woods for hours, even though it had probably been less than half an hour. Neither Rosi nor Angie could read the sun with any skill. The only thing they noted was that it was giving off precious little heat.

"My feet are sore. Perhaps we should rest for a little while," Angie suggested. "It will get a little warmer."

Feeling foolish, they wrapped themselves around each other as tightly as they could and tied the blanket to cover both of them as much as possible.

No longer having the hike to distract them, they began to get scared again. Angie must be really terrified, Rosi figured. She herself was scared, and she at least had some idea what was going on. Of course, she was generally forewarned, briefed, and often armed when she traveled, even when she was with Uncle Richard. *Armed might be nice*, she thought. *What with a crazy Kirk roaming around with a knife the size of a small sword.*

Angie was dropping off, Rosi noticed. She decided that she should stay awake, but the steady pounding of the sea eventually rocked her into an uneasy doze.

The sun rose a little higher and the temperature dropped.

* * *

ROSI awakened first. It was later morning. She could tell that much from the sun.

She then disentangled herself from Angie, who flopped over on one side and mumbled in her sleep.

"Shh," said Rosi. "Sleep."

Angie curled up into a ball and continued to sleep.

After having retreated into the woods for nature's call, Rosi

ventured up and down the dunes. She was surprised to see a
sailing ship standing to the south a short distance out. She
thought about trying to get their attention, but figured the ship
was too far out. She walked a bit north before she saw some
figures walking along the beach. She sat down and waited for
them to approach.

As they got closer, she counted five people in the group. Rosi
was about to stand up and give a shout, when she noticed that
two of the men were treating the other three roughly. They were
pushing the others—with guns. The two men wearing red jackets
were carrying rifles. Rosi hunkered down and watched a little
more carefully. No one acted as if they had seen her.

The two men with rifles were apparently guards, Rosi
guessed. They were rushing their prisoners, who tripped and
stumbled along the beach, to the south. They seemed to be in a
hurry.

About the time they reached a spot just below her, Rosi
realized that the three prisoners were Kirk and his pals. She also
recognized the uniforms that the two guards were wearing.

This is not good.

Something out to sea caught Rosi's eye. There was some
activity aboard the ship. Rosi squinted and tried to see as far as
she could. All she could tell was that a boat was being lowered
into the water.

Rosi decided not to call out, but to follow the small group
and see what was happening. After a minute or two, Rosi drew
ahead of Kirk and the others below. This gave her time to look
around and try to figure out where she might get down to the
beach.

The ship's boat seemed to be headed for a spot some
distance ahead of Rosi, so she decided to head for the same
point. If those guns were real, then Rosi could not do anything
for Kirk. But maybe she could find out something about what
was going on.

About a quarter of a mile down the coast Rosi found where
the ship's boat was heading. There was a small inlet where the
beach broadened and the surf was further off the beach. The

bluff hooked around to protect this little area.

Now, if Rosi could only find a way down. It did not look like too difficult a climb, but Rosi did not want to be seen. She needed some sort of path.

Like the one just over there. It looked like it could get her to the bottom quite nicely, and give her time to find some cover.

Her father had given her an invaluable lesson on downhill skiing. "Getting down the hill is the easy part," he explained. "Gravity will do it for you." Climbing cliffs, Rosi decided, was much he same. The path ended suddenly about half way down the cliff. Rosi slid much of the rest of the way. Her butt, or what was left of it, was going to be pretty sore. *Thanks, Daddy*, she thought.

Rosi tried to remember if her father had given her any follow up advice for when the slope ended as well. The final twenty feet were done in free fall, with a landing cushioned by a low dune and its sharp, stiff grass. She would have landed quite easily, but her left arm had caught briefly on a root and had spun her around. The arm gave out when she tried to push herself up. There was blood on her hands and she could feel that her upper arm had been badly cut or torn but did not have the time to investigate. It was only luck that had kept the men's eyes from turning and seeing her.

Rosi shook some sand out of her eyes and realized she was half buried in the dune. She raised herself up and glanced through the tall blades to see Kirk and his friends being led right to her. She dropped down, hoping no one had seen her, and dug herself down into the sand. She gave herself just enough room to shake her head, breathe, and listen.

Rosi could hear them trudge through the sand. She heard Kirk and the two silent boys being pushed, none too gently, down. Kirk, by the sound of things, was not happy with his treatment.

"Easy, you clod!" he snapped. "And get that thing out of my face or I'll shove it up your—"

"'Ere!" cried out one of the guards. "None of that language, you little brat."

"You'll be sorry," Kirk yelled defiantly.

He was obviously scared, and Rosi was surprised that he was speaking so boldly to the men with the guns. It crossed her mind to wonder if they were carrying rifles or muskets. She had not really thought about it during the last few minutes, but she was beginning to get an inkling of when they were. The lecture from Andypedia probably should have clued her in.

"Shut your gob," the other guard snarled.

At that moment, Rosi realized that her foot was not covered. She squiggled it under, causing some sand to slide down.

"What was that?" the first guard said.

"Yer hearin' things, Connor," the other man said. He sounded nervous.

"I'm hearin' nothing. You check that out, Paulsy." They both sounded a bit apprehensive.

"Check it out yerself, Conner"

"Y'see these stripes? That means you check out what I tells you to."

Someone climbed to the top of the dune and came to a stop, standing on Rosi's hand. "There's nothing 'ere," he called back. "Probably some fish stuck in tidal pool. Do y'have tea? Could use tea. Is cold." He stomped to warm his feet and Rosi bit hard on her cheeks to keep from screaming. She was sure she heard a crack. The sharp pain was almost a relief from the dull throb from the now freely bleeding gash in her arm.

"I don' like being this far from camp," Connor said. "See rebels in every tree. Thank God they cannot shoot straight."

"Start bloody fire, Connor. Put kettle on. Make tea."

"I ha' better than tea, boyo. I got rum. Sergeant Major give it me. Keeps body warm in morning. Come on over."

Paulsy spun on Rosi's hand, tearing the skin, and stomped off. Rosi carefully pulled her hand back in. In moments the two of them were enjoying their drink and loudly complaining about the fool officers who had sent them here with the prisoners to meet with someone from the navy. They were not too pleased with the assignment. They could have taken these boys to a ship much closer to camp and been done with them, but word had come back that these boys were to be kept quiet and out of sight until the admiral's man saw them. It was all mysterious and sounded somewhat like spying to the two soldiers, who clearly did not like spies, whoever they might belong to.

"Boat approaching," Paulsy said finally. "Y'owe me a shillin'!"

"Spit!" Connor said. Then he called out "Oy!"

"Ahoy there!" Someone called back.

"'Bout bloody time, Paulsy."

"Trust sodding Royal Navy to be late and leave us out here in cold."

"Thank God for Jamaican rum."

Someone else was approaching. The man from the boat, Rosi supposed.

"We received a signal to meet someone here," the man said. He certainly sounded more educated that the first two.

"Aye, sir," Connor snapped out loudly, confirming Rosi's suspicion that the other man was an officer.

"Quiet, man. Do you want every man-jack local to know we're here?"

"Miles from any town, sir," Connor said. "Sodding commandant sending us out to middle of nowhere."

"Quite. I suppose you can tell me why we were sent to the middle of nowhere," the officer said.

"No, sir. I can na' do tha'. 'Bring those boys' is what the commandant says. So we bring 'em. I don't know much about them exceptin' they were found about a week ago."

"And what are these odd garments? Some sort of injun clothing. At least the shoes."

One of the men, Rosi supposed it was Connor as Paulsy had not said anything since the officer arrived, grunted.

The officer hemmed and hawed for a moment. "Do you have any more of that rum, Sergeant?"

"What rum, sir?" Connor sounded truly confused at the question.

"The rum in the bottle in your friend's hand, you fool."

"That rum!" Connor said sounding genuinely surprised. "It

was here when we got here. Must ha' been left by smugglers.
Devil's drink, you know. Never touch the stuff, of course. Bad
for morale."

"You and your man go over to the boat and share out your
rum with the members of my crew or I'll have them shoot you
and they'll still get the rum."

"I was just thinking about offering them some, sir," Connor
blustered. "Come along, Paulsy."

Rosi heard footsteps move off and some unintelligible words.
There was a soft cheer.

"Young man," said Mosley.

"Who the hell are you?" Kirk demanded.

"I am Lieutenant," he said, pronouncing it *leftenant*. "The
Honorable Beaumont Mosley."

"What kind of fairy name is that? Beaumont!" Kirk sang out
mockingly.

"Who are you?" Mosley asked.

"Wouldn't you like to know?"

"Young man, the Royal Governor signaled my Admiral that
he, or rather, you, had important information for us. I was sent
here to get that information."

"I would rather speak to your Admiral." Rosi had never heard
Kirk this aggressive.

"I am the Admiral Cromwell's aide. You speak to me, and the
words go straight to the Admiral's ear."

"I would see his face when I spoke to him."

"I see." So far, Lieutenant the Honorable Beaumont Mosley
had been quite charming. Now his voice turned hard and cold.
"Young man, you and your friends are wasting my time and that
of the Admiral. I have no idea why, other than, perhaps, to
hinder our progress. You must be spies. I realize that spies are
generally hanged, but I see no trees. Shooting you would make
too much noise. I shall have my men drown you. Good day."

"Wait, lieu—lieutenant," Kirk was clearly terrified.

"What?"

"I—I have information for your Admiral."

"What sort of information?"

"I'd rather—"

"I'd prefer if you told me." Lieutenant Mosley had a piercing, commanding voice. "At the very least you could tell me the nature of you information."

Kirk seemed to be considering his situation.

"Boy," said Mosley companionably. "If your information has real value, you will find Admiral Cromwell most generous. If the information is volunteered. If necessary, however, we can find ways of encouraging you to tell us what you know. I prefer the first option. It is more… civilized."

"I can get you into New Richmond," Kirk said. "By sea," he added.

"That is interesting. You know the reefs?"

"I can find you the charts. There are secret ways into and out of that area. I know some of them. I can help you find out the others."

"And what is it that you want in exchange?" Mosley asked. Rosi could tell Kirk had the officer hooked. If he could provide access to New Richmond, then Mosley would pay handsomely.

"There is something…."

"What?"

Rosi felt like echoing the Englishman.

"A…family heirloom. A family treasure. It has been stolen from my family. Cromwell can help me find it."

"What is this heirloom?" Mosley pushed. "Does it have any real value? You are betraying your people—"

"They are no people of mine," Kirk said, his voice getting excited. "Let them all die, I say. When I find my heirloom, there will be other treasures. Great wealth. I'm sure even your Admiral could share. Or you."

"All Admiral Cromwell wants is to take New Richmond."

"I know." Kirk giggled.

How much will you give away? You idiot? Rosi bit her tongue.

"How do you know?" Mosley snapped. "His plans have been kept secret."

"All ships leak. Will you take me to your Admiral?"

"Yes. Sergeant!"

Rosi could hear Connor puffing as he sprinted over.

"Untie this boy. He will be coming with me."

"And the other boys?"

"I have no need for them." Mosley left, taking the giggling Kirk with him.

Rosi heard the Lieutenant bark some orders to his sailors and the boat being dragged out to deeper water.

"Bloody officers," Connor swore. He kept his words under his breath, even though the boat had had plenty of time to get some distance from the beach. "That's a strange one even for the Navy."

"Watch it, Connor," Paulsy hissed back at his friend. "I've heard of this one, Connor," Paulsy's voice shook a little. "Don't cross him."

Connor hawked and spat loudly. "'Ere, 'elp me search these two." After a minute, Connor groaned. "Junk! Rubbish! Any rum left?"

"A swallow for each of us, Connor."

"Give it to boys."

"Connor!"

"Ungag them and give them swallow. They deserve that much."

"Yer soft touch, Connor."

"Be quick 'bout it, boyo. The tide is coming in fast now."

Rosi heard the two boys gasp for air. Paulsy forced some rum into them, which made at least one of them cough and choke.

"Easy does it," said Connor kindly. "Sorry 'bout this, lads."

One of the men grunted. Rosi heard someone gargling and some wet thrashing.

One of the boys cried out and apparently tried to run away.

"Connor!" Paulsy cried out.

"I've got 'im. Give me a hand."

There was another grunt.

"Let's get out of here, Connor."

"Aye, Paulsy. Let's go. It's a bit of a hike back to town."

The two soldiers whistled as they walked off. Rosi could hear them splashing in the fast rising water.

Rosi had needed to cough for the last fifteen minutes, but she held it in. *Better safe than sorry*, she thought. Finally, when she figured that Connor and Paulsy would be around the bend, she dug herself out of the sand. Rosi tried to stand, but her legs gave way and she rolled down the dune and came to a stop half under water in a tidal pool.

"Crap," she said. A stranded fish took one look at her and scurried as far away as it could.

When Rosi put her hands down to stand up, she almost screamed. Tears sprang to her eyes. She jerked her left hand up and looked at the bloody skin and the awkwardly bent and mangled fingers. Her upper arm looked like half of it was missing. She had no idea how bad it was, but it could not be good. She tied the tail of her t-shirt in a loop and stuck her hand in it. The movement caused her excruciating pain, but, once it was done, she was able to let her arm rest.

Rosi looked out to sea. The boat was being hoisted aboard the ship.

She thought about what she had witnessed over last half hour. Rosi had not had any idea where the door in her bedroom led. Actually, she had thought the doorway extinct. Somehow, it had escaped Uncle Richard's notice. Or, he had not commented on it for some reason. Somehow, events from the doors other side had bled through into Rosi's time so that she and Angie could see them. This she knew happened from time to time. She had never before experienced anything quite so vivid. There were the red coated soldiers. There was this Admiral Cromwell. She thought about what Andy had been speaking about earlier.

"Kirk, you've screwed us all, you creep," Rosi muttered under her breath.

She hunkered down for a few more minutes until the ship had started moving on. Rosi climbed to the top of the small dune and looked around. Below her, at the water's edge, the two silent boys lay. A river of red flowed from each of them into the ocean and dissolved in the incoming tide. One's face was turned towards her. His eyes were empty, silent. The other boy had made it only about ten feet before he had been caught. Whoever had slashed his throat had all but decapitated him. Rosi hoped it had been fast, but she remembered hearing them die. She could not look.

At her feet, a length of cloth that had gagged one of them lay next to a pile of the junk Connor and Paulsy had decided not to take with them. Panting to keep from throwing up, Rosi shoveled the silent boys' junk onto the cloth and tied it closed. It was difficult with one hand and her teeth, but she managed without swallowing too much sand. She looped it around her good arm and started back to the cliff when her foot hit something.

Looking down, Rosi saw the bottle of rum. There was half a swallow left. It burned her throat and lay heavily in her empty stomach, but it warmed her slightly.

She looked up at the cliff. Sure enough, the path was clear and easy to maneuver, if only she could get the twenty feet or so straight up to it. If only she had not been so stupid as to leave Angie. If Angie knew where she was, she could help. One thing Rosi did know about Angie was that she was not stupid. She would wait for Rosi. She would not want Rosi coming back from exploring to not find anyone.

Eventually, of course, Angie would move. But who was to say that she would come south. Rosi seemed to remember that the ground up there sloped downhill slightly to the north. Angie would most likely go north.

There did not seem to be any way to get up the cliff other than the way Rosi came down. What about moving along the beach? To the south the beach ended. To the north? Connor and Paulsy were bound to stop at some point to rest and eat lunch. What would happen if Rosi stumbled onto them?

She had a pretty good idea. The two boys half floating in the water nearby had been lucky.

Rosi felt sick to her stomach. She wanted to throw up. She wanted to sit down and rest. The tide continued to rise. Soon, most of this little inlet would be under water. Rosi could not stay here.

She had to get to New Richmond somehow. She had to warn the people there. She had to figure out what to say. How could

Kirk change anything? Ships could either get into the harbor or not. Kirk certainly could not alter that, could he? What were these ways into the New Richmond harbor Kirk had spoken about? And what was this stupid treasure he wanted?

Angie would know what to do. She always knew the right thing to do. Rosi wished Andy were here. He would know exactly what was going on. She wished Dan were here. He could get her out of here and take care of her.

It took about twenty minutes to reach the foot of the path. One foot per minute. Actually, it was several bad falls, a bloody nose, at least one loose tooth, cracked shins, banged knees, skinned elbows, and more than one blinding jarring of her left arm before she was able to scramble up, gripping at any and every conceivable foothold, and some inconceivable ones, with her bloody fingers and toes, and reach the narrow path that led to the top of the cliff. Even once she reached the path she did not so much climb as throw herself up, foot by foot.

The sun was high by the time Rosi reached the top. Dripping with sweat, coughing, spitting, retching, sobbing, and freezing, she collapsed on the top of the cliff and looked out to see the ship slip around the wall of land and out of sight.

Rosi looked down at the inlet. Her sand dune was the only thing not covered by the rising tide. One silent boy's body was floating gently with the water, bouncing against the sand, and looking blankly into the sky. The other body was not there. Rosi found it a few moments later. It had been carried out and was being pulled south by the current. Rosi wondered if she could have done anything for them. She had not even closed their eyes. She had been too startled by the sight of them.

Rosi, like her father, believed in God. Like her father her faith was little more than an abstract belief, perhaps based more on the hope for the divine than in a concrete belief in a Christian God. This whole idea of romping through time suggested to her that even this vague hope was misplaced. For some reason though, Rosi said her first prayer since she had prayed in vain months ago for her father.

These silent boys had meant little to Rosi. Indeed, the only time they had ever interacted with her, they had threatened her. However, they had done no evil so great that they deserved this death. She could imagine the fear, the sense of abandonment, the despair, the loneliness they must have felt those last few moments on the beach. The terror the one must have felt as he made his futile yards' long dash for freedom. Perhaps worse was that they faced death at the hands of men who were so completely devoid of compassion or remorse.

Did these boys, silent outsiders, have mothers? Fathers? Siblings? Girlfriends? Who loved them? Who would miss them? Would anyone sit up late at night and weep to see their boys once more? Once more to hold them in a tender embrace and kiss away their fears? Who would post their photographs? Who would mourn them? Who would lay flowers on their empty graves? Who would hear a doorbell and be filled with a sudden rush of joyous hope, only to be crushed on the opening? Who?

Perhaps, Rosi prayed, someone, somewhere, somewhen, would. Perhaps somehow, these boys would be at peace. Whatever their sins might have been, as far as Rosi could tell, their deaths could be laid at Kirk's feet. Once Rosi got Angie home, she would deal with Kirk.

She stood up and spent a moment collecting herself. She was somewhere near New Richmond. Rosi figured that much from the conversation between Kirk and Mosley. She looked around and swore loudly. There, a couple of miles to the south, an easily recognizable, oddly shaped building rose above some surrounding trees.

Rosi knew exactly where she was.

Rosi knew when she was.

They were going to need help. But how? She had better get to Angie.

"And where would you be going, boy?" came a voice behind her.

Rosi spun around to see the barrel of a rifle pointed right at her face.

* * *

THE makeshift braid Rosi had woven a few hours ago took that moment to unravel. Rosi had not cut her hair in months and it was getting long. The hair served to reinforce the gravity of the mistake.

"I beg you pardon, miss."

It was a young man. Indeed, Rosi noticed right away that it was the young man with a scar on his face whom she and Angie had seen earlier in her room.

"Who are you?" Rosi said.

"Miss, I'm the one asking questions here. Where are your clothes?"

"What are you doing here?"

"Answer me first."

Rosi stared at the barrel of the rifle. On closer inspection, it looked like one of those muskets she had seen at museums. Whatever it might be, she did not want it pointing at her face. "Get that thing out of my face."

"What?"

Rosi reached out and slapped away the barrel. "I told you to get that thing out of my face!"

The young man was nonplussed, but before he could speak, Rosi went on. "Now, if you want to ask some questions, ask them nicely." She closed her eyes. "I have had a bad day."

"Do you need to sit, miss?"

Rosi did not bother answering. She let her legs collapse and sat heavily. Pain shot through her hand, up her arm, and through the entire left side of her body.

When she opened her eyes, she saw that the young man had set aside his musket and had dropped to one knee beside her.

"You aren't well," he said.

Over his shoulder, Rosi could see Angie tiptoeing up, holding a large branch.

"I'm feeling much better," Rosi lied. "Could you give me a hand?" She reached out and, grabbing one of his arms for support, threw her weight to one side. She was not able to knock him over, but she was able to screw up his balance.

Angie seized the moment to leap forward and bring the

branch down on his head with a satisfying thump.

"Run!" Angie screamed.

Rosi forced herself to her feet and stumbled towards the tree line.

"Miss!" she heard after a moment.

"Miss! I will shoot your brother!"

Rosi stopped and turned.

Angie was lying on her back and the gun was pointed at her stomach.

"I will shoot him. Come over here and help him up."

Rosi moved slowly over and held out her hand. Angie waved it away, standing up on her own, her eyes flaming. "Boy?" she snapped, reaching out and slapping the young man on the chest.

"Angie," Rosi warned.

"Boy?" Angie snatched up a clump of dirt and threw it at him.

"Watch it!" he cried.

"I'm no more a boy than she is."

"He thought I was one, too," Rosi said weakly, taking that moment to sit down again. She was feeling positively dizzy.

"You thought she was a boy? You're not only stupid, you're blind!" Angie reached out and slapped the young man's chest again.

"You know…miss," he started. "I am the one here with the gun."

Angie slapped the barrel away and kicked him in the shin. "Ouch!" she cried out, dancing around until the pain in her toe abated.

"What are you doing?" the young man cried.

"You broke my toe!"

"I did nothing!" he protested.

"You broke a girl's toe!"

"Hey!"

"And what did you do to Rosi?"

"Her?"

"Look at her! If you hurt her…."

"I found her like that! Hey!" he cried out as Angie threw

another clump of dirt at him. "That was a rock."

"Good!" Angie thumped him on the chest again.

"Look! I will shoot you."

"You will not!"

"I won't?"

"No!" Angie reached out and punched the back of his hand sharply with the knuckles on her right hand. With her left hand, she snatched the musket away.

"Hey!"

Angie pointed the musket up into the air and pulled the trigger. The powder flared, there was a dull crack and a puff of smoke came out of the barrel. The musket ball shot harmlessly over the trees, whistling through some of the higher branches and scaring a few birds to flight.

"What do you think you are doing?" the young man demanded.

"Just a little trick my father taught me," Angie crowed. She dropped the musket and turned to Rosi. "Rosi!"

Rosi could barely follow what was going on. Her hand was constantly throbbing and her arm felt like it was on fire. The rest of her felt like she was encased in ice.

"Rosi?" Angie took the blanket and wrapped it around her friend. "You! Boy!"

"It's Will," the boy said.

"I don't care. Give me a hand with her. Give me your coat. Now!" Angie took the coat and wrapped it around Rosi. "Do you live far from here?" Angie asked Will.

He thought for a moment. "Not too far."

"I'll carry the gun. You carry her. Gently!"

Rosi felt herself being lifted up.

Will started off, walking along the tree line for a few minutes, and suddenly turning into the trees and following a path Rosi and Angie would never have found on their own.

Soon, the ocean was out of sight as they moved deeper into the forest.

CHAPTER 7

THEY were in a room. It was dark, even with the candles on the tables and the fire that burned cheerfully.

Rosi lay on a cot on the floor near to the fire. One side of her was too hot, and the other ice cold. Her arm was throbbing, and fingers of heat streaked up the side of her head and down along her back. She bit back a scream. It would not serve any purpose.

"You're awake," said Angie.

With difficulty, Rosi turned her head and looked for her friend. Angie was walking toward her. She was wearing the stupidest, bulkiest, most shapeless dress Rosi had ever seen.

"What is that?" Rosi asked.

"It's a dress." Angie said, clearly not happy with the idea.

"I figured that out," Rosi laughed weakly. "I mean, you look like Hester Prynne."

"A hundred points for obscure references, but I'll dock you ten—no letters on me anywhere, no matter the color." Angie helped Rosi sit up a little, and shoved a hard pillow under her head.

"What's going on?"

"You wouldn't believe me if I told you."

"Try me."

"Eat some first," Angie said, as she moved to an old looking stove and taking a wooden bowl from inside it. "I know it smells pretty bad, but it doesn't taste much better." She started to spoon some into the ailing girl's mouth.

Angie was right. The food tasted little better than it smelled. However, it did even out the warmth a little.

"We have to get to New Richmond," Rosi said as Angie took the bowl away. She started to get up.

Angie rushed over and gently shoved Rosi back down. "You're not going anywhere," she said.

"I have to warn them."

"You're not strong enough."

"I'm plenty strong," Rosi protested weakly.

"Besides," Angie laughed. "You're naked."

Rosi lifted the blanket a little and looked. Angie was right.

"Give me my clothes."

"I would. Look, your stuff was ruined. We practically had to peel it off you."

"Angie!"

"Don't worry, Will didn't look."

"Will?"

"The guy who found us."

Rosi remembered. "The guy you beat up?"

"Yeah," Angie giggled. Rosi tried to join in but only started coughing. "Your arm's pretty messed up, Rosi," Angie said, sobering suddenly.

"Yeah. I got that."

"Will thinks it is infected. He's gone to find help."

"How long have we been here?"

"A few hours. Not too long."

They sat for a few minutes, trying to enjoy the fire.

"Angie?"

"What is it?"

"What is today?"

"March 25th."

"I see."

"Rosi, it gets worse. The year. It's seventeen—"

"Eighty," Rosi finished for her.

"How did you know that?"

"I saw Kirk." *Well, in for a penny.* Slowly, carefully, haltingly, Rosi told Angie what she had seen and heard. Before Angie had a chance to respond, Rosi told her what she knew about the Carol family secret.

"Jesus!" Angie hissed when Rosi was done.

"You believe me, don't you?" Rosi asked. She was afraid Angie would be angry.

"Well," Angie started. "That explains a lot. I think.

Somebody's got to have figured it out by now."

"Uncle Richard explained that to me. He said that on an emotional level, most people are simply unable really to comprehend the idea of being in another time or that linear time is not right—"

"But there are all sorts of books and movies about time travel."

"They are fiction. Anyway," Rosi went on, not sure if she was explaining this correctly. "It's a kind of collective repression. You come up with stories and tall tales and myths to explain something you otherwise wouldn't be able to accept."

Angie had a lot of questions and Rosi tried to answer them as best she could. However, she did not know the answers to most of them.

"So," Angie said finally. "Who have you met?"

"Nobody, really."

"You've been traveling through time with your uncle, and you haven't met anyone. C'mon!"

"He usually goes to country houses and buys furniture. Obscure French aristocrats, Chinese mandarins. I don't speak the languages, so I really don't know who they are." Uncle Richard had told Rosi that she needed to start studying languages. "I met Mozart, once. Uncle Richard needed a piece of music for a collector."

"What was he like?"

"Mozart? Drunk. We went to the *Titanic*, but left before it hit the ice berg. Beautiful ship. The clothing, though. How could women dress like that? At least Uncle Richard never makes me wear a corset. So many layers. Trust me, women never needed to be given the pill for equality, all we needed was pants. And Shakespeare tried to kiss me. Even offered to write me a sonnet."

"And. I mean. Shakespeare!" Angie's mouth was agape.

"You realize these people never brushed their teeth. They bathed maybe once a year. Yuck! Uncle Richard doesn't really like to associate with artists too much. Says they're vulgar and low. The few once-in-a-millennial geniuses I've met make me kind of agree." It struck Rosi that her father had never socialized with his stable of writers that much. He would go to business events, publication parties, and the like. They did not, however, often come to his home.

"Anyway," Rosi said, determined to come back to the present, or the past, or whenever they were. "We need to get to The Castle. I need to get you back home. Then I need to come back and warn everyone before Kirk does whatever he's going to do and screws everything up."

"Kirk's not stupid," Angie said. "By now he's figured out what is going on. At least to some degree. Why does he need to get into New Richmond at all? At least with an army."

"He still thinks the family Carol treasure is a physical treasure. Gold. Paintings. Money. Or perhaps he thinks there is some sort of machine or object that sent him back here."

"When all along it's you."

Rosi shrugged. "Yeah. Perhaps his greed will keep him from figuring it out before I can fix everything."

"If you can."

"If I can. Kirk being here is bad news. So, you have to get me some clothes!"

"This was all that was here. I mean it. Look around, there's only the one room."

The room was simple. It was a square made of logs. There was no ceiling, just the roof and its supports. Whoever these people were, they were poor. All they had was a couple of cots, a rickety table, tree stumps as chairs, and some firewood. There were only a few knickknacks and small handful of books.

"Will is coming back soon with someone to look at you. Maybe he can find a doctor."

"Are we in a big village?"

"Didn't you see anything when we came? There's no village here. Three cabins of some sort. Lots of trees. Not even a proper road."

"Then he's not gone to find a doctor."

"Probably not," Angie agreed.

"He'd better get here soon. We don't have time." Rosi sat up, but she was weak. Tired.

Angie pushed her friend back down. "You just lie back and rest some. We'll warn them when you're better. We have a week and a half," Angie smiled, trying to make the best of it.

"That long? Then I definitely have time to rest." Rosi leaned her head back, intent on not falling asleep. She was asleep in seconds.

Angie pulled up the one real chair in the room, the one with a back, and sat next to the fire to keep warm. If and when Rosi awoke, she would be sure to see a friendly face.

* * *

ROSI awakened to renewed pain. Someone had put a damp cloth over her face and she could not see anything other than a dull red glow.

"Leave, child," a woman commanded as she grabbed Rosi's arm to stop her from removing the cloth.

"It's okay," she heard Angie tell her. Someone, presumably Angie, took her right hand.

Someone else, presumably the woman, began exploring her left hand with calloused yet gentle fingers. If Rosi knew anything about medicine, and she really did not, she knew that the examination was expert. The fingers probed and moved carefully up the arm. Rosi winced and moaned, but tried not to make too much noise.

Finally, the probing was done, and Rosi felt her hand placed down on her stomach.

The woman took the damp cloth from over her eyes and wiped Rosi's face carefully.

"That is not so bad, is it, child?" The woman asked loudly.

"No, I guess not. Is that it?"

"I haven't yet begun." She dipped the cloth in some warm water, wrung it out, and wiped Rosi's face again. "I will begin, by and by."

She was a tall woman. Rosi thought she had once probably been quite nice looking, but time and toil had taken their toll. She could not be more than thirty or thirty-five, but she looked much older. Her straight black hair was flecked with gray. Her skin was unwrinkled, but her kind brown eyes were tired and looked to have not been happy for a long while. Her nose was broad and flat and her lips slightly thicker than they should have been. Her complexion was too dark for a New Englander in March. Perhaps she was Hispanic somehow. Were there Spanish in the colonies? There must have been.

"My name is Zilla," the woman said. "My boy Will told me who you were."

"I'm Rosi."

"Yes. And you are Angie," Zilla said turning towards the other girl. "Will told me you gave him a right good beating."

"Yes, ma'am," said Angie.

"Don't be embarrassed, little girl. I have no doubt he deserved it. If not from you, then from me. You saved me from the effort. For that I am grateful."

"Ma!"

Rosi craned her head around and saw Will standing on the far side of the room, trying to be as small as possible.

"What are you still doing here, boy?" Zilla had the most peculiar accent. It sounded familiar, Rosi thought, but she could not place it. "Didn't I tell you to fetch some water?"

"I'm goin' Ma."

"And fill the pot, boy! Fill it all the way. And heat it on the fire outside."

Will left, slamming the door on his way out.

"And bring the water in when it is boiling, boy!" she shot out after him.

"Ma!"

Angie and Rosi could not help but smile to each other. They liked Zilla already.

Zilla turned her gaze on them. "He's a bright boy, don't get me wrong. But he does not listen. Like his father, he is. But don't you go telling him I said that. I taught him to read when he was a lad and I ruined him for useful work and chores. Always drifting back to his books. They are over there," she announced proudly, pointing at a small shelf on which were maybe six thick books. "He's a good shot, I'll give him that. But for field and house he's as useless as a child. I'll never find a wife for him if he can not push a plough."

"I'm sure you have plenty of time for that, ma'am," Angie said.

"He's seventeen years of age, little girl. He's ripe. He should be plucked before he gets soft around the edges. And don't you go calling me ma'am, little girl. I was born Zilla and I'll die Zilla and I'm content with what I am and don't go pretending to be someone better. But I've raised myself a bit of a wise fool in that boy Will."

"He seems very nice," Angie protested, laughing.

"To be whupped by a little thing like you? Begging your pardon, little girl. And then to be taken in by your story. No! I can tell a story when I hear one. I've been told enough of them in my lifetime. I may have done some foolish things in my life, but I could always tell when I was being told a tale." Zilla looked at the two of them for a moment. "To begin with, you are not sisters. I cannot believe even someone as knuckle headed as my boy could have believed that."

"We could have had different fathers," Angie tried.

"Yes, you could have. But you didn't. He said you lived on a farm in the Maine Territories and were being sent to Boston by relatives."

"Yes."

Angie, you're a genius, thought Rosi.

"Have you ever pushed a plough, little girl? Can you tell wheat from chaff? When do you pick the ear? When the weight has bent the stalk or before?"

"It was a dairy farm?"

Angie! Rosi could have screamed. *Don't give in so easily!*

"Have you ever grabbed a cow by her teat? Tell me, how do you castrate a pig? What is whey?"

Angie was turning slightly green around the edges.

"Do not worry, little girl. I'll not tell anyone you are here, at least unless you give me a reason to."

"No, that's all right, ma—Zilla."

"You girls are well born. I could tell that at first glance." Zilla ruffled Rosi's hair. "Only a very fine family could produce such teeth as yours. So, see if you can tell me a story that sounds a little more likely. I certainly won't expect you to tell the whole truth, but if you could end up in the general neighborhood, I'd be appreciative."

Rosi decided that sticking close to the truth would probably be best. "Do you know The Castle?"

"Rosi!" Angie gripped Rosi's hand tightly.

Zilla said nothing.

"My uncle lives there."

"Your Uncle would be Beatitude Carol."

Beatitude? What a name!

Zilla looked long and hard at Rosi. "I see some resemblance. Go on."

"Our father, sorry my father sent us to live with my uncle. He felt that we should not be living…he felt we should be…safer in a more secluded spot. We were on our way there when we were separated from our traveling companions. Two men tried to rob us. Angie ran to get help and I had to fight them." Rosi looked down at her hand.

Zilla looked carefully at both girls. "That's much closer to the truth. Thank you."

"The men who attacked me," Rosi went on. "Were talking about a danger to New Richmond. Can you get word to my uncle?"

"If Mr. Carol was at The Castle, I would certainly. You'd be much better off there than here. But your uncle has gotten himself involved with the fighting that's been going around. He and some men, last I heard, were somewhere to the south raiding the English supply routes. No one has been at The Castle for over a year, child."

"Well, could you send someone to New Richmond? Couldn't your son go?" Rosi was beginning to get excited.

"It's okay, Rosi," said Angie, holding her hand.

"It's not okay!"

"You just relax, child," Zilla ordered. "You are not going nowhere for a few days. I will consider what to do, but believe me that I will not be sending my boy into that fight. It is not his concern. You just relax now."

Rosi and Angie tried to convince Zilla of how important it was to send word to the town, but Zilla waved off their arguments. Finally, she turned. "Hush, now!"

They hushed.

Zilla spent some time rooting around in small boxes and drawers, humming to herself. Soon, Will returned carrying a small steaming cauldron. Zilla took a cup and scooped out some water. Carefully, she crumbled some old bark looking things up and dropped them in the water.

Rosi balked when the strong odor hit her nostrils. "What is that?"

Zilla did not answer. She swilled the cup around and blew on it. After a few minutes, she stuck her finger into the water. Taking her finger out, she nodded. "Cool enough," she said. "When I was a child, I used to get cut up something powerful. My da would make me drink this. It chases away the poison in your blood. Now drink it, child." Zilla did not actually give Rosi the option. She put one hand behind Rosi's head, and with the other put the cup to Rosi's mouth and tilted it up.

The hot liquid burned as it went in Rosi's mouth and down her throat. It tasted horrible, and she tried not to swallow it, but Zilla held her head in such a way that she could not close her throat.

"How was that?"

"Oh, God!"

Zilla and Angie laughed at Rosi's reaction. Will stood awkwardly near his mother.

"Boy!" Zilla snapped suddenly.

"Yes, Ma?"

"You're standing in my light. Move over to the table and sit down. Now, child, I need to clean you. Little girl, you hold on to her."

"Yes, Zilla."

"I will be as gentle as I can be, but I am afraid this will hurt a little."

"I understand," Rosi said.

"Before I start, I would like you to drink something else." Zilla reached somewhere and produced a large jug. She pulled out the cork and slopped an amber gold liquid into the cup. Quickly, she held the cup to Rosi's lips and poured its contents in. Again, Zilla made the girl swallow. Again, the contents burned, but it was different.

"What is it?" Rosi coughed.

"It will help with the pain."

Rosi felt the warmth swell through her. She tried to say something, but her tongue could not form the sounds.

"Don't bother thanking me, child, until I'm done," Zilla said, amused. She turned to Angie. "Hold on."

The cleaning must have been painful for Zilla. She had to dip the cloth in the boiling water and wring it out. Zilla was as careful as she could be, both Rosi and Angie could see that. As careful as Zilla was, no one could have stopped it from hurting.

Rosi held up as best she could. Finally, she ended up with her head in Angie's shoulder, crying softly.

After Zilla had wiped Rosi's face, she gave her some more of the burning liquor. Sniffling, Rosi tried to stop crying. Angie's eyes were watering as well.

"See," Rosi laughed through her tears. "That wasn't so bad."

Rosi was feeling dizzy. She remembered something Angie had said earlier. "Dog from a Volvo," she giggled.

"Maybe you should give her some more of that," Angie suggested to Zilla.

"She's had plenty for now. When we are finished, little girl, we will all have some."

Zilla took a deep breath. "Are you ready, child?"

"Hmm," Rosi hummed.

"Good."

"Boy!"

"Yes, Ma?"

"You want to help?"

"Yes'm."

"Good. Take hold of her legs. No! No! Not through the

blankets. You have to keep her feet from kicking out." Zilla pulled up the blanket a little. "Grab her."

Will didn't so much grab her as tickle her. Rosi laughed out and kicked his hands away. "No fair t'tickle a girl," she said woozily.

"Grab her legs, boy, and be quick about it. Little girl, hold her shoulders and head."

Rosi tried to say something clever but Zilla shoved a stiff piece of leather between her teeth.

Not wanting to give the girl time to worry, Zilla quickly lifted Rosi's hand, grabbed her broken fingers, and jerked them straight.

Angie and Will used the weight of their bodies to keep Rosi from thrashing around too much. Rosi bit through the leather and spewed forth a stream of expletives that frightened Angie and confused Will.

As Rosi arched her back and tried to wrench herself away, Zilla twisted, pulled, and forced the fingers back into shape. By the time she was finished with the second finger, her patient was lying still. The other two fingers were so much easier with Rosi unconscious.

Finally, the three were able to step away. Zilla poured each a jot of liquor. "We should know in a day or two," she informed Angie. "You get some sleep now. I'll watch her. It's going to be a long night." She put her hand on Rosi's forehead. She thought it a little warm.

CHAPTER 8

ROSI woke up, but kept her eyes closed. What an extraordinary dream she had been having. Then she felt a dull throbbing running up her arm.

"Oh, nuts," she murmured.

"What is it, child? Are you awake now?"

Rosi sighed and slowly opened her eyes. The room of the rustic cabin was dark, even though she could see shafts of sunlight streaming in. The light gave the room a little illumination, but was unable to reach the dark corners. She turned her head one way and saw that the windows, or what she supposed were the windows, were open and the door stood ajar allowing in not only the feeble light but also a gentle cooling draft. The wood fire burned low.

"Are you awake now?" Zilla was sitting on her rickety chair on the other side of the fire. She seemed to be sewing something.

"Hey, Doc," Rosi said weakly. She tried to sit up a bit, but could not quite make it.

"You are awake," Zilla said. "I thought it would be about now." She leaned toward the fire, grimaced, and sent a stream of tobacco juice into the embers, which sizzled and popped for a moment. Then she moved over and helped Rosi raise her head a bit, shoving some pillows under her for support.

Rosi lifted her hand. It was splinted and wrapped in not particularly clean bandages, and it still hurt, and the memory of Zilla's first aid came flooding back. Tears sprang to her eyes.

"Keep still, child. You have a ways to go." Zilla brought her jug over to Rosi. "Drink some."

"Maybe not."

"Have some child."

"I'm only fifteen."

"And it's time you learn to hold your liquor. A lightweight

like you will never find a husband if you can not drink." Zilla did not wait for Rosi to answer, but poured some of the fiery liquid down her throat.

"Why does everyone want to get me drunk?"

"Because this will hurt again, child." Zilla began unwrapping Rosi's arm.

Zilla was right. It did hurt. It was probably the mixture of weariness and booze, but Rosi was able to take the pain without crying too much.

Zilla tossed the bandages to one side. She took out another length of cloth and put it into a bowl. "Your friend has some strange ideas about fixing people, but she was very insistent." She took the jug and poured a healthy dose of the liquor into the bowl. Then, she took a long stick from the fire and blew on it until there was a small flame. She touched the flame to the cloth. The alcohol in the bowl began to burn a bright blue. After a moment, Zilla snuffed out the flames and shook out the cloth.

"Now, let's take a look at that arm of yours." Zilla leaned in and sniffed at it carefully. "I think it will be all right."

"Thank you."

"Now don't blame me for this. It was not my idea." Zilla took the jug and splashed the liquid liberally on Rosi's arm.

It stung, and Rosi flinched.

"That's not the worst of it, child." Zilla brought the burning stick close to the arm. "Stay as still as you can."

Rosi swallowed, but nodded. She took a corner of the blanket that covered her and bit on it.

Zilla touched the flame to Rosi's arm and the alcohol flared up. It was really quite lovely, and if Rosi had not been so scared she would have been fascinated. Zilla then quickly took up the new bandage and wrapped it around the arm, putting out the pretty little flame.

"There," Zilla said, looking at her handiwork. "Again, your friend was quite adamant. I cannot remember the word she used."

"Sterile?"

"That could be it."

"It means clean."

"Like I would have a dirty cloth in my home. It's clean enough for the dishes. It's clean enough for a little cut. But, child, I feared you would lose that arm. I may know a few tricks, but I'm not up to doing that and Lord knows where there is a doctor around here."

Rosi shuddered at the thought. She did not think she would look nearly as cute with only one arm. "We have some strange ideas about cleanliness where I come from," she said simply.

"And will you be telling me where that is? The truth?"

Rosi thought for a moment. Zilla was being kind, but Rosi did not want to push it. The woman would think her a witch. *Don't they burn witches*, Rosi reminded herself. "I'm sorry," she said softly.

"That is all right, child. You will tell me when you will." Zilla spat into the fire again as she carefully placed another log on the coals. After a few minutes, there was a nice little flame going and Rosi could feel the warmth against her cheeks.

"Where's Angie?" Rosi asked finally. She supposed that Angie had merely gotten out of the stuffy cabin, but Rosi could not hear anything other than the occasional bird outside and Zilla made no move to fetch her.

"She and my boy went into New Richmond," said Zilla, not very happy about the answer. "They left yesterday morning before light. We were sure then that you would pull through."

"They went where?" Rosi tried to sit up again.

"Stay you down, child," Zilla commanded.

"She can't. She won't know who to talk to. I have to help her."

"You are not going anywhere, child. You would not make it a stone's throw, and I would not want to have to carry you back here. Lie back down." Zilla pushed Rosi softly back, her gentle touch belying her tone. "They'll be back when they are back and not before."

"I wish she hadn't gone."

"I wish they hadn't, also," Zilla agreed. "As I recall, it was your idea."

Zilla had a point. If she had been able, Rosi would certainly have gone. She had the feeling that she would have been more effective. It was odd that she was clearly expecting Angie to fail.

"What is so important about your friend going to the town?" Zilla asked. She was over by the stove, ladling something into a bowl. "Are you up to some food, child? Because if you aren't, you still have to eat," the woman added, putting the bowl next to Rosi and helping her sit up a little more. She then moved the bowl to Rosi's lap and handed her a spoon. "You aren't a baby, child. You can feed yourself."

It was a stew of some sort. There was a little meat, a few pieces of vegetable, quite a few bits of potato, and lots of thin broth. Tentatively, Rosi sniffed at a spoonful.

"It is food, child. Not perfume."

Rosi tried it. It did not taste like much but she was able to chew it until she could swallow.

"That's very nice," Rosi lied, using her most convincing voice.

"Nonsense, child. The meat is tough and the vegetables are from the bottom of the barrel. I haven't had salt for three weeks. But it will give you strength and you have got to eat it. Finish it and I'll give you another drink."

Rosi thought that a fair exchange. She realized that she was beginning to like this drink Zilla kept giving her. Even though the food was not very tasty, once she started she wolfed it down, mopping up the last of the broth with a hunk of stale and moldy bread. Remembering penicillin, she did not pick the mold off.

"You look better already," Zilla said.

"You'll notice that I heal very fast," Rosi said. "It's a family thing. We all do. Don't know why." *It is certainly becoming a useful skill, though 'condition' might be the better word*, Rosi thought.

The family also benefited from longevity. Once they reached a certain age the aging process slowed down. Uncle Richard had explained that there was no way of knowing at what age the 'condition' would kick in. He had thought it was usually early adulthood. When she asked Uncle Richard how long guardians lived he told her that no one knows because very few have ever died of natural causes.

Zilla was pouring some of the liquor in a cup, to which she added a liberal amount of water. "Just to help you sleep."

"You wanted to know why we have to warn New Richmond."

"Yes, child. You are much too young to be involved in all this nonsense."

"Don't you realize what will happen if the British take New Richmond?"

"I'll be selling my crops to the English, then. Just as I always do."

"No, no, no. Look, New Richmond isn't really all that tactically important. But, we have to keep the British from gaining too strong of a foothold in the northern New England colonies."

"Foothold, child? We're their colonies."

"But we declared independence. Didn't you know that? On July 4th, 1776." Rosi thought for a moment. "In Philadelphia. The Continental Congress signed a document stating that we were declaring ourselves free. Don't you realize how important that is?"

"No. I know nothing about that."

"But it's one of the most important events in world history. Certainly it made the newspapers."

"Child, we're ten miles from the nearest town. This isn't a city like Boston with broadsides and town meetings. It's a small farm with two people."

"But it explained, for the whole world to see, why we were fighting the British. It proved that we had the right to rebel. It started the United States of America."

"I've never heard of that. Not a very pretty name, whatever it is."

"There's a revolution going on. George Washington and Thomas Jefferson and men like that are forging a great new country out of the colonies. A great new experiment with no kings or parliaments and no taxation without representation."

Zilla laughed. "Go on, child!"

Rosi was quickly running out of social studies lessons to talk about.

Zilla considered what Rosi had been saying. "Just because a group of men in Philadelphia say they are their own country, doesn't make it so."

"Washington and Jefferson are great men."

"Being great does not make them right. Child, Philadelphia is a thousand miles away. Let them be their own country if they want to be. It means nothing here."

"It will. It will. Trust me. Thousands of people are rising up against European tyrannies, trying to create a nation based on the values of truth, justice, the American way." Oh, God! Did she just say that? "Based on the belief that all people have the right to life, liberty, and the pursuit of happiness."

"I see that you believe that. But that is just philosophy. We aren't living in a fine drawing room in Boston or Charleston. Truth and justice are all well and good at the theater among all the fine people with their carriages and fancy wigs. Here, child, truth is a row of turnips that do not rot. Justice is enough wood to burn through the winter. The likes as me will always have to pay our tax. I do not care who gets it as long as he leaves me alone the rest of the year."

"America will be different."

"So I won't have to pay tax?"

"No," Rosi conceded. "You'll still have to pay taxes. But you'll have more freedom. You'll have freedom of speech."

"I say what I like in my house. No man has ever tried to stop me from doing that."

"But," Rosi pointed out. "You'll be able to say it outside your house."

"I can walk into the middle of the town and say what I like?"

"Yes," Rosi said. "Unless—"

"Unless?"

"Well, unless it offends someone."

"And no one will take away my boy to fight in the army."

"Of course not!" Then Rosi remembered the Draft. "Except sometimes. When the government needs to"

"And this new country of yours will feed me if I'm hungry?"

"Well, no."

"And pay for a doctor when my boy is sick?"

"You'll have to pay for the doctor, of course."

"Will you be paying me, child. I doctored you pretty well."

"You won't be allowed to do that. I mean, you're not really a doctor."

"I'm doctor enough," Zilla grumbled. "And they'll be no poverty with this great experiment?"

"Of course there will be," Rosi laughed.

"Crime?"

"Well, there will still be crime. But you'll have a say in government."

"I'll be in government? Imagine me in the House of Lords," Zilla laughed at the idea.

"There's not gonna be a House of Lords. They'll be a Congress. Like in Philadelphia."

"I can waltz into Philadelphia and join this…Congress."

"You'd have to get elected."

"How will I do that?"

"Well…." Rosi thought for a moment. "First of all, you need a lot of money." She decided not to elaborate.

"I can't see how I'll be better off, child. I certainly do not want my boy dying so that his life can stay the same."

Rosi was confused. She was not sure that she had come out ahead in the discussion.

"You say your son Will is a smart boy?" Rosi asked.

"Yes, he is a smart boy. More's the pity. He is not made for the sort of life he's been born to."

"There is where this revolution can make a difference. With the British gone, Will can do what he likes. He can make a life for himself. He can be anything he's capable of. He'll be free. Don't you see? That makes it worth fighting for." Rosi felt that she had made a good point. "No one wants to die, but some things are worth taking the risk."

"What part of Cloud-Cuckoo Land do you come from, child? Do you know who I am? Do you know what Will and me are?"

Zilla sat down next to Rosi and looked at her intensely. "Do you know where I am from?"

"No," Rosi answered. "South America?"

"I was born in Jamaica. My mam was a cleaning woman. A slave. My da was the foreman on the sugar plantation where she lived. A white man, he was. Look at me. I'm fair. I'm almost acceptable. So I was taken into the big house and taught to take care of my master's girl, Frances-Anne. She was a pretty girl. And she grew up lovely, like you. And we were fast friends, even though she had a fierce temper and was fast with the crop. And she taught me many things I was not supposed to know like how to read and how to act like a lady. It was great fun. But what was I but just a toy for her? A toy she brought with her when she married. Her husband is a preacher in Portsmouth. An important man in the town. And his drawing room is often filled with all sorts of people who speak about freedom and equality. It was surely exciting to hear such talk."

Zilla went on. "But Frances-Anne was a spoiled girl. And she grew up to be a spoiled woman. And it was sad to see such a pretty girl become such an ugly person. And her husband noticed it, too. And he noticed me."

Zilla stopped, but Rosi did not know how to respond, so she sat there silently, nursing her toddy.

Zilla spat again into the fire, and wiped some juice from her chin. "And then I was with Will. I begged Reverend Scranton to find me a husband. The coachman was a good man and would have me. So I was wed. When Will was born, there was no doubt who the father was. Frances-Anne beat me and threatened to kill the child. Who would have blamed her? Who would condemn a woman for taking the child of her slave and her husband and exposing it in the woods? I had cuckolded my mistress. I would be turned out into the streets and left to freeze in the first winter."

"But the reverend was fond of me. He sent my small family out here and told us to live off the land and he promised we'd never be thrown off. But he is an old man and his wife and their white son might not be so generous to me and mine. I pray every day that Reverend Scranton lives to be a hundred. Three years we lived here. Three cold years with little food and this shack for a home. I'd grown up in the big house, mind you. I was used to nice clothes and a warm bed."

"On the third year, about this time of year, I went searching for my man, who had not returned from hunting. I found him by the creek. Some Indians had come by and he hadn't been fast enough. They shot him. I think they were Indians. Perhaps there were trappers or thieves or Frenchmen. Who knows. I buried him by the creek. That is where I was when Will came looking for me the other day. I visit my man from time to time to tell him what a fine boy the child he had taken for his own was growing to be. So we live here. Most years we have enough food. If we're lucky, there's some to sell and put a few pennies in our pockets. Everyday I half expect the fat Scranton boy to come here and tell me to leave my home. What could I say? What could I do? I'm just a slave, as is my Will."

"I'm sorry," Rosi took Zilla's hand. "I didn't know."

Zilla shook off the hand. "How could you not know? Look at me!"

"We don't have slaves where I come from."

"Then it must be a wonderful place. But they have slaves everywhere else."

"They won't always," Rosi protested.

"They always have, child. Why would that change?"

"But it will. Someday, slavery will be a thing of the past. Even the word will be considered one of the ugliest in any language. Black people will be treated like everyone else."

"The word may change. The color may change. But that don't mean the institution will be gone. That don't mean people like me will be thought of or treated any better. Might even be worse. I lived in the city and saw the poor free people freezing in the streets. No, child, I'm not having my boy fight and maybe die for some pretty drawing room notions. Maybe...maybe Eric the pig farmer two miles over might care about your nice theories. But English or no, he'll probably never be much more than a pig farmer. Reverend Scranton is loyal to the King. I know that. If the English are beaten, what will happen to his land? Will it be given to a slave woman? If I help your cause and you lose, what will they think of me? Will they let me stay? Will they understand some colorful talk about liberty? I don't see most of us around here caring what happens to your fancy ladies and gentlemen and your concerns about freedom and rights. You can have them. Don't go giving my boy ideas. He'll never be more than just a black man. His children will be black. You might not have seen it. Our neighbors might not care. But in the real world, they will. And we cannot hide our color. We cannot scrub it clean like dirt from the hands of a spoiled city girl. No matter how kind you white people are, I can see the way you look at us. Like we are stained by our blood. When push comes to shove, someone will always remember who and what we are. No one is fighting for my Will's freedom, so just leave him out of it."

They sat there and watched the fire burn and Rosi finished her drink. Suddenly, she felt tired and her eyes couldn't stay open. Zilla took the cup from her hand and helped her lie down.

* * *

THE next morning was bright and sunny and it seemed to Rosi as if the temperature was rising.

Zilla had found Rosi some clothes. "It was the best I could do, child," she said, laying them out on the cot. "I gave your friend the only other dress I had."

Rosi considered Angie in this larger woman's clothing and had to laugh. Zilla did not need to ask, she simply joined in. "At least she won't need a tent at night," Rosi laughed.

"That is true. It took a lot of rope to make it fit. But I had a little time and some thread to make yours better. "It is an old suit of Will's."

After conscientiously following Angie's instruction for changing the bandage, Zilla carefully helped Rosi into the blouse, which was far too large and hung down to her knees. Then, she slipped Rosi's legs into a pair of ridiculous looking knee britches, which reminded Rosi of Capri pants. To top it off, there was a vest, a waistcoat Zilla called it, that looked to be patched together by bits of nice cloth that Zilla had picked up piecemeal.

Actually, Rosi thought, Zilla had done a fairly decent job of altering it. The girl was not sure about using a rope as a belt, but she certainly did not want the britches falling down even if she did look like a hillbilly.

"There's not much I can do with the boots," Zilla apologized.

"I'm sure they're fine," Rosi assured her.

They were not. The old leather boots looked like they had spent a couple of years outside, which might have been the case. After several tries, the two of them were able to stuff enough pine needles wrapped in cloth into the toes of the boots to give them something akin to a decent fit.

"Which is left and which is right?" Rosi asked, looking down at her feet.

Zilla did not understand the question. Then Rosi remembered a class trip to a museum once where they had been told that shoes did not have lefts and rights in this time period.

"Do you have a piece of string or a ribbon?" she asked.

"I think I do." Zilla rummaged around for a minute in an old box and pulled out what once might have been a pretty red ribbon.

"Can you tie my hair back in a pony tail?"

After Zilla had fashioned a pony tail Rosi looked at the nonexistent mirror and checked herself out. "Wonderful," she said cheerily. "I look like a boy."

Zilla looked her up and down. She sighed. "I wish you didn't look so much like a woman, child." She took another length of cloth and fashioned a sling for Rosi's injured arm.

"What's wrong?" Zilla asked a minute later.

Rosi was busy trying to scratch her back and her hips at the same time. "It itches."

"It's clean. I checked for lice myself."

Lice!

"Um, it's just that. I mean—"

"I know it's not the fancy silks you're used to, child. But there's naught wrong with the cloth. You will get used to it, by and by." Zilla could not, or would not, hide her amusement at

Rosi's discomfort. It was infectious, and Rosi had to smile as well.

"What are you doing, child?" Zilla asked sharply, as Rosi started to sit down on the cot.

"I was just going to rest for a minute."

"This isn't an inn. You sit at the table. It's time for breakfast."

Rosi realized that she was indeed hungry and stood back up. All of a sudden, some images from movies she had seen about people in big wigs and tailcoats sprang to mind. Rosi kicked out her leg and gave a formal bow. "After you, madam," she said.

Zilla smiled, placed a hand against her heart, and curtseyed low. "It isn't my place to sit in the presence of such a great gentleman," she replied. She danced over to the stump and brushed it off with a rag.

Rosi glided over and sat down gently.

Zilla again curtseyed. "I suppose you'll be wanting cakes and a pie," she said.

"Naturally, lass." Rosi affected her best very upper crust British accent. She waved her hand in front of her.

"I had the kitchen maid up before dawn to prepare. Be careful with the china, it's very fragile."

"We throw away our plates after every meal," Rosi said aloofly.

"And the silver has been in our family for generations."

"It's lovely." Rosi took up the wooden spoon and inspected it expertly. "Made by Paul Revere, I see."

"Only the best for our young gentlemen, sir." Zilla went over to the stove and brought back the pot. "Strawberry tart, lemon cake, and quail pie."

It looked an awful lot like the stew.

"And to drink, young sir? Turkish coffee?"

"I think champagne would be in order don't you?"

"Of course, young sir. Very good choice." She dipped a cup in a pail and brought it over. "Notice how the light shines through the very fine crystal."

"I do." She sipped at the stale water delicately. "Ah! A very fine year."

"The young sir shows excellent taste."

Rosi laughed. "And the young sir likes a saucy wench!" She reached out and slapped Zilla's bottom.

"Oh, sir." Zilla's hands flew up to her face. "You'll make a girl think above her station."

"I don't care what happens above your station, just what happens below stairs," Rosi replied archly.

Zilla let loose a loud laugh.

While Rosi ate, Zilla cut a sliver of tobacco from a large wedge she kept wrapped in a piece of cheesecloth and slipped it in her cheek. When Rosi was finished, the older woman took the bowl and plunked it in the water pail. "Let the kitchen staff clean up."

"Let them eat cake," Rosi crowed.

"Shall we promenade, young sir?"

"But of course."

Zilla snatched the blanket from the cot and wrapped it around Rosi's neck, attaching it with a rusty pin. "What a fine cape you have, fine sir. Tailor made in London, no doubt?"

"Heavens no," Rosi sniffed indignantly. "Made in Paris, of course."

"Of course." Zilla stepped to the door and opened it.

"No, no," Rosi said, bowing low. "After you, lass."

Zilla threw an arm out in front of her and held her nose up as she slid through the door. Rosi followed and closed the door behind her.

Whatever Rosi thought of the inside of the cabin was washed away once she saw the outside. The inside was the Ritz compared to the farm. There were three buildings, as Angie had said, if you could call them buildings. One of them was little more than a stall containing a mule of some sort. The other building was clearly supposed to be a barn, but Rosi could see through to the other side. And the structures were not really made of logs, but of logs, stones, twigs, and mud. They looked hastily thrown together and about ready to collapse if you sneezed too loudly.

The cabin itself had been built against the side of a small rise. The roof was covered in dirt and grass and had weeds growing out of it. There was even an anemic looking chicken strolling along the top, apparently looking for worms. The chicken had presumably walked from the small rise to the roof without breaking its stride.

Zilla tossed a rock in the direction of the chicken. "Go on, bird!" she yelled. "Back to the others!" The chicken squawked, spread its wings, and half ran half flew back to solid ground, where it relaxed and began wandering back to the roof. "Now we begin your healing," Zilla said.

"Fresh air?"

"If you like. I was more thinking hard work. They do that in Cloud Cuckoo Land?"

"Of course. We put our pants on one leg at a time like everyone else," Rosi laughed. "I'd love to help, but I've only one arm at the moment."

"One arm will be plenty, child. Your friend has taken my boy, so you can do some of his chores."

"But—"

"No buts. You can feed the animals, can't you?"

So Rosi slowly carried slops to the two sorry looking pigs, who were only too happy to eat whatever it was they were eating. Rosi found a few berries on some bushes and, with Zilla's okay, tossed them in for Quarky and Bob, as Rosi christened them. Quarky was the bigger one, liked girls, and wanted to be an accountant. His plan was to embezzle a lot of money, move to Argentina to avoid extradition, and live with a former supermodel name Jezell who was really only using him to pay for her coke habit. Bob did not care much for girls, or anyone for that matter, and was looking forward to moving to Greenwich Village, living on his trust fund, smoking cigarettes, drinking coffee and absinthe, and talking about writing angry poetry, even though he would never actually put pen to paper. The true artist could not be expected to conform to the bourgeois stereotype of the artist as producer who kowtows to the dictates of a capitalistic consumer economy, nor could he sully himself with hard work, for the artist had to reject complaisant acceptance of the oppression the proletariat endured at the hands of the factory owners.

"Don't go making friends with the pigs, child," Zilla called over from where she was repairing something. "We'll be eating them come autumn."

"Sorry boys," Rosi called over to Quarky and Bob as she tossed corn to the chickens. "But if you want my advice, South America is that way." She pointed.

"You are pointing to Quebec, child."

"What?"

"South America is to the south." Zilla pointed south. "You have some strange notions of direction where you come from."

Rosi did not bother naming the chickens. They might be eating them sooner than autumn. Considering the way the chickens looked, they might have welcomed the pot. She was able to collect three or four eggs, which Zilla snatched away and took inside.

The mule actually had a name: Mule. Perhaps it wasn't as creative as Quarky and Bob, but he answered to it with a tired look and a groaning yawn. Rosi gave him a good brushing.

Zilla was not sure why Mule needed to be brushed, but Rosi was intent on it, so she simply grumbled a bit.

It took Rosi's mind off her arm and was busy work, if nothing else. After a light luncheon of bread, Rosi started the hard chore of going down to the feeble stream to collect buckets of water.

At first, Rosi could not figure out a way to fill more than half a bucket, the water was so low. She finally moved down stream a couple of hundred yards and found a place where the stream went over a rock. She put the bucket below the rock and let the stream do the work. If only the stream could have floated the bucket back to the homestead. Rosi had never realized how heavy a bucket of water could be. *This is easy*, Rosi thought in the beginning. But it took her almost twenty trips to fill up the barrel.

Then she had to fill the water troughs for Quarky and Bob, the chickens, and Mule. Next, she had to dump some water on a small patch of ground on which Zilla was trying to grow tomatoes. Rosi's left arm was throbbing, but she tried to ignore it.

Now, her right arm hurt.

Before Rosi realized it, after possibly the longest day in her life, it began to grow darker.

"In you go, child," Zilla said, taking the bucket from her and turning her to the door.

Inside, Rosi collapsed on the bed and barely felt it when Zilla took off her boots. Zilla then, carefully, took off Rosi's vest and blouse and changed the bandage.

"It will heal," Zilla said, sniffing at the wounds. "But I don't know how well. But you are right, it is healing much faster than it should. But Carols always was strange people."

She took a look at Rosi's other hand and smiled. "Tomorrow will be worse."

Rosi looked at her right hand and groaned. She thought working for Nellie had ravaged her hands. It had been nothing compared to this day of work.

"Don't worry, child," Zilla laughed. She took a handful of lard and massaged it into Rosi's palm and fingers.

Zilla let Rosi eat in bed, which was nice. After stew, Zilla had a chew and they both had toddies as they watched the fire begin to burn low.

"You did well today."

"Thank you, Zilla."

"I'm surprised a city bred little thing like you would do so well."

Rosi blushed at the compliment.

"I've been thinking, child."

"Yes."

Zilla spat. "Perhaps I was a little hard on you last night."

"No, not at all."

"Yes, I was. You mean well. I do not think much of those men in Philadelphia, but I know you. You mean well."

They sat silently for a minute, with only the sound of the crackling fire to keep their thoughts company.

"I've also been thinking, child. I treat my boy Will like a child. I worry about him. I don't want him to get hurt. Or used. But he's seventeen. He's a man. Sometimes I forget that." Zilla looked strangely at Rosi. "Don't you be forgetting he's a man, either, child." Her hard gaze went back to the fire. "He's the man of this family and he can make his own decisions. He decided to help your friend, because of you. If he wants to help you when he gets back, I'll not stand in his way." Her look shot back at Rosi. "But remember this, child. Men may be stronger than us women, but they can be much more fragile."

Rosi tried to hold the older woman's gaze, but soon she was forced to lower her eyes. "Yes, ma'am."

"You sleep now." Zilla took Rosi's cup from her and covered the girl with the blanket. "I took you into my home. It may not be much, but it is mine for the time being, and I am mistress here. You can stay until you are well. Then I suggest that you and your friend try your best to go home. Will and I will help you do that as much as we can."

Rosi lay back and let sleep catch up to her. She thought about what Zilla had said. She wished Angie had not gone into New Richmond. It was not her friend's problem. She would not know what to do. For that matter, Rosi was not sure what to do.

Could she find Kirk? If she found him, would she be able to get to him, surrounded as he was by the whole British army? If she could get to him, what would she do to him? And if she did anything, it might be too late anyway.

Rosi needed her uncle. He knew what to do. He knew how to look through the tears in time and see what the possibilities were. It was always possible that Kirk simply would have no lasting effect on history. Perhaps his advice would not help the British. Perhaps the rebels would win the battle anyway.

Rosi had always heard that history could be affected by relatively minor circumstances. For lack of a nail, the battle was lost, etc. Uncle Richard argued that most major events would not be significantly changed by trivial occurrences. Certainly, though, the loss of New Richmond would have to be a major blow to the Americans. It would have some sort of effect. This would be something that Rosi would have to fix.

"Our role," Uncle Richard was fond of explaining. "Is to adjust the results so that the events unfold as closely as possible to our history while making as little personal impact as we can. Showing up in an odd photograph is one thing. Being mentioned in the history books is another thing and quite unacceptable."

"Shouldn't we try to make the world a better place?" Rosi had countered once. "There are so many things in our history that should not have happened."

"What is written is written," he had responded. "Do not try to improve on the world. You are a Guardian, not God."

In this situation, Rosi was afraid, she would have to do some heavy revision to history. Angie could warn whomever she liked in New Richmond, but unless she ran into the current Carol, Beatitude, no one would believe her. Worse, they might listen and decide she should be locked up. If Angie ran into Beatitude Carol, what would happen?

Uncle Richard had explained that the Guardians had to consider certain possible outcomes.

If the person was likely to forget about their jaunt into otherwhen, then it was simpler to drop him off on a secluded road as close as possible to when they went through the doorway. If it was likely that they might remember bits and pieces of the event, then some flashing lights would have to be used and unconscious memories of alien probes would have to be created.

If they had been too involved in the events or had been there and then long enough, then there were hundreds of islands in the South Pacific where no outsider had ever gone and tribes on them that had very little contact with the outside world. Sometimes, it was even convenient to have someone appear to help a primitive culture take a few big developmental steps quickly.

Even if this Beatitude Carol believed Angie, he might simply choose not to help. Guardians generally did not interfere with other Guardians. If he wanted to help, would Beatitude Carol be able to? If he were somewhere fighting, he could be hundreds of miles away. Rosi had no idea how to go about hunting him down.

It was possible that they might have to wait another two or three years before she saw him? Could she wait at The Castle? It was her home. Or was it?

And if Kirk succeeded? Rosi would have to fix that.

Rosi needed to talk to Angie. *Think about it in the morning. That would be better.*

Rosi and Zilla both awakened at the same moment. It was still black as pitch outside and all that remained of the fire was just a few glowing embers.

Rosi looked over to Zilla. "What is it?"

"Someone's outside."

They listened for a moment.

"It's just the pigs," Rosi said, hearing them scratching at their fence.

"No. They never make any noise at night. They sleep like babies."

There was a soft rustling from somewhere not too far away.

Zilla was up and over by the door before Rosi knew it. Rosi tried to slip her feet out from under the covers. "Stay down, child. You'll not be doing any good."

Rosi's left arm banged against the wooden frame and it took all of her strength to keep from screaming or fainting.

Zilla came back to Rosi and put something in her hand. It was a pistol. "It's loaded. If someone comes in without me telling you it's all right, pull back on the hammer, point, and pull on the trigger."

All of a sudden, Rosi was terrified. "Where are you going? Don't leave me here alone."

Rosi heard the sound of metal being dragged across metal. When Zilla turned, Rosi realized that she was holding a mean looking sword, the type d'Artagnan might have used.

"It was my Da's." And Zilla was through the door.

CHAPTER 9

ANGIE and Will left Zilla's before sunrise. Six o'clock, Angie guessed. She did not have a watch. She should have brought a watch. Angie did not like not knowing what time it was. She had saved up her allowance and birthday and Christmas presents for a year to get a really nice watch that could tell time in ten different time zones at once and had a perpetual calendar and set itself by satellite and looked really good on her, and now where was it when she really needed it? Probably in her desk drawer at home. Who wore a watch anymore?

Zilla and Will had no watches or clocks. They even seemed surprised that Angie would ask. They said they had no need for them. They knew when the sun rose because they could see. They knew when the sun set because they could not see. They went to bed when they were tired and the work was done. They woke up when it was time to get to work.

They had not even been positive about the date. When Angie had asked, when she first got to the shack, the two of them had tried to count back to the last time they had actually known the date for sure, and they had disagreed about what the count came up with. It could be late March. It could be early April. They did not understand how important the difference might be.

"How do you know when to sow and plant?" Angie had asked, appalled at this show of ignorance.

"Ma tells me," Will had shrugged.

"We plough when the frost is gone and the ground is thawed," Zilla had offered.

It sounded terribly inefficient.

Zilla did not know the first thing about sanitation. Oh, she had cleaned Rosi's arms well enough, and straightened her fingers, but then she had been about to wrap Rosi's arm in filthy rags.

Angie had put a stop to that right away. She had taken care to change the bandages after that. And she had done the best she could to keep things clean. Andy might be a braniac, and Rosi was pretty smart too, but Angie was not stupid. She certainly knew that the biggest threat to Rosi right now was if her arm became gangrenous and the infection killed her. She also knew that a common treatment for gangrene at this time was amputation, which generally killed the patient as well.

Angie let Zilla do most of the doctoring. The woman seemed to know what she was doing. But Angie stood firm on the issue of cleanliness. She was not about to trust the water, though. When she thought about it later, it struck her that creek water at this time was probably pretty clean. She did know that fire would help clean the wounds, so she improvised.

At least, she figured, Rosi was in bad enough shape that nothing Angie did could actually harm her. Zilla said as much when she agreed to Angie's "harebrained notions," as she called them.

Once it was clear that Rosi was going to come through, Angie had given thought to their predicament. There was certainly something weird going on. 1780? That was impossible. From the first day, Angie had kept looking around half expecting to see a camera and someone hiding in the bushes to jump out and explain the joke for the viewers. But there were no cameras, no producers. This was real.

It was this area. Strange things happened from time to time around here. They seemed to have intensified when Rosi came.

Some of the older people looked at Rosi strangely. Andy had said something about it one night when they were outside on the swing. Angie never really cared much about those old stories the old people told which fascinated Andy so much. Angie worried about important things like how to get Andy into a good university so he could get a good job and get her to a real city where you did not have to lock yourself inside on certain nights so some boogey man would not get you.

Her mother knew exactly where Angie got those ideas. Mom came from Pittsfield and was not as *stupidstitious* as everyone else.

Her father, who had gone to college in Boston, was not bad either, but he made sure she followed the silly rules everyone else followed year in year out.

Somehow, the Carol family always showed up in these stories. So if Rosi felt that getting to New Richmond was important, then it probably was. Angie might not have listened to the local legends, but she did study for class at school.

On April 8, 1780, the British, commanded by Admiral Nathan Cromwell, attempted to land at New Richmond and take the harbor. He was unable to take his ships through the reef. He lost two ships on the reef. However, by this time, he had already started the attack and had no way to call it off. Cromwell was forced to land his men in ship's boats. Cromwell lost the element of surprise. His men were exposed to danger much earlier than they would have been had they been aboard ships of the line instead of boats for crossing the harbor. The British were not able to use the ships' guns to full effect. It had not been an easy victory for the locals, but the Lobsterbacks had been beaten off. By the time Cromwell had regrouped his forces and reconsidered his options, the rebels had gathered together a large enough force to watch Cromwell's naval forces from shore, harass any landings, and reinforce coastal defenses wherever Cromwell might attack. In short, he had his moment and lost it. It was a great moment for New Hampshire. The victory had indeed stopped the British from having any real control in the region. It was a story known by every schoolchild in the area. And it was a subject for endless debate and anger, yet there was no mention of it in any history books. It was almost as if the rest of the country was trying to pretend it had not happened.

If Kirk really was trying to give the British information, it could change a lot of things. And this confused Angie. She knew she was here and now. She could feel it and see it. There was not much she could do about that.

There was some rule someplace that said you could not change history. If you could not change history, then Kirk would not be able to do anything. So then why was she trying to find a way to stop him? If Kirk did change history, that would mean

Angie would never be born and would simply disappear, in which case she could not do anything to help. That meant that Kirk would never be born and he would disappear. Then he could not come here and change history?

It gave Angie a headache just thinking about it.

What was there to do but go to New Richmond and try to find a way to fix what might not be broken? Angie had to do something and she figured that she had to do it right away. If it was now March 31, as Zilla and Will had said, she had little enough time. But they had been unsure. It could be the 6th or 7th of April or the 24th or 25th of March.

Zilla was not happy at the idea of Will getting involved, but she had let him go. She probably thought it would get rid of the girls faster. Or, at least it would get Will away from Rosi. He kept looking at Rosi and not looking at her at the same time and Zilla was clearly not happy about that.

"Go, boy," Zilla had said. "Help her find the town. Wait for her. But don't go in to the town yourself. You hear me, boy?"

Will had mumbled something, but agreed. So they had woken up far too early in the morning and set off. Will had a musket. They gave Angie an old knife. "It won't help you much, little girl," Zilla had said. "But a blade is a blade. However dull, it can still hurt someone if they fall on it." Just before they left, Zilla gave Angie a bag of food to keep them. And off they went.

As a guide, Will was a mix of incredible competence and unbelievable ineptitude. He led her skillfully through the woods. He seemed to have a sixth sense about where the ground was unsafe or where there was a tree root or other obstacle. It was dark for the first leg of their journey, but Will made sure that Angie did not stumble.

By late afternoon they had not reached The Castle. Angie was not sure about the geography, but she was pretty sure The Castle was no more than five or six miles from wherever it was they started, and she was pretty sure that it was vaguely southeast from the little farm. Will had led her north then west then south then north then east then west. She had become confused as to which direction they were going.

Angie knew enough from math class that the shortest distance between two points was a straight line. She tried to explain this to Will. He merely shrugged and said that they were going the only way he knew how.

Zilla had given her this horrid dress. No wonder Will did not look at her the way he looked at Rosi. *What am I, chopped liver?* She had asked herself several times. As much as Angie loved Rosi, she wished she was not so...look-at-able. Angie was pretty. Andy thought so. Lots of boys did.

There was definitely something odd about *this* boy.

Angie's feet hurt. She should have brought her sneakers. She was hungry. They had stopped for lunch, which had consisted of a chunk of stale bread, some sorry looking vegetables, and some dried meat.

They came upon The Castle so suddenly that Angie was surprised. She had expected, somehow, to recognize the area. She did not. She was in the woods, and then she was on a long, un-mown lawn. She had thought to come here first. Zilla had said that Beatitude Carol was not in the area, but she might be wrong. Even if he was not around there might be someone else. A relative, perhaps?

The sun was already lowering, and the trees and shadows looked like they were bowing to the building that seemed to shimmer ever so slightly. The Castle was built to conform to the shape of the coast, so it was not flush with the sun. Given the odd angle, the shadows gave the front door the appearance of being a great, gaping maw waiting to devour all comers.

Holding her breath, Angie stepped up to the front door and knocked. "No one's there. Let's go." She started to move off.

"Where are you going?" Will stepped up to the door and banged on it a couple times.

"No one's there," Angie insisted.

"Hello? Is anyone home? We got your niece at home. Hurt her arm. Can you let us in?" It was then Will noticed, in the gloom of the doorway, the knockers. He used them. The noise was muted, but the whole house seemed to vibrate.

Angie had never actually used the knockers. If her father

drove her out here, she would call Rosi from the police car radio. If she came out on her own, she would call Rosi in advance and have her waiting out front. She did not really like being alone when she was at The Castle and avoided it as much as she could.

The house rumbled for a bit, moaning quietly. Then nothing.

"I guess you were right," Will turned to Angie.

Angie was not looking at him, but rather, she was staring behind him.

He turned back to see that the door was swinging open.

"Thanks," he called out.

Nothing.

"Hello?" Will stepped into the foyer. There was no one around. He shrugged his shoulders. "Come on in, Angie."

Angie was not sure she wanted to go in. She was nervous enough when she was with Rosi.

"I don't think anyone is there," she called back to the disappearing Will.

"I'm going to look around."

Angie could barely see Will for the shadows even though he was only about ten feet away. His voice, however, sounded distant.

Maybe Angie should just wait here. The door began to close. She had a choice. She could be alone in the dark next to The Castle or inside in the dark with Will, who had no idea what he was getting into. Angie threw caution to the wind and edged through the door at the last moment. Right after Angie passed by, the door slammed shut with a resounding thud.

Will spun, pointing his musket at Angie.

"Put that thing down, Will," Angie snapped. "Or I'll take it from you again."

Will lowered the barrel.

"This way," she said, starting off to Rosi's room.

"You've been here before?"

Oh, nuts! She thought quickly. "No. But the door this way is open."

"There's more light up the stairs." Will pointed. He was right. Angie was not about to go upstairs in The Castle without someone who knew what was going on, so she grabbed Will's arm and pulled him along with her. The doors led the way, rudely opening and closing with regularity and purpose. They seemed to have a perfect idea of where they wanted Angie and Will to go. Angie thought about it, at one moment when they paused to rest, they seemed to be going in some ever decreasing circle.

Will appeared as terrified as Angie felt.

Somewhere, they could hear doors opening and closing, but always in another room, just out of sight. The slamming doors seemed to be getting closer. Soon, they heard scuffling feet and whispered conversations just out of range, but close enough to almost be understood.

Finally, they entered one room with no other doors. Will spun and tried to grab the door through which they had entered, but was not fast enough to stop it from closing.

Angie had never seen this small room before. There were no windows in it, so she could not guess where they were. After a moment, it dawned on Angie that she could see because there were a handful of lit candles sitting on a small table in the center of the room. Why would there be lit candles in an empty house, Angie wondered briefly.

Suddenly, Angie realized they were being spoken to. A great voice, or was it a hundred different voices speaking from a hundred different directions, each word coming from different directions.

"Who are you? What do you want?"

Will was speechless.

"W-w-we're trying to get some help," Angie forced out.

"Why come here? Why bother us?"

"We don't know where else to turn." Angie looked around the room they were in. It was a relatively small room. The one door was not open. "Someone has to help us. I can't do it on my own. Is, is, Beatitude Carol here?"

"Haven't we done enough?" The voices were getting angry, though some of them sounded a little tired more than anything else. The voices and the doors and the footsteps were getting closer.

"Please!" Angie begged.

"Do we have to do everything? Can't you help yourselves?"

"I don't know," Angie called out. They were being forced to the floor by the power of the voices. "I'm not supposed to be here."

"How did you get here?" the voices demanded. "Why did you come to The Castle? Why did you go through the door?"

"It wasn't my fault!"

"Are you a thief? Did you come to rob us?"

"No!"

"We know how to take care of thieves!" The voices were right on top of them. Neither Angie nor Will could see anyone, but they could feel the hot air of angry talk on their faces. The candles flicked in the conversation. The room darkened ominously. "We keep you for a time. And we have all the time in the world!" Some of the voices laughed. Some of them sounded sort of sad.

"I'm not a thief. I didn't do anything wrong!" Angie was yelling into the floor. "I was trying to help my friend Rosi. Rosi Carol. She brought us here! Rosi brought us here! Rosi! Help us!" she screamed.

The voices were gone. It happened so fast the air forgot to puff as they left.

After a few minutes, Angie and Will raised their heads. There was now a cheery light to the room. A door to one side slid open politely. They agreed it would probably be best to take that door. They both stood up, but Will dropped to his knees. Angie reached out for him, but realized he was praying softly. She closed her eyes and waited.

Will whispered to himself. Angie caught very little of it, but one phrase struck her.

"Angels and ministers of earth defend us," Will mumbled just as he stood.

Who was this boy?

They followed the doors. Gradually, the rooms got lighter and lighter and it was not long before Angie realized that they were in Rosi's rooms. None of Rosi's things were there and the floors were covered with dust and there were signs of rats or other critters. But at least it was something familiar.

Angie had no idea how long they had been wandering around The Castle. It could have been ten minutes. It could have been ten hours. It was definitely nighttime outside. The rooms were empty save for the old cannon, not so old at the moment, on the top level. Angie could see much of the harbor and some of the town, depending on where she stood.

"That's New Richmond." Angie pointed to the small village. "I think." The moon was not up yet, so Angie could not see if there were any boats on the water. "That's where we're going."

"Not tonight. We should sleep and go in the morning." Will finally spoke.

"Good idea." Angie thought for a moment. She did not want to sleep here.

Angie walked to the top of the stairs. "We're leaving!" she called out to the house. After a moment, they heard the doors. Angie led an increasingly nervous Will along the path and out of the house. The front door closed behind them.

"Come with me," Angie said, starting off.

"Wait." Will jogged to catch up with her. "I'm supposed to be looking after you."

"And you're doing a fine job of it."

Rosi had shown her the old watchtower. That was where Angie had decided they should stay the night. It was in much better shape now than it had been when Angie had seen it the last time. Or *would be* she reminded herself.

Angie let Will go in first. It made him feel better. She did not think there would be any real danger, so why not let him lead the way. If there *was* any real danger, then so much the better.

When Will stormed through the door into the first level, the only things he stirred up were dust and dirt. This place had not been used in a while.

The two of them tiptoed up the stairs. Each level was furnished. Or rather, the frames of the furniture were there. Anything that might biodegrade or have any value had been stripped away. The only thing useful they found was a neatly stacked bundle of wood on the top of the tower.

"At least we'll be able to get warm," Will said, squatting down and starting to arrange some of the wood into a fire.

"What are you doing?"

"Building a fire," Will said.

"Are you mad?"

"What else to do with the wood. Besides, it's cold." He continued arranging the logs.

"But if you build a fire, you'll be telling everyone in sight that we are here."

"You were wanting to warn them. Perhaps this will do."

"I don't want to warn everyone," Angie argued. "I want to warn the right someone."

"Ah. And who is that?"

"I don't know." Angie said.

"So, this is not a well thought out plan of yours, is it?"

"No," Angie sighed. "I guess not." She had an idea. "Wait here." She popped down the stairs and came up seconds later. "I got it."

"What?"

"The next level down. There is no aperture facing the town."

"Aperture?"

"Aperture. Opening," Angie sniffed.

"I know what it means. What an odd word to use. Why not say opening? Or window? You thought I didn't know the word."

"I—I suppose so," Angie confessed.

"Then why use it?"

Angie had no idea. She helped Will carry down the wood, and in minutes, there was a nice fire burning. The apertures, or openings, in the walls and the shape of the tower created a wonderful flue that kept the flames dancing well into the night.

They were able to heat up some water to go with their miniscule dinner. Will had seen the occasional game during their journey, but Angie wanted to make as little noise as possible. Angie tried to get Will to talk. He did not say much, which she found annoying. She supposed some girls liked the quiet type, but she preferred someone who could carry on a conversation. Like

Andy.

"So, what's the plan?" Will finally asked.

"We're going into town tomorrow. Not too early. We want people up and about so we don't stand out."

"And who do you talk to?"

"I haven't figured that much out yet." That was something that had been bothering Angie the entire day. "But we'll find someone."

"You." he said.

"What?"

"You will go into town. Ma told me to stay out of sight."

"Fine." *What a momma's boy!*

Angie settled down near the fire hoping to be able to get some sleep.

"Should we set a watch?" Will asked.

"If you want to watch, go ahead. I want to sleep," Angie yawned. "We made a lot of noise coming up here. I suppose anyone else would, too. Get some sleep."

CHAPTER 10

THE morning was briskly cold. It took Angie a few minutes to straighten out her limbs, but eventually she was able to get moving again. Will did not seem too discombobulated by the chill. The water flasks had all but frozen. Will had to build up the fire so they could heat up the water enough to drink it.

By midmorning, they could see that people were coming into the town and milling about. There actually seemed to be quite a large number of people.

They smothered the fire and left. The sun had chased away the chill and it was getting nicely warm. It appeared not to have rained in a while and the traffic on the narrow road had made quite a cloud of dust and dirt. There were moments when it was hard to see. This would be a good thing, Angie decided. It would make her less conspicuous.

A couple of hundred yards from the town Will dropped out. "I'll find us some food and meet you back here in a while," he said.

Before he left, they agreed that Will would make sure he was at this spot every hour on the hour once the bells started striking noon. If they still were not able to meet, he would go to the watchtower, which would be the next best place to find each other.

Angie went into the town. She hoped she did not have to buy anything. Zilla had slipped her a few pennies before she left, but she suspected a penny was not worth much more now than it would be in the future.

Parts of New Richmond had clearly not changed that much. The same types of fisherwomen who went from a stunning gay twenty to plump gray wizened sixty in a matter of months ran the booths and tried to convince you that last week's catch had just arrived yesterday.

Everyone called her *thee* and *thou*. This seemed funny to Angie.

A couple of the fishing boats appeared not to have gone out for the day. They looked just about the same as the ones used by people like Andy's father. Indeed, slap a few coats of paint on and add a small engine, and some of these could be the same boats! Change the material of the clothes and these were essentially the same folks who lived and worked by the harbor. One old woman even looked a lot like Nellie.

Angie shook her head. She was getting carried away. Besides, she had a mission to accomplish. She wondered what the rest of 'then town' looked like. The area she lived in would probably be woods or someone's farm. The Country Club and the golf course would not have yet been built. The school? She remembered that the school had met in a church until around the time of the Civil War.

The church was still standing, would still be standing, and all of the kids had visited there at some point on a field trip. It was one of the dullest field trips they ever took. The preacher, who was about eighty if he was a day, talked for over an hour about the wood and the architecture and then got really quiet as if he was imparting some deep secret and led the kids down to the basement where there was an old school room with several long tables and a podium. There was an apple, looking spotted like it had been forgotten from yesterday's lunch, on the table.

The kids found places to sit on the uncomfortable benches and the preacher told everyone how they had taught the kids here. There had even been a couple of the old textbooks lying around. One of them was a Latin primer.

The church would be here. That might be a place to start.

Angie cut into town, following small streets that would not have changed very much over the next two hundred years. In Angie's day, the old church was not very impressive. It was dwarfed by the city buildings and the newer churches. Its one claim to fame was that it was still around. And there it was, much more impressive now, towering over the other buildings around it.

There was a crowd standing in front of the church. A preacher looking man was holding another man by the arm and haranguing the crowd.

"And to think that this vile infamy would be exacerbated by being committed on sacred ground, under the very roof given to us by the Lord, under the very eyes of the Lord himself. This spawn of the devil and his harlot succubus," the preacher pointed at a woman who was being held by some of the men. The men stepped away from her. She was a pretty girl and looked terrified. "They have violated our Holy Church with their sinful and wicked kisses."

The man tried to pull away from the preacher. "But I haven't seen my fiancee in two years," he protested.

"And when was the last time you saw Jesus?"

"Amen," someone called out.

"Does Jesus violate your house?" The Preacher asked.

"No!" someone called out.

"Does Jesus engage in profane and unspeakable acts under your roof?"

"No!" several in the crowd yelled.

"This is Christ's house. Jesus' house! The house of the Son of God! And you bring your whore of Babylon inside the House of the Lord? The Lord God who gave you life. Who breathed part of him inside you and gave you a soul. And you pervert your soul with this Jezebel? The Lord God created the heavens and the Earth, the Sun and the Moon, the Night and the Day. The Lord God created the winds and the oceans. These very same winds and oceans kept you away from your fiancee these two years. As you can see, it was God's plan to separate you. He was testing you. Lord, yes!"

"Amen!" the crowd responded.

"And you failed! You failed the test of the Lord! He asks you to come to His house. To His house. To thank Him for your salvation. And how do you thank Him? By sinning with your woman before the eyes of man and God."

"I only kissed her."

"He only kissed her?" The Preacher laughed.

The crowd laughed.

"It was only a kiss?" The Preacher turned on the man. "Satan's kiss. It was a kiss that could have led to fornication. Therefore, it is the same as fornication."

The crowd spoke its agreement.

"And did you fornicate with heathen women on your journeys? And while you were fornicating with devils' children and pagans, what of your woman? Have you so corrupted her that she throws herself at unmarried men? Has she dropped so low that she would engage in unlawful kisses? Has your abandonment ruined her chances for salvation?"

The woman screamed and dropped to her knees. "Praise God!"

"Has this man tempted you from the true path?"

"He has tempted me from the true path," she cried.

"Has he prostituted your body through kisses and...worse?"

The crowd mumbled.

"He has violated me. He has raped me with kisses."

"Premarital kisses?" The Preacher demanded.

"Yes."

"Do you repent?"

"Yes!" The girl was weeping.

"Do you condemn him?"

"Yes! Yes! Yes!"

The crowd cheered.

"Take him away!" the preacher yelled.

The crowd cheered, lifted up the man, and carried him off. Angie followed them. She was curious. The crowd didn't go far. They stopped at what must have been The Common and two of the men led the guilty party to a platform where they stuck him in some stocks and people started pelting him with fruits and garbage.

Angie went back to the church. There, the crying girl had collapsed on the church porch. The preacher was standing over her saying something. Slowly the girl stood up and let the Preacher lead her around the side of the church.

The church was not the place to go for help.

What about the town hall? But that was not built yet. Not for a hundred years. The town council always met and did business at the Dancing Cavalier. Everyone knew that. The Dancing Cavalier had been around since 1649. And that meant it would be here now! Angie should have thought of that first.

It was a fairly short walk to the Dancing Cavalier. Both the church and the inn had been built soon after the arrival of the English settlers. Because the priest had objected to the presence of an inn with a pub in it so close to the church, the leaders of the English had decided to build the church and the inn out of sight of each other. Even in Angie's time, the town was fairly small. In 1649, it barely reached the low hills that ran parallel to the coastline and much of that was farmland. There was almost no way for the two buildings to be built out of site of one another. One of the English, a man named Rupert Marston, set up a matchlock on the site of The Dancing Cavalier and fired in a random direction, but not too random, because the church could have ended up in the middle of the harbor. As long as Rupert Marston could hit a playing card tied to the end of a stick, the distance was too close. When he finally missed, the English decided the distance was appropriate and built the church there. It was about 150 yards from the inn. To further insure that neither church nor inn corrupted each other, the town leaders agreed that they would have no windows or doors facing each other. That was why the Dancing Cavalier only had windows and doors facing to the east, and the church was built facing north by northwest. The Anglo-Catholic church built by the early settlers mysteriously burnt to the ground in 1688 and was replaced by a much more acceptable puritan meetinghouse. Now, Angie's now, it was Methodist. The rebuilt church also faced north by northwest. As the years passed and other churches joined the community, they too followed the old town rule and were built facing away from the Dancing Cavalier. Even the schools were built at such an angle that none of the windows directly faced the offending inn.

When Angie reached the inn she was disappointed to see that there was no outdoor cafe. A few men lounged near the front door. A couple of them more lay than lounged. One man came up to Angie, tipped his hat and smiled at her, showing that he was missing about half his teeth.

"Fancy a drink, molly?" he slurred.

Angie was repelled. "No, thank you."

"Thank ye? Yer a lady, are ye?" the man laughed. "Come an' jine me." He grabbed her and pulled her to him.

"Oy! Leave 'er be," another man broke in, grabbing Angie by the arm. "'Er came see me." He started dragging her away from the first man.

"Leave off. Molly's mine."

"Sod you, mate," the second man cried. He produced a long, wicked looking knife. His other hand pulled out a length of rope with a wicked looking knot on one end.

The first man grinned and dropped Angie on top of the barrel that he had been using as a seat. "Yer waits here," he said with a leer. A short length of chain appeared in one hand and a knife appeared in the other.

He and the other man began circling around each other, snarling and laughing.

This would be a good time to make a getaway, Angie thought.

She made it about two steps before the second man grabbed her, lifted her up, and plopped her on the barrel. "Yer stays 'ere, lass," he laughed. "We'lls be wi' yer when we're doon."

Before he had the chance to turn around, the first man was lunging at him. Had the second man not twisted violently, the little scuffle would have ended at that moment. As it was, the first man's knife nicked his opponent's hip causing him to howl in pain and lash out with his rope, catching the other man on the chin and sending him back and into several of the onlookers. This drew the onlookers into the fray and soon it was a veritable brawl. Mugs and beer were flying as freely as fists and oaths. The two men who had started the fight were, Angie was surprised to note, soon helping each other against the newcomers. They threw one of them so roughly against the barrel Angie was sitting on that she was sent sprawling. She ended up stumbling through the front door and into the taproom of The Dancing Cavalier.

If anything, the taproom was noisier than the outside. There was very little light in the large open room, and what little there was had been obscured by the fog of smoke. The room was packed with men drinking and singing and shouting at the tops of their lungs in a number of languages. The floor was covered in sawdust and small puddles of what Angie hoped was spilled beer.

A woman carrying a tray came up to Angie. "Are you working here, girl, or do you need anything." The woman repeated her question louder, shrugged, and wandered on. There were several waitresses squeezing their bodies through the masses of men, many of whom groped and fondled the women. Both the men and the waitresses were laughing.

Angie noticed the other women, who were wearing less than the waitresses, garishly made up, and were drinking and swearing as raucously and loudly as the men. One man caught Angie's eye and winked at her, slapping at the seat next to him.

Oh, God, Angie thought. *What am I doing here?*

At that moment, two of the brawlers from outside rolled into the room, right past Angie, and into the middle of the room.

Chaos erupted. Angie was shoved roughly against a table and felt something glance against her head. She ducked down and slipped under the table. She hastily crawled away from the riot. Sliding along the wall, keeping her eyes covered, her ears as closed as possible, and using her hand to find her way, she eventually found a hallway that led away from the noise. Finally, she found a door that felt like it would open. She knocked on it loudly. Not sure if there had been an answer, she edged her way inside.

"Aye, what is it, lass?" came an oddly familiar voice. "Are ye the new girl?"

Angie peered through the dimly lit room. It was Young Captain Sam! It had to be.

"Young…Captain…Sam?" Angie ventured.

"Aye, lass. Have we met?"

"Aye…I mean yes."

"I don't remember ye."

"Well, I mean, we haven't met yet."

"We haven't met yet?" Young Captain Sam looked at her oddly. "Who are ye, lass?"

Angie's eyes were getting use to the gloom. Young Captain Sam was doing paperwork, something she never thought about in connection with him, and she could swear that he was using an electronic tablet.

"Where did you get that?" she asked, pointing at the little computer.

Young Captain Sam tossed it in a drawer hurriedly and approached Angie quicker than a man his age should be able to. Angie noticed that he actually looked older than he did in her time.

"My name is Angie Kaufman," she said hurriedly. "My father is Sheriff Kaufman."

Young Captain Sam grabbed her and shoved her roughly against the wall. "Where do you come from, lass?"

"New Richmond," she said.

"Yer not from here, lass!" He was shaking her. "Where are you from?"

"Brook Road," Angie yelled. "I'm from the 21st century. You know what I'm talking about. I know you know."

"Ye should be careful what ye say and to whom." Young Captain Sam dragged Angie over to the door.

"You have to help me."

"Talking to the wrong person can be very dangerous."

"New Richmond is in great danger."

Young Captain Sam opened the door and dragged her down the hallway. "Ye should be very careful. Ye have no idea what yer dealing with. Get ye gone!"

He shoved Angie into the ongoing brawl.

"What are you doing? You have to help me!"

Young Captain Sam turned away from Angie and said something to one of the men, who rushed into the crowd and lifted Angie up. Angie felt herself carried across the room, passed from hand to hand like in some colonial mosh pit. Then, she was unceremoniously dumped out the front door into the blinding sunlight.

Standing up and brushing herself off, Angie rushed back to the door, but it was locked.

There were still a few men lolling around. Angie tried to convince them to help her back inside, but they simply refused to speak to her.

"Run along, girl," one of them finally said, giving her a shove.

* * *

ANGIE was stumped. It was not as if she really had any idea of what to do in the first place, but it would have been nice if she had been able to figure something out.

At noon, she went back to the meeting place. Noon was easy enough to figure out.

No Will.

She sat around for a while.

No Will.

Angie thought about going back to the watchtower, but the idea of being any closer to The Castle scared her a little. And she was getting hungry. She went back into town and bought some cooked meat on a stick from a stall. It was half undercooked, half overcooked, needed salt, and was of curious origin. It was wonderful.

Not knowing where she was going, Angie wandered around a bit. She found herself on the common. She was just about to sit down under a tree and watch the setting sun when she heard someone calling her name.

"Angie!" the voice called again.

She looked around. It was Kirk. Relieved to see a familiar face, even if it was his, she waived.

"Angie. What are you doing here?" He was running to her.

She noticed that he was wearing britches and a triangular hat. By the time Angie recalled why she was in New Richmond, Kirk was next to her and holding her arm.

"What am I doing here?" she asked, incredulously. "What are you doing here?"

"I dunno. One moment I was in a room, and the next, I was standing in a creek surrounded by British soldiers."

"We've got to get out of here."

"You know how? I don't know how."

"If we can get back to Rosi, maybe she can figure out how."

"She's here, too?" Kirk wouldn't let go of her arm. "Good. You know how much we can make here? We know everything that's gonna happen. We can make out like bandits."

"You can't do that Kirk."

"And who's gonna stop me? You?" Kirk turned and called out to a man who was standing nearby. "Beaumont! Come over here."

The man who swaggered over was dressed poorly, but he was clearly well born and obviously military. This must be the man Rosi saw Kirk with, Angie concluded. "What are you doing? Are you crazy?"

"Like a fox. Beau, this is a friend of mine. She's gonna try to get in the way."

"We can deal with her. Connor!"

Another man close at hand snapped to attention. "Sir."

"Watch it, you slag!" Beaumont said harshly. "You're not a soldier here."

"Sorry."

"Take this girl back to the camp and hold her there."

Connor leered. "Aye, captain."

Angie did not wait. Growing up, she had had a lot of friends who were boys. That meant she had learned to fight boys. The secret was not to try and be pretty, but merely to be devastating, which she was by kneeing Kirk, shoving him at Beaumont and Connor, and fleeing. Hoping to lose them in the crowded streets of market day, Angie fled into the town.

She did not lose them, but was able to put some distance between her and them. Finally, ducking around a corner, Angie came to an empty street. A dead end! She could hear them coming up to the corner, so she dove under the raised sidewalk. She saw four sets of legs come around the corner. Two sets went in one direction. The other two sets, a young man and an adult stood there for a moment. They were just approaching the spot in the street where Angie was hiding, when some of the dust from the dirt road made her sneeze. Her pursuers stopped, Angie was sure they would look under the sidewalk, but they turned and ran off.

Another set of legs came up to Angie. Will poked his head down."You all right?"

Angie almost wept.

"Let's get you out of there," Will said, holding out a hand. "They've gone after their friends. They'll be back soon."

They ran off, ducking down several side alleys and thoroughly losing themselves.

"What are you doing in town?" Angie asked when they had stopped to catch their breaths.

Will coughed for a few seconds, and spat. "I was finding us some food. Saw these men. They were dressed like the rest of us, but they were soldiers. And they had this boy with them who talked like you do."

"Kirk."

"That was his name. They said they were coming into town to look for someone who knew the charts for the reef. I thought that if they saw you, there would be trouble. So I followed them."

"Thanks. What did they do?"

"Helped some man down from the stocks. You know who he was?"

"An angry sailor."

"Were you able to warn anyone?"

Angie shook her head again.

They were breathing easily again. "I left my musket out of town, with some hares for cooking. We should go get them and get back to the farm."

"There's got to be someone we can warn," Angie insisted.

"Maybe," Will began. "Maybe I can—"

"Oy!" a man said. He had popped out from a doorway and was standing next to them and pointing a nasty looking pistol at Angie. "Don't you be movin'!"

He stepped down into the alley. "Ye are the girl my mate Connor be looking fer."

"I don't know any Connor," Angie said, edging to one side.

She glanced over to Will and tried to signal him to edge the other way, hoping that in the dusk the man did not see the gestures.

"I'll be taking you to Connor and the officer and they'll know what to do with you." The man glanced back and forth between the two of them.

The only thing Angie had with her was the stick her food had come on. She had not wanted to litter, so she had stuck it in the rope she used as a belt. She drew out the stick and slashed it across the man's wrist like a knife. It was not sharp enough to cut him, but it made him jerk his hand away.

Will took advantage of the opportunity to lunge at the man. Will was a tall boy, much taller than the man, but the man was stockier and used to fighting. He sidestepped, grabbed Will and threw him to the ground. Will's long legs saved him. He wrapped them around the man's legs, tripping him. On the dusty ground, they wrestled, cursing and grunting, each trying to get a good grip on the pistol.

Angie dove to one side. Will broke away from the man and came to his knees shakily pointing the pistol at him. The man laughed and lunged at the boy. There was a flash and a bang and the man tackled Will. The two of them lay there for a moment, until Will rolled the man to one side. Will stood up shakily, still holding the pistol.

Angie ran to him. "Are you okay?"

They both looked down at the fallen man who had a rough charred hole just under his left eye.

"Never...."

"It was self defense."

"Paulsy!" The man named Connor ran into the alley. "Paulsy!"

"Run!" Will commanded, shoving Angie away.

Connor raised his pistol and took aim. The pistol Will had was spent, so, instead, he threw it at the other man. Connor ducked to avoid the flying gun, just as he pulled the trigger. The shot went wild, though Angie felt the heat as the ball passed inches in front of her face.

Will ran to catch Angie and grabbed her arm. "Come on!" He

pulled her around the corner.

"Paulsy!" they heard. Then came a different cry. "Murder! Help! Murder!"

In minutes, the whole town would be looking for them.

"Which way?" Angie asked.

"To get out, we have to go back. Don't you know any way? You're from here. Your friend lives at The Castle. You have got to know a way."

Angie did. At least she hoped it would work. "Follow me." And she took off as fast as she could run in those shoes.

The sun was well behind the hills when they reached the Cavalier. Much of the time had been spent hiding. Some, too much, had been spent running. Angie hoped that they had, at least temporarily, lost the mob.

The Cavalier was crowded, but no one paid them any attention. Angie found the hallway and pushed through the door to the office.

"Young Captain Sam!"

"Lass, I told you not to come around here."

"We need your help."

"Yer dangerous to us, lass." He stepped forward and grabbed both of them. For such an old man, he was surprisingly strong. "I did warn ye, lass." Instead of pulling them out into the main room, he was dragging them deeper into the inn. "I apologize," he said. "I'm sure yer a nice lass, but I have rules t'follow."

"This is important," Angie said, desperately.

"I'm sure that it is."

"Rosi Carol sent me!"

Young Captain Sam stopped. "What was that?"

"Rosi Carol. From The Castle."

"Rosi Carol." Young Captain Sam thought for a moment. "What be she doing here?"

"We don't know. It was an accident."

"And where be she now?"

"She's hurt."

"Bad?"

Will broke in. "She's at my ma's farm. Not too far from here.

A few hours walk."

"We're in trouble, Young Captain Sam," Angie said.

"Aye," he responded. "Whole town's after ye."

"Can you help us?"

"Aye."

"And can you get to Rosi Carol?"

"Nay. Don't leave the Cavalier." He let them go and started off. "Follow me."

Young Captain Sam led them a circuitous route. Angie did not think that the inn could possibly be so big. Finally, having gone along dark, little used passages, through cobwebs, and passing through rooms both small and vast, they came to a door.

"In here." Young Captain Sam opened the door. It was a room filled with barrels.

They entered the room, and he closed the door behind them.

Young Captain Sam went to the middle of the room and easily shifted a large barrel to one side, revealing a small trap door. He lifted the door. The odor that sprang from below was indescribable.

"Into here," Young Captain Sam said shortly.

"Oh, God. Yuck!" Angie was barely able to stop herself from running out of the room.

"Lass, get ye in here. Wait until you hear the search ended, and then go that way," he pointed. "It will get you to harbor. Inside fast. People are coming."

They could hear an angry crowd not too far off. Both Will and Angie slid through the trap door and dropped. There was water below. Or, at least, it was kind of like water.

"Watch out for rats," Young Captain Sam called down, shutting the trap door. They heard the barrel being shifted back onto the space.

* * *

ANGIE and Will stood in the chest deep water, their feet sinking slightly in the muck on the bottom.

The water was cold, but that was not why Will was shivering. "I never—"

"I know," Angie said.

"—Killed a man before."

"It's all right." Angie put a hand on his arm. He was quivering violently.

"I never done that before."

"You didn't have a choice."

"I never even met him before."

"He was going to kill us."

"But why?" Will pulled away. "What's so important about New Richmond?"

"I don't know. All I know is that what is going to happen here, should not be happening." How could Angie tell Will that she had come from 200 years in the future?

Above them they could hear people moving around. There was some yelling, though Rosi was not sure who was making the noise. After a while, the sounds moved off.

"You can't just go around killing people in the streets and not get hung," Will said. "Maybe you can do that where you're from, but not here. Ma will kill me."

"There's a war going on and that man was the enemy," Angie said, a little harshly.

"Ma's not going to be happy if you get me hung."

"I'll explain it to your mother. That man was going to kill me."

"Ma told me not to come here."

"She also told you to look after me. You were just doing what you were told. It isn't your fault." Angie felt they had probably waited long enough. "Come on."

"Where to?"

"We have to get out of here. We have to get back to Rosi and your mother. They need to know that Kirk knows we're here." Will was not listening. "It wasn't your fault," Angie said, shaking his arm.

"He just lay there," Will said. "Looking at me. His eyes weren't moving."

"You did the right thing. Your mother and Rosi will tell you that when we get back."

"You think?" Will was relaxing a little.

Angie held out her hand and Will reached out and took it. "I'm sure of it," she said.

The trudge under the inn and to the harbor was another of those events Angie would try not to remember. The muck sucked at their feet, making it difficult for them to move. The smell of whatever it was overwhelmed them, and they both had to stop every few seconds to retch. And there were rats. Angie wasn't sure how many, but they were on the beams that served as handholds. They were swimming on the water. They were under the water. Angie and Will splashed, hoping to keep the rats away, but their efforts had little effect.

Finally, after traveling much further than they should have for just going from the cellar under the Dancing Cavalier to the harbor, they reached the open air and water. It was dark, but they hugged the boardwalk and made their way along until they could safely climb up onto land without being seen by the townspeople.

The search was clearly still going on, but the mob, complete with torches and dogs, was on the other side of town. It reminded Angie of one of those *Frankenstein* movies Rosi had made her watch. That girl had strange taste in movies for someone who lived in a haunted house.

* * *

ONCE they were out of the water, Will relaxed noticeably. He led Angie along the edge of the town until he found the place where he had hidden his musket and his game.

"I'm famished," Angie said, hopefully.

"No time to wait here. Those are hound dogs. They'll pick up our trail soon. We have to put some water between us and them. We have to find some streams to wash away our smell."

Will kept a fast pace going, slowing down only when Angie was so exhausted that she was about to fall over. Even then, he only slowed down long enough for her to catch her breath.

Angie was again impressed with how well Will seemed to move through the darkened forest. They only stopped once, to drink some water and to finish off what little was left of the bread.

"Can't start a fire to cook anything. We'll eat when we get home." Will assured her.

How long that would be, Angie did not know. After a while, Angie was moving on autopilot, numbly following Will's twists and turns, her legs burning as they ran through the trees.

Angie did not even notice when Will stopped. She blindly continued on, walked into something, and found herself sprawling among a couple of very angry and confused pigs.

"Shh!" Will hissed at her.

"Where are we?"

"Someone's place."

"Thank God. They'll help us."

"Shh. Not sure whose, yet. Got a bit turned around. People can be a bit suspicious of strangers lying in their pigpens in the middle of the night. You stay here and stay quiet. I'll be right back."

"Where—"

"Shh!"

It was so dark Angie could not make out anything. She could feel a pig or two nuzzling her curiously. She was not sure if Will was still nearby. She was pretty sure she did not want to get shot for a trespasser. She was absolutely sure that she wanted to get out of the mud.

She thought she heard a door open. Was that a footstep?

Someone grabbed her from behind.

"Will!" Angie screamed.

A hand was clamped over her mouth and she felt cold steel pressed against her throat.

PART III

The Castle

CHAPTER 11

IT seemed like hours since Zilla had slipped silently through the door. The pistol was heavier than Rosi thought it would be. Gradually, it dragged down the poor girl's arm. Not only her arm, but her eyelids were drooping as well. If she fell asleep....

I can not do that, she thought, blinking her eyes and shaking her head to stay awake. Rosi put down the pistol for a second to rub the sleep from her eyes. The jarring pain as her left arm bumped against the pillow woke her up fast enough. She snatched up the gun and pointed it at the door.

Yeah, Rosi thought. *I'll shoot anyone who comes through that door.*

Being able to use her left arm would certainly have helped matters tremendously. Everyone in movies used both hands to shoot. At least the women did. Rosi practiced holding the gun sideways and thought it probably a lot cooler than barrel up. It also made the gun lighter for a minute.

Zilla sure has been gone a while. Maybe she was been captured.

Maybe the intruders were actually behind her looking at her though the window about to shoot her in the back of the head. Rosi closed her eyes and waited for the shot that did not come. She opened her eyes when her head fell forward and her chin was jolted. *Stay awake! Stay awake!* Carefully, she turned around and saw that the shutter was closed.

If those were footsteps outside, Rosi was going to get her chance in just a minute.

There was a knock on the door.

"Yes!" Rosi yelled out nervously.

"It is me, child. I'm coming in."

"Okay." Rosi lowered the barrel. Then the barrel was up again. "Wait!"

"What is it?"

"What's the password?"

"Password? There is no password, child."

"It's us," came Angie's voice. "Let us in!"

Angie was back! And Will. "Just a sec." Carefully, Rosi lowered the hammer and placed the pistol on the foot of the bed.

Being careful not to jar Rosi's injured arm, Angie was finally able to embrace and kiss her friend. In seconds, both of them were crying and holding on to each other.

Angie gave Rosi and Zilla a rough summary of what had happened. When Angie told about Will's fight with Paulsy, Rosi leapt to her feet, ran over, and kissed Will on the cheek. She expected Will to blush or do something like a normal boy. He merely sat there and scowled.

"Sorry," she said.

Will stood up and left the cabin.

"What did I do?"

"You did nothing," Zilla said. "I told you this wasn't his fight. He's not prepared for what has to be done. It is time for you two girls to be getting to sleep. Now that Will is back, I will let you sleep late in the morning. But be prepared for some chores."

Rosi groaned as Zilla tossed a log onto the fire, and then went off to look to her son.

Angie and Rosi spooned on the cot and watched the flames of the fire.

"Do you have any ideas?"

"No." Angie yawned. "I'm tired."

Zilla came in softly a few minutes later to find the two girls fast asleep on the cot. She adjusted the blanket to cover both of them, then went and sat on the chair. They were sleeping in her bed, after all.

* * *

"THE real question is," Angie pointed out. "Whether or not we should get involved."

"Of course we should," Rosi argued.

"Why?"

The two girls were at the creek filling buckets of water. Zilla had allowed them to sleep late because the sun was up when she awakened them. Will was nowhere to be found, so they did his chores as well as some Zilla created for them.

"Because Kirk isn't supposed to be here," Rosi pointed out.

"We don't know that."

"Of course we do. The British lose the battle."

"Who's to say that Kirk will help them win it?" Angie pointed out. "Perhaps he's the reason they lose."

"But he's trying to get them maps of the reef. He said he knows secret ways in and out."

Angie thought for a moment. "I don't know about secret ways in and out. If he takes the British in the way I got out? Well, I wouldn't go that way. I doubt I could find my way back that way."

"What about the sailor and the reef?"

Angie thought for a moment. "The sailor hadn't been here for two years. And I'd be surprised if Kirk actually would know how to pass through the reef. It's dangerous enough for the men who have been fishing the waters all their lives. Look, Rosi, It's your decision."

"My decision?"

"Yeah."

"Why is it my decision, Angie? We're equal partners on this venture."

"No, we're not. How about the way Young Captain Sam reacted? Rosi, if you are some sort of mystic Guardian of Time and Space, we are anything but equal partners."

"But I have no idea where I would even begin."

"Do you have to *know*? You know Kirk is here. You know he needs to be stopped. Stop him."

Rosi sighed. Angie had a very simple way of looking at the world.

"It may not be simple to do, but it is a simple answer. You, however, are the person who has to make this decision. Trust me, if I had any ideas, I'd tell them to you."

"And you got nothing?" Rosi laughed.

"I got a great idea," Angie said, laughing as well. "Find an army and go and beat the British."

"Angie, you're a genius. I'll get right on it."

"Ladies!" Zilla called from a short distance away. "Get back to work!"

"Yes, Zilla," they both called back.

Silently, they carried their buckets back. It was only the first of many trips. By sundown, their three hands would be badly blistered, and Rosi still had not come up with a solution.

When they were finally finished with their chores, they washed up and changed Rosi's bandages. Angie might have known everything about sanitary conditions, but Zilla had a much gentler touch, so Rosi grinned and bore her friend's ham fisted nursing.

Rosi was healing so quickly that it even surprised her.

"It's unnatural," Zilla groused. But she clearly liked Rosi, and seemed pleased that she was getting better. "I never saw someone heal so fast, child. You must have the devil's own blood in you."

Rosi started to laugh at the image, but then realized that Zilla might actually believe it. She caught Angie's gaze and stopped her from laughing as well. Zilla was the one ally they had at the moment and it was best to keep on her good side.

By the time they were done with dinner, Will was still not back.

Rosi was not sure whether to be worried or not. Angie was clearly worried. Zilla was silent.

"The boy has things to do," his mother said quietly.

Rosi was not sure, but she had the feeling that Zilla was blaming her and Angie for Will's absence. The two girls had tried to find out why Will had walked out so suddenly last night, but Zilla said little.

"He's not used to such excitement," she finally said, as if that was an answer.

Rosi had not come up with an answer to her more pressing problem. What if she and Angie were able to help New Richmond? What if by interfering, New Richmond lost the battle?

It was possible Kirk was the reason that they attacked in the first place. Angie had told her that the British had tried and failed to breech the reef. What if they would have attacked another way without Kirk's advice and information? What if?

There were too many what ifs. This could not be that hard.

Rosi knew Kirk should not be here. Neither should she and Angie. The logical thing would be to do something about it. Right? But what?

She desperately wanted to talk to Angie about it, but she could hardly talk about a battle that had not yet happened in front of Zilla. If they told Zilla whence they really came, there was no telling how she might react.

* * *

IT was well into night when the pigs started acting up. Zilla, Rosi, and Angie heard someone trying to quiet them. Zilla handed the pistol to Rosi. Angie drew her knife. The two girls sat there quivering while Zilla slipped out carrying her sword.

A few seconds later, they heard a yell, followed by a great many more yells, and then silence.

It was a long silence. Too long.

"What's going on?" Angie asked.

"How am I supposed to know?" Rosi snapped back, regretting her tone at once. "Shh."

The waiting made them even more scared. Finally, Rosi stood up shakily.

"What are you doing?" Angie asked.

"I'm going out to see what is going on."

"Are you crazy?"

"Probably. Are you coming?"

Angie sighed. She stood up and followed.

It was almost pitch black outside. There was a slight glow of the moon trying to break through the clouds, but little of it reached the ground. Rosi noticed that there was light flickering through the walls of the pseudo barn. "Come on." She tiptoed over to the door and waited for Angie to catch up to her. There were people inside, but she could not see more than shapes and shadows. "On three."

"What on three?" Angie whispered back.

"We go in on three."

"Okay."

Zilla kicked the door open from the inside. "You two are louder than a screaming baby," she yelled. "Come on in. Good, you have your gun. Now shoot one of these boys."

It took Rosi's eyes a long moment to adjust to the light. There must have been fifteen or twenty men in the barn. They weren't moving, rather, they were eying Zilla and her menacing sword suspiciously.

"I said shoot one of them," Zilla repeated. "Take aim, and shoot."

"Shoot?"

"Yes, child. Shoot them. Kill them." Zilla stepped forward, grabbed one of the men and threw him to the ground. "Start with this damn fool!"

"Ma!" the huddled figure cried. It was Will.

Zilla kicked him and he rolled over. The other men shied away. "Go ahead and shoot him," she snarled. "Then reload and shoot another. Angie, go and get more shot. We've got a lot of killing to do tonight."

"Zilla," Rosi tried to go to Will, but his mother stopped her. "I'm not gonna shoot Will."

"Then give me the gun and I'll shoot the fools."

"Why?" Rosi looked around at the men. They seemed terrified.

"Because they want to die."

"What are you talking about?"

"Tell her, boy!" Zilla ordered. Will opened his mouth, but nothing came out. "Go ahead, boy. Talk!"

"Ma," he started. "These men are—"

"I know who they are," Zilla snapped. "Lazy good for nothing local boys who think they're too good to be farmers."

One young man stepped forward, raising his hand. "My pa's a blacksmith, Miz Zilla."

"Shut up, Tom!"

"Yes, Miz Zilla." He faded back into the group.

"Go on, Will," his mother said.

"You are always telling me how this isn't my fight." Will was nervous, but seemed determined to have his say.

"It isn't." Zilla insisted.

"But I—we've been talking about it. Maybe it is. I mean, these girls say—"

"You won't listen to you own mother, but you listen to these little girls?"

"Yes, ma...I mean, no." Will looked around at his friends nervously, as if he expected one of them to step in and help him. "We've been talking about it for a while. For a couple of months."

"Behind my back?" Zilla roared.

Will hung his head. The others did as well. "Yes, Ma."

Zilla appeared to think for a moment. Rosi was afraid the woman might use the sword. Finally, Zilla lowered the point. "Go on."

"Perhaps this is our fight." Will held up his hand to stop his mother from interrupting. "One way or another, we're going to have to choose sides. At some point we will have to. All up and down the coast, everywhere, everyone is getting involved. Can't stay neutral any more. We thought to fight the Redcoats."

"Why?" Zilla kept the point of the sword down, but it looked like it might come up at any moment.

"Because...because...Ma, we know what our lives'll be like if the Redcoats win."

"You stay out of the fight, then your lives will go on like before."

"You're right, Ma. Our lives will go on like before. But if they lose—"

"You think your lives will get better? Are you such great fools?"

"We don't know, Ma. We don't know." He was silent for a moment. Rosi thought he might be done. So did Zilla, who turned away and was about to leave when Will spoke again. "But they can hardly get worse. And, who knows...they might get better."

Zilla turned back and held her son's eyes for a long moment.

"You might be right," she finally conceded. "I'm still not sure we shouldn't shoot you. Get it over with. Did you bring some food?" she asked everyone.

Several of the young men nodded. At her direction, they brought it up and Zilla had Angie gather it together.

"We'll be busy tonight, little girl," Zilla said. "Take the food inside and start cooking. These men must start their brave venture on a full stomach. Go on!"

Angie bundled the food into a blanket and carried it off.

"Child!" Zilla turned to Rosi.

"Yes, Zilla," Rosi answered.

"You get some rest." Zilla began pushing Rosi out the door. "These boys may have been talking about it for some time, but they'd still be talking if you hadn't come and got Will to thinking above his station. These boys may mean well, but they haven't a brain between them. I'm making you their captain. So you get some sleep, and we'll decide what to do in the morning."

"Me?"

"Yes, child. Go to bed."

Rosi left. The men were grumbling and she thought she heard one say something about "not following no stupid girl."

Zilla followed her in a few minutes later. "I told you to sleep, child," she said. "Who knows, perhaps your command will have drifted away in the night."

Rosi almost laughed. "So that was your plan. They won't want to follow a girl and will go home."

"No, child." Zilla was sad. "But I've given them the opportunity. I locked them in the barn. I don't want to make it too easy for them. If they're smart enough, maybe they will have figured out how to get out by morning. I doubt it, though. Will hasn't figured it out in seventeen years. They won't figure it out overnight."

Zilla turned to Angie and they started going through the food.

Rosi tried not to sleep, but to no avail. She blinked once too often and opened her eyes to see sunlight streaming in through the windows.

Angie was standing next to the bed, stifling a yawn. Silently, she changed Rosi's bandages. "Your company awaits you, Captain," she said with a wary smile.

"*Et tu*, Angie?"

When Rosi stood up, Angie wrapped an odd looking belt around her waist.

"What's this for?" Rosi asked.

"Zilla says that an officer needs a sword." Angie shoved Zilla's sword into a makeshift scabbard and handed Rosi the pistol. "There. You look ridiculous."

Rosi laughed. "It could hardly get worse."

"It does," Angie giggled. She produced a hat wrapped in ribbons and plopped it on Rosi's head. The hat was much too large, and practically covered Rosi's eyes. "The hat was my idea," her friend said. "So they can see you in battle."

"*They* being our guys or the enemy?"

"Not sure."

"Thanks. I owe you one."

Angie opened the door and bowed Rosi out.

The men had been let out of the barn and were sitting around on the dew-damp ground eating. There had not been enough plates, but the men had made do with pieces of bark and old bits of leather to serve as dishes.

"We were up all night cooking," Angie said proudly, handing Rosi a plate of stew and eggs. "I made the eggs."

Zilla came up to the two of them. "Little girl, I hope you stay pretty, because you'll never get a husband with your cooking."

There was a generally laughing agreement to this sentiment.

Angie blushed brightly and scowled. "My eggs are fine. My father loves them."

Rosi took a bite and had to try hard not to spit them out. Rosi knew she had to say something for her friend. "Angie, perhaps Andy can do the cooking."

Angie glared at her, then her face broke into a smile. "He can't do any worse."

"No," Rosi agreed. "He can't."

The two girls had a loud laugh together.

Soon, breakfast was over, thank goodness. The young men gathered together in something resembling a line and waited for Rosi.

"What's going on?" Rosi asked.

"Your company," Zilla said.

"You're not serious!"

"Child, you're the best one for the job."

"I'm a fifteen year old girl."

"You're a Carol.

"What does that have to do with anything?"

"Don't you know anything about your family? Your family have been leaders since the area was settled. Whatever your age, your name means something." Zilla leaned in, as if to maintain confidentiality. "What's more, these boys think they're playing a game. I trust you to remember that this is serious business."

"Yes, Zilla."

"Besides, you seem to know what's going on. Most of these boys have never been more than a few miles from their homes. They need someone in charge who knows the world a little."

"Why don't you lead them?" Rosi asked. "I'll tell you where to go. I'll tell you what needs to be done."

"No, child, I'll not get involved. I'll be here to sew them up when it's over. That's all I'll do. But I told them last night to listen to you. They will. Don't ask me exactly why, but I know you should be in charge."

Most of the men had gathered around and were listening.

"You'll do as Miss Carol says," Zilla said gravely.

Will, and a few others nodded. Seeing them agree, the others nodded as well.

Rosi picked up a stick, stuck it under her arm, and marched up and down the line, pretending to inspect her troops.

Angie giggled.

Rosi really had no idea what to do. She hoped that the men thought she looked sufficiently professional. She counted the men. There were thirty-one men. A few had come in the night to join the others, Zilla explained.

Rosi decided to split them into three platoons of ten, keeping

Will as her lieutenant. Each platoon would have two squads of five including a sergeant and a master sergeant. She had seen enough war movies to know that this was necessary. She was not sure why. Soon, they were standing in six small groups.

"What do we do now?" Will asked. "How do we choose sergeants?"

Rosi did not know. "Who's the best shot here?"

Every man raised his hand. Then they started arguing among themselves as to who actually was the best shot. One had shot a rabbit at two hundred yards. One had hit a flying bird. It went on. Voices rose. Rosi worried for a moment that the posturing might get out of hand. Finally she had to raise her own voice, multiple times, and resolve the issue. "Why don't we just say that the oldest two men in each platoon are the sergeants?" she said, after she was able to get the others to be silent for a moment. "One for each squad?"

The men discussed this for a few minutes. Finally they agreed, after Rosi explained to one man that September did not come before August. This, of course, made the older men happy. The younger men were not so pleased, but were generally smaller than the older men so they stayed quiet. Finally, the talk quieted down and the men stood facing her expectantly.

Rosi had no idea what to do until Angie suggested she actually have the men show her what they could do. Rosi called over to her Lieutenant. "Take the company a quarter of a mile," she told him. "That direction and then come back and—" She thought for a moment. "Storm the farm."

"But the farm is already ours."

"I know that!" *Jeez*. "I just want to see what you can do with the men."

The men shrugged and started off.

"Will," Zilla called out.

"Yes, ma."

"Tell them not to shoot. There aren't actually any Redcoats here."

"Do you think they got lost," Rosi asked about twenty minutes later.

"No, child. No such luck. There they are." Zilla pointed across the clearing that made up her small farm, where a long line of men were straggling out of the trees and beginning to amble toward the buildings.

"Stop!" Rosi called out. "You'll all be gunned down if you walk up like that. You're not going to church. You're attacking the farm. Go back and do it again."

Grumbling, the men disappeared into the trees.

A minute later, Rosi, Zilla, and Angie heard a great yell. The men charged from the trees and ran across the clearing, racing to the farm. A couple tripped and a few tripped over them, but soon, most of the men were standing in front of Rosi, gasping for air and clapping each other on the backs.

"Pathetic," was all Rosi could say.

"What?" several of them exploded. They clearly thought they had done a great job charging the farm.

"All wrong. You'd still get wiped out. Gather around."

Rosi stooped down and drew a rough outline of the farm and its buildings in the dirt. "Here's the farm. I know, Tom," she said, when the young man started to speak. "It's a drawing of the farm. You don't just charge out in the open. One platoon comes from the east and attracts fire. The others come in from the north and the south. And you don't just charge. Send one squad forward to hold an area, those trees over there. Then the second squad comes forward and takes that clump of rocks, and so forth and so on."

The men seemed to think it was an odd way to fight a battle, but they gave it a try. They did pretty well, Rosi thought. She could still hear them five minutes away, but it was a beginning.

The rest of the morning was spent storming the farm. Rosi knew little about tactics other than what she had seen in movies, but she was far ahead of her company. Angie and Zilla seemed to think the whole affair rather amusing and tried hard not to laugh.

For a couple of hours after lunch, she had the men practice sneaking up on each other. Finally, she had a contest to see who had the best aim. The men had been pretty honest. They were all fantastic shots. Rosi redistributed the squads, making sure everyone had a sniper, one of the better shots, and recon, the quietest.

By late afternoon, Rosi felt confident about her company. Confident was a little strong, but she had added a few men. Her troop was now thirty-seven men and eight horses. The time had now come for Rosi to come up with a plan. Rosi summoned Will, Angie, Zilla, and her sergeants, and asked that they attend her at headquarters.

"That means follow me into the house," Rosi explained, sticking her head out the door when she realized that no one was coming in.

Jeez!

* * *

ROSI stood before her staff. "We have to decide what to do."

"Fight the Lobsterbacks," one man said, as if that was the obvious answer.

"We are all agreed that we have to fight the Redcoats." It struck Rosi at that moment that most of these men considered themselves to be British. She would have to be careful with her choice of words. "But exactly what are we going to do? Where do we engage them? How do we engage them? I suggest we try to help New Richmond. We know that the Redcoats are coming and we know when."

"How do we know that?" asked another.

Angie and Rosi looked at each other. Zilla came to their rescue. "Don't ask stupid questions, Tom. The girl says they're coming to New Richmond, then they're coming to New Richmond."

Rosi realized that Zilla's response was not actually a very good one, but the men did not.

"So," Tom tried, hesitantly. "We go to New Richmond?"

"Sort of. Angie, my recon," Rosi smiled at Angie, who blushed. "Tells me that there is a cannon at The Castle."

The men paled at the mention of that place.

"Now, don't you worry. I know The Castle. I swear that it won't hurt you. We hold the high ground there. Harass the enemy with artillery, and wait for reinforcements."

"What reinforcements?" Will asked.

"Can any one tell me where the New Hampshire Fourth Regiment is?" Rosi looked at Angie triumphantly. *I remembered! Good girl.* Angie gave her a thumbs up.

"Last I heard, child," Zilla ventured. "Was that they were over Concord way."

"Excellent." Rosi looked around the room. "Will. I hate to lose you, but I need you to take a squad by horse and find the Fourth. Tell them that the commander of the Carol Company sends compliments and requests relief at The Castle and New Richmond."

"The Carol Company?" Angie asked, smiling. "Why not Rosi's Raiders?"

"With any luck, they will think it is Beatitude Carol who is asking for their help."

Zilla spoke up. "That's a good idea, child. Beatitude is well known. They might come to help him."

Might was the word that stayed with Rosi. Might. They might not, too. Then this would be a short command.

Rosi sent Will out to find enough men who could ride to form his squad, while Rosi went over her plan of approach to The Castle. She was almost done when she heard a commotion outside. Rushing outside with Zilla close behind, she saw that everyone was gathered around two men who had rode up on one horse.

Rosi and Zilla rushed up as someone helped the breathless men down.

"The Redcoats," one of them gasped. "The Redcoats."

"What is it, John Thatcher?" Zilla demanded. She stepped in and took his arm.

"The Redcoats. The English" He could not go on. Someone gave him some water, which he drank greedily.

"Catch your breath, boy," Zilla said. "And tell us what is going on."

"There are soldiers over to the village. They've dogs. They're looking for a boy and a girl who killed one of their men."

"How many are there?" Rosi asked. Angie was turning pale, so Rosi took her hand.

John Thatcher thought for a moment. "Couldn't be more than ten. But they're angry. Asking questions and beating those that don't answer. They burned down Eustace's barn and chased his wife into the woods."

"Is she all right?" Eustace leapt in and grabbed the exhausted man.

"She's fine. She's fine, Eustace. Went over to Parson's place. Even Redcoats wouldn't burn a church."

"Which way are they going?" Zilla asked, in an attempt to get the conversation back on track.

"They'll be here by tonight. They heard somewhere that everyone's come here. They'll be here by nightfall."

Zilla took Rosi and Angie away from the others. "That gives us a few hours, and that's all."

"That means we have to leave now," Rosi said.

"No, child. They have dogs. Tracking dogs. They'll be following her smell." Zilla pointed at Angie.

"So what do we do?"

"You clear off as much sign of all these men and then start off for New Richmond. Little girl and I will distract them. We'll lead them a chase."

Rosi insisted that she and Angie take some men with her. Zilla tried to disagree.

Angie took Rosi's hand. "Well, we're split up again."

"You're gonna be fine." Rosi said.

"I know," Angie said. "You better be fine, too. I gotta get home somehow. I don't want to end up on some deserted island."

"Think I have a chance?"

"No," Angie laughed. "Your men have only trained for a day. It is crazy. We should run and find some real soldiers. Find this Beatitude fellow and have him get us home."

"I can't do that." Rosi knew Angie would understand. "But, hey, these guys can shoot. They know the area. There aren't enough of them for a pitched battle, but if we can hang onto The

Castle long enough for reinforcements—"

"If? Rosi, I don't like that if."

"I don't either. What else am I supposed to do?"

They were both crying. There was not much to be said. They held on to each other until Zilla came out carrying a small bag of food for her party. "Come on, little girl," the older woman said.

"You bring her back to me," Rosi said through her tears. This was not fun any more. "You hear me, Zilla."

"Aye, Captain." Zilla quickly chose three men to go with her, and she led them and Angie off to the west. Just before they disappeared into the trees, Angie turned and snapped Rosi a quick salute.

"You come back, Angie," Rosi whispered to the wind.

"Ma'll take good care of her." Will rode up next to her. He looked pretty good on horseback. There was a confidence in his eyes. "We'll see you at The Castle in a few days."

Rosi held out her hand to shake his, and was a little surprised when he bent over it and pressed his lips against her palm.

He started off, but she stopped him with her hand on his knee. "You come back, too, Will Scranton." He nodded and rode off with his men.

Now Rosi was alone. Except for the thirty or so young men who had never seen a woman wearing trousers before and were enjoying it perhaps a little too much.

"All right, you men," Rosi bellowed. "Gather together everything you can! Get all the supplies on to the horses! Form squads! We leave in ten minutes! *Didi mao! Didi mao!* Move it!"

CHAPTER 12

ROSI watched from the tree line as the three platoons approached The Castle separately. They did it in textbook fashion, she supposed. Each platoon set up a sniper, out of sight, to keep an eye on the area as far ahead as he could shoot. Then, with one squad covering, the other squad made its way forward. That squad would cover while the second squad caught up and then moved ahead. Then the sniper moved up and the process was repeated.

They had had a fair amount of practice since sunup, for Rosi had them run through the sequence every time they crossed a stream or a road or a clearing they could not go around.

It had taken Rosi and her men somewhat longer to reach The Castle than it had taken Angie and Will a few days earlier. Rosi was not quite sure why, but thirty-odd people moved a lot slower than two. Of course, most of the journey had been made in the dark. *These guys must eat a lot of carrots,* Rosi thought. No one ever seemed to walk into a tree or any obstacles. But Rosi's face was scratched by leaves and the not infrequent branch that got in her way.

Rosi had kept busy on the march. She had restructured the platoons. Minus Will's squad, and Zilla and Angie's escort, she now had thirty-four men. Eustace had shown himself to be hard working and, more importantly, extremely popular. So Rosi made him head sergeant for the First Platoon.

The next platoon went to the oldest man in the group, who probably was in his thirties. He had the unlikely name of Spartacus. He had been a trapper in his earlier years, until he had lost a hand to a bear. His wooden hand had a pipe carved into it, from which he puffed smoke almost incessantly. He was also the only one who had ever even seen combat. He had been in a caravan that had been attacked by Indians about seven years earlier. Rosi was pleased to note that he was honest enough with the others. "I ran and hid in the bushes," was how Spartacus described his involvement. The Second Platoon held the right flank.

The left flank was held by the Third Platoon, led by a younger man named Robin. Two of the remaining three horses belonged to him and he was indignant at not being allowed to ride. He neither understood nor cared that the horses were needed to carry supplies and saved in case Rosi needed to send a message to the Second or Third Platoons. She kept a close watch over the First. Because Rosi was afraid Robin might leave the company and take the horses, she gave him the Third Platoon to keep him happy. Robin was probably the one man in the company least happy to be led by a girl and grumbled whenever Rosi said anything.

Spartacus and Eustace kept him from anything more severe than insubordination. Spartacus, like Zilla, with whom he stepped out from time to time, realized that the average member of the company was a few pints shy of a full intellectual gallon. Rosi might not be qualified to lead the company, but was less unqualified than anyone else. Eustace was smitten with her and had already been in two fights with boys who had impugned her honor.

The men were generally happy to follow Zilla's instructions and let Rosi play captain. Rosi could tell they were thinking that perhaps Rosi might do something right. She might actually be as smart as Zilla thought. If things really got bad they could just leave and go home.

With the four men left over from the three platoons, Rosi had a Headquarters' staff. She liked the idea of having an HQ staff. John Thatcher, who was a fine horseman, was her runner and personal scout. She dubbed him Director of Intelligence. John's younger brother Harry, who was Rosi's age but looked much younger, was put in charge of the horses and the meager supplies and had the title of Wagon Master.

The third member of Rosi's staff was named If-Christ-Had-Not-Died-For-Thee-Thou-Hast-Been-Damned. *Really!* Another of those Puritan names like Beatitude, but even worse! He was known by his last name, Essex, but Rosi had the feeling that he had been delegated to her staff because of his name. If-Christ-Had-Not-Died-For-Thee-Thou-Hast-Been-Damned Essex was a quiet young man and just about the ugliest person Rosi had ever seen, who, rumor had it, was married to the most beautiful girl in the colony. She was also the biggest nag and If-Christ-Had-Not-Died-For-Thee-Thou-Hast-Been-Damned Essex had married her because no other woman would marry him and she had married him because she had driven off every other prospect. He was one of the few people in the company who knew why he was here. "I need the rest," he said when Rosi had asked him.

Essex had the best eyesight in the group and a very gentle touch. It was, at least in part, because of him that Rosi had made it this far without killing herself. He had even carried Rosi across a couple of deep streams. Rosi was not exactly sure how to thank him. She knew a hug or a kiss on the cheek was the traditional way a girl thanked a guy when she came from, but he was so ugly! And she was afraid the pimples on his face would explode if she touched them. She could hardly even look at him. He took it all in stride. Whenever he had to move her or lift her, he did it so gently her arm barely hurt, any more than it already did. By the time they caught sight of The Castle, her arm was throbbing and she had been forced by Essex and John Thatcher onto one of the horses.

Finally, A-Squad, First Platoon reached the front porch. The whole company stood there proudly, waiting for praise, as Harry led her up. She looked around and nodded. "Fantastic," she said. The men grinned. Then she gave them what they were waiting for. Rosi smiled brightly, showing off all of her teeth, and flicked her hair out of her face. That made everyone happy, except for Eustace who scowled at them. *Men are so easy!*

But now was time to give some more orders.

"Spartacus. Down the drive a bit," it was more of a path, but Rosi was not sure what else to call it. "You'll see a watchtower to the left. Station some men there and keep an eye on the town and the road below. First Platoon, you're with me. We'll secure the building and the towers. We'll be able to see the harbor and the straits. We'll have the only cannon unless the New Hampshire Fourth brings some."

Spartacus had suggested that Robin would respond better to questions than to orders.

"Robin," Rosi asked, "what would you say to keeping an eye of the approach from the woods? That way you can keep an eye on the First and the Second and serve as support for both?"

Robin agreed.

"On the other side of the main house are cliffs. I'd like to see the British try to get up them." Rosi laughed at the idea.

The men spread out and went to their stations, except for Eustace and his men. They stood, looking at the front door.

"What's wrong?" Rosi asked.

"Castle haunted," one man said.

Rosi scoffed. "Go on in."

"Door won't open," he said, demonstrating the door was indeed firmly closed. When he touched the door the house seemed to moan slightly. The men stepped back a few feet.

This is ridiculous, Rosi thought. She walked up to the door and kicked it. "Shut up and open!" The moaning stopped and the door swung open. Rosi might be getting the hang of this.

Voila, she gestured, waving the men in. They entered, all who had them removing their hats at the threshold and giving a little respectful bow to Rosi before going in.

The Castle was behaving. The doors leading to Rosi's tower were open. None of the other doors were open, and they would not budge, but this was a start. Rosi set up HQ in her once, and, future room and sent the men to work clearing up the place and preparing the cannon.

Eustace suggested they post men on the other towers, which were higher, but Rosi rejected the idea. "I don't want to disperse the men over too great an area," she said, hoping he would accept the reason and not need to know that Rosi had never been able to find the other towers.

Rosi noticed the door in her room. She wondered what would happen if she touched it or opened it. Would it take her home? If it took her home, what would her home be like? Would it be the same world she had left? Would she be able to come back for Angie? Best not to risk it.

* * *

THROUGHOUT the day, the men got themselves and The Castle ready.

They found some powder in the stables. They had, perhaps, ten shots for the cannon. That was a beginning. Rosi had no idea how much powder to put in. It could not be that difficult, could it? Eustace seemed to be quite comfortable with it.

Spartacus had done a wonderful job setting up ambushes along the path. The watchtower and Rosi's tower gave them a view of the whole harbor and the village.

Robin had gathered his men together by the stables. It took all of Rosi's patience to refrain from yelling at him. He had not stationed men in the trees.

"Just keep an eye on the tree line," Rosi finally said, stalking off in a huff.

Rosi thought about riding into town to talk to the locals. What could she tell them? Zilla might be able to convince her neighbors to listen to her, but Zilla was not here and probably did not have the kind of influence needed to convince the townspeople. Angie said that Young Captain Sam had refused to help. So what could Rosi do but hold the heights until the New Hampshire Fourth arrived?

"How can you be so sure the Redcoats will come?" John asked.

"I am." Rosi could not tell anyone how she knew.

He shrugged. He was not going to argue.

A couple of hours after the sun set, the sliver of moon followed it behind the low hills to the west. There was almost no light, for clouds obscured most of the stars. The land, the sea, and the sky were merely different depths of black.

Rosi would not allow the men to build fires, so there was some grumbling.

Robin's men were able to clear out enough space in the

stables to make a small fire and they all hovered around it. Rosi was not happy about this, but she could not think of any reason to forbid it. "Just don't burn down the stables," she said.

About two in the morning, some men straggled through the trees. Robin's pickets nervously challenged them and discovered they were an advance party from the New Hampshire Fourth.

Thank God, Rosi thought.

Over the next couple of hours, the men streamed in steadily.

Rosi called her platoons together and consolidated them around the main building. She let the new troops take the watchtower and the drive. There were a couple of officers who were not too happy about this arrangement. Why was some little girl dictating the disposition of their men?

The presence of the New Hampshire Fourth, and their rather condescending attitude towards the company and its leader instilled Rosi's men with an *esprit de corps* that they had not had before. Even Robin stood up to one of the captains who tried to ignore Rosi's instructions.

As Rosi had pointed out, it was her family's house and if she did not want the others in it, they could go away!

Finally, Brigadier General Pierce arrived. "I know your uncle," he bellowed to Rosi. He was a large red faced man who smelled of gin. His clothes were tailor made and fancy, and Rosi felt a little foolish around him. He was a real general, and she was just a kid playing soldier.

Rosi only halfway paid attention to him, because Will and the others had ridden up and Rosi was very happy to see him. Them.

Pierce's captains ran to him and started complaining, but he waved them off, taking Rosi's arm and allowing her to guide him around the area and explain her set up. He was quite impressed and clearly thought one of the men had told her how to do it.

Rosi kept her mouth shut, because he quite solicitously called her captain and made his men do the same. There were some grins. Rosi merely grinned back.

"If you'll permit, general," Rosi said as he guided her back to the main house. "The view from the inner tower is as good as anywhere else. Why don't you let my men hold the main building as your headquarters as well as mine?"

Rosi was just trying to be polite, but Pierce's eyes practically popped out of his head.

Oh, God, she realized. *He thinks I'm propositioning him! And he's about to say yes!*

Just then, an aide rushed up with an important message for the general. The cannons were arriving.

"Thank God!" Pierce shouted, momentarily forgetting the girl's apparent offer.

"Thank God," Rosi sighed.

Pierce left Rosi and went to inspect the big guns. Rosi followed.

"Take them into town and set them up in the port," Pierce ordered.

Rosi knew this was wrong. "General."

"What is it, m'dear?"

"May I make a suggestion about the artillery?"

He was not going to let some little girl tell him how to dispose of his artillery, his body seemed to say. His face turned even redder. "What," he said tightly.

Rosi knew the warning signs. Perhaps she had gone too far. She knew, however, that the cannon would be more effective from the heights. She knew what to do. If only Will and the other men were not just standing around watching everything!

Indeed, everyone in the area stood and watched, aghast at the idea of this little girl telling their general anything.

Rosi stepped in closer to the general, tilted her head, and lay her hand on his arm, letting her index finger run along the gilded braids. "Don't you think," she said sweetly, looking down and drawing a little circle in the dirt with the toe of her boot. "That the range might be more effective if the cannon were placed up here? It would also put them further from harm's way?"

Brigadier General Pierce, who would one day be Lieutenant Governor Pierce, thought for a moment. He took her hand, bowed over it, and kissed it sloppily. "Out of the mouths of babes!" he cried, laughing. All of the other men laughed as well. "We'll put the cannon up here." He reached behind Rosi and pinched her rear firmly, and staggered away to see to his men.

Rosi fled into The Castle and hid in a corner to cry. She had never been so humiliated in her life! Will and Spartacus and Eustace and John and most of the others had had to watch her make a complete spectacle of herself. Clara Barton and Susan B. Anthony would be rolling over in their graves, if they had been born, lived, died, and been buried yet.

"It's all right," Will said, sitting on the floor next to her.

"I'm not really a bimbo," Rosi said, wiping her nose on her sleeve. He looked confused. "I'm not really a bad girl," she explained.

"I know that." He took her hand. Her arm went tingly. "You were right. General Pierce knew that."

"He should see that I'm right because I'm right, not because…."

"Don't worry about it."

"I don't want the men to think…I don't want you to think…."

"I don't." He stood up, but kept her hand in his. "We should be getting back. We don't care what Pierce is doing. We want you. You're our leader." He helped her up. He reached out and gently wiped her eyes with his thumb, letting it linger on her cheek.

"I'm scared," Rosi said.

"I am, too."

"What if I did the wrong thing? What if we're not supposed to be here? What if Kirk—"

"No one knows what's going to happen until it happens, Rosi."

She looked into his eyes. "I wish I could tell you…."

"Tell me."

"You wouldn't understand." Rosi said quietly.

Will's eyes were sad, but they trusted her. She turned her head and kissed his fingers. "Let's go back."

Hand in hand, they went back to her tower.

* * *

IT was a quiet night. A strong breeze blew out to sea. Not good, Rosi knew.

A few lights burned in New Richmond, but most of the town was asleep.

General Pierce came by once or twice to inspect the men. He winked at Rosi each time, which Rosi did not like. She kept her mouth shut, though.

He also sent a couple of gunners to take control of the cannon, which she did like. Rosi'd had a recurring waking nightmare that one of her men would blow up the battlement and kill all of them. She had calmed her fears by convincing herself that a cannon was simply a large musket, but after about five minutes of watching the gunners prepare, she realized that she had been wrong and that one of her men would most likely have blown every one up.

Rosi had a pretty good grasp on American History, but the history books and the philosophical treatises of great men were hardly a good introduction to what life had really been like. Books, even by those alive at the time, and paintings made the Revolutionary War seem like it was fought by men of noble sentiment and heroic bearing. From what Rosi could gather, the average soldier thought the British were responsible for all of their lives' ills and had little or no idea of the philosophy behind the war. Few of them had even heard of the word *democracy*. They certainly did not look like heroes. They looked like they were starving. Rosi knew that quite a few members of the New Hampshire Fourth had disappeared during the winter. It happened every winter. Some would come back. Some would not. General Pierce hardly looked the dashing leader. His fancy tailor made clothes were stained, by what Rosi did not even want to guess. Tobacco juice dripped from his chin. And she listened to him talking with some of his soldiers. His description of what they would be doing to the British was not just graphic, it was pornographic and scatological. At least this Mosley fellow had the veneer of sophistication, even if he was little more than a thug.

Rosi had made a point of trying to discuss the reasoning behind the war with her men. Their attitude was odd. They considered themselves Americans. They also considered themselves British. But, they also considered the British the enemy. They liked the idea of getting rid of the King, but mostly because it was a poke in the eye of the *haves* by the *have nots*. Like Zilla, they seemed to take the philosophy with a grain of salt. None of them felt that their inalienable rights had been violated. None of them cared about their right to vote. Rosi realized few if any of them would ever have that right. Spartacus, whose father had fled Scotland in 1746 in the wake of the Forty-Fives, simply hated all of the English and George III. His King was Charles III, and he let everyone know it.

Rosi wondered what was more important, soldiers who knew how to fight or soldiers who knew why they were fighting. She understood her men followed her orders out of respect for Zilla, and perhaps, because Spartacus and Eustace seemed to accept that she was in charge. Indeed, like Zilla, they insisted on it. It was not just because she was a Carol. It was also because she was an outsider, Will explained. None of the local boys would accept one of their own as the leader.

Right now, Rosi figured she was more of a mascot. They had dressed her up, given her a sword, and put some boots on her. They might insist that everyone else treat her with respect, but they were her men as long as she amused them.

That might change if Rosi were able to help keep the British out of New Richmond. *Might* being the operative word. If she failed, her command might disperse like dandelion seeds in a hurricane. For now, she would do her best to keep her men alive and at least doing something vaguely soldierly.

Rosi had a great deal of respect for the military. Yet she knew almost nothing about the military except what she had derived from movies, books, and video games. She could bellow, bluster, swear, storm, preen, and pose. She was also fairly bright and had some common sense. She owed it to Zilla and to her men to try her best. If that was not good enough, then so be it.

Rosi had the men redistribute their ammunition, so that everyone had roughly the same amount of powder and number of shots. The First Platoon stayed on Rosi's tower. Not much they could do. Their muskets would never have the range. The Second took over the watchtower again when Pierce moved his men down closer to the road and the entrance to the town. If the British did indeed attack, and Pierce doubted they would, he wanted to be able to get his men into the fight as quickly as possible.

"You'll serve as reinforcements," he told Rosi.

Pierce took the Third Platoon to act as powder monkeys. Quite a few of Pierce's men had still not arrived. Also, there was some sort of action going on to the north and he had sent some of his others to investigate.

Most of the men slept. They took the idea of a British attack very seriously, but did not really think it would happen any time soon. Pierce's men knew who Beatitude Carol was, even if Rosi did not, and suspected that if there was any real danger he would have warned them.

Rosi could not sleep. She was nervous. She was scared. She was excited.

Beatitude was not supposed to look to the future, so he might not have any reason to think there was any danger.

Rosi did not have the ethical dilemma. She knew the attack would come.

CHAPTER 13

THE farm was dark. The three small buildings were merely darker shadows in the middle of a greater shadow. Occasionally, starlight peeped through the clouds to give objects more shape, but not often.

The men inched their way forward.

One man crawled forward and hid behind a low table which had been knocked over in the hubbub earlier in the day. Carefully, he looked over the edge of the table and listened. He crawled back.

"Hear anything?" he was asked.

"Aye. Som'un's inside."

One of the dogs whimpered.

"Shut that mutt up," someone snapped quietly.

"Sorry. Sur."

Connor looked at the buildings for a moment, letting his eyes become adjusted to the change from the darkness of the woods to the darkness of the clearing.

He made hand signals to two of the men. "Go around to the side," his hands said. "Stay out of sight."

It was his turn to approach the building. That was why he was the sergeant and got the extra pay. *Rot that*, he thought. He did not care about the two women. He wanted the man who had killed Paulsy. You do not kill a man's mate and not expect to pay the price.

He was frustrated further by the wasted running around the woods. They had been to this small farm the night before. Now their prey had come back to it. They might just as well have stayed here and waited for the women to come waltzing right into their arms. There was little that Connor hated more than doing something the difficult way. Much as he wanted to kill the boy who had killed Paulsy, Connor would much rather have stayed in camp.

But the sailor and his boy had different ideas. "Bring the girls," was what they said. "Do what you want with the man, but bring the girls."

He would bring the girls, and he would follow orders and not hurt them. Too much. He grinned. Not many women at the camp. At least not for the men. Bloody officers!

Almost there.

The other dog whined.

Connor turned and waved for quiet. That was his mistake, for in turning, his foot went wide and landed on a small stick. Any other time, and the noise would have been ignored. Tonight, though, the breaking of the stick was as loud as an explosion.

Connor froze.

His men froze.

The shutters covering one of the windows flew open, the barrel of a musket appeared, and there was a pop, a flash, and a puff of smoke. Connor dove behind the overturned table, feeling the musket ball tear through the air just over his back.

Gunfire erupted.

Connor tried to raise himself to call out for his men to hold their fire, but they were tired from slogging through the woods all day and arguing with uncooperative settlers. They were screaming as loudly as they could and firing as fast as they could. They had been at it hard for the last day and a half since they finally located the trail. *They even almost caught them twice,* Connor thought. Now, he was so close. *If only these idiots would stop firing.*

"Hold your fire!" he bellowed. No one heard. Or, at least, no one listened. "Hold your fire," he tried again.

The women inside fought back admirably, Connor could tell, but the barrage of bullets soon put an end to their resistance.

Finally, Connor was able to restore order. In the renewed silence, he approached the cabin again. "It's all right, ladies," he called out. "No one wants to hurt ye. Just come on out and we'll be along with ye."

There was no response.

God help me if they're killed, Connor thought.

Then he saw the red glow inside.

Who knows how these things start. Perhaps a bullet hit the fire and caused some sparks to fly out and catch. Perhaps a ball itself hit a piece of cloth or struck the grassy roof. Perhaps the women inside knew they were lost and did it deliberately. Whatever the cause, there was a fire inside. It grew quickly, from a small flame to a regular inferno.

"Come on out. No one will shoot ye," Connor yelled. "No one shoot!" he called back to the men. "Ye hear me? Any man shoots will deal with me!"

No one came out.

Connor rushed to the door and kicked it open. Flames shot out, forcing him back. He looked in as best he could. The flames would hurt no one. Maybe one of his men was a better shot than Connor thought. More likely, a couple of the lads had gotten lucky.

The two women lay in each other's arms, covered by skirts and bonnets that were already smoldering. They did not move.

"Bloody hell," Connor grumbled.

"Come on lads." He stomped back to the tree line. "There's nothing t'see here. Let's get on back t'camp. Get some grub in ye." Mosley and his boy were going to be furious.

What a waste, he thought. Connor had no problem with killing. It was what soldiers did. Except these women were not soldiers. *Bloody shame to kill them.*

They left. In minutes, all that remained of them were the odd barks of the bloodhounds, growing fainter.

The cabin burned. Sparks flew out and, catching a light breeze, drifted over to the barn and the shed. No one was around to hear the chickens and Mule and Quarky and Bob cry out for help. Well before the sun rose, the fire had died down to glowing embers.

The few eyes that came to see the cause of the fire, drifted off silently on errands of their own. There was no reason to stay.

* * *

THE early hours of the morning grew cold.

About five in the morning, Pierce sent an older man, one Colonel Bailey, to the tower to take command of the headquarters.

Rosi stayed by the parapet and looked out into the blackness. Will had come up behind and put his arms around her. She snuggled up to him to keep warm.

The sunrise came as suddenly as if someone had switched on the light. There was no false dawn. One second, it was pitch black. The next second, the rim of the sun soared over the horizon and revealed the harbor. What Rosi saw sent a chill up her spine. Will gripped her tightly.

The harbor was filled with ships.

"Barges," one of the men muttered.

"What is it?" Rosi wondered.

Bailey explained. "Flat bottomed barges." That was how they beat the reefs.

The barges, filled with men, were sailing steadily towards to the shore. A few of the larger ships had braved the reefs. One had failed and was listing to one side and would soon, Rosi was sure, succumb to the waves.

Rosi barely had time to take the sight in when the British man-o-wars opened fire on the town. The ships were far enough away that she saw the puffs of smoke long before she heard the reports. She could even see the black shot flying through the air, pounding into the buildings along the boardwalk. In seconds, several of the buildings erupted in fire.

"Fire!" someone on the battlement above yelled. There was a great noise and soon there was a splash in the water.

The other cannons were firing as well. Huge plumes of water filled the harbor. One of the barges shuddered as a shot went true. A mast collapsed and Rosi watched as men dove off of the barge and into the water.

Rosi could tell that the artillery would not stop the landing. There were too many barges and too few big guns. Furthermore, it was only a minute or two before the British realized where the attack was coming from. Two of the large ships tacked or jibed or whatever it was they did, and turned their broadsides on the bluff and The Castle.

The air was filled with distant screams and the British sailors proved true to their reputation as marksmen. Once or twice, the tower shook slightly.

Rosi's cannon responded, soaking the British ships but doing little else.

Rosi watched as British soldiers landed near the harbor and formed up and Pierce's men rushed to meet them. She watched as one platoon of colonists tried to hold on to the old ruined lighthouse, where the country club would someday be, but they were quickly routed by overwhelming numbers of redcoats. The faint popping of musket fire reached her ears.

The town below was bursting into flames. Fires were raging out of control.

Colonel Bailey grabbed a younger man. "Go and warn Major Hanley," he bellowed over the noise. "Tell him to watch to his artillery and pull it out of range of those 50s. Beg his pardon and ask if he would be so kind as to regroup his cavalry by the lighthouse to form a flying unit."

"Yes, sir!" the man yelled back. He turned and ran up the stairs.

Everyone ducked as an explosion shook the tower. Rosi screamed and held on to Will, who covered her from the flying rock splinters with his own body.

Bailey rose and brushed himself off. "Charlie!"

"Sir!" A very young boy carrying a bucket of water paused just to throw the water onto one man's burning shirt, then turned to his superior.

"You must," the older man began, before the two were forced to duck as a cloud of rock dust blasted through the room. "You must," he continued, helping the boy up. "Find Mr. Phillips. My compliments to him and beg that he look to his flanks. You have that, Charlie?"

No one would ever know what little Charlie's answer would be. The older man stood there looking at the stump that was once his hand, and the lower half of Charlie's torso. Charlie's torso collapsed to one side, while the older man slid to the other.

The metal ball that had so ravaged the two bounced off the other wall, dropped to the floor, and slowly rolled across the inner room, its fuse still burning.

All the men in the room and on the parapet froze and stared at the unexploded shell. Screaming, they dove for cover. Will pulled Rosi to safety just in time.

After that, shot after shot pounded into the tower. Even though she had not been hit, Rosi was shaken and bruised. She was also terrified. Stooping over Colonel Bailey, she put her fingers to his neck and checked for a pulse. He was dead.

The tower shook again. Dust and shards of rock covered her. *I have to get out of here. I want to go home.*

There was the door. Waiting for her. It was calling for her. Come home, it said. Come home and you will be safe. Rosi's hand reached out on its own accord and touched the doorframe. The door cracked open.

What would it be if Rosi went home? What sort of world would it be? Would it be the same? Would it have changed? What of Angie? Where was Angie? Would she be able to get home as well?

The door inched open a little more. Rosi tried not to move, though she could feel her feet being pulled forward.

There was a loud explosion and the screaming of dying men. "It's not time, yet," a voice inside her head said. Could she stop it? The room began to swim in and out of focus. How? She had to stay. She tried to close the door, but it wanted to open, to pull her in.

Rosi felt something hit her in the small of the back and knock her to the floor. "Get down," Will cried.

The door was closed.

Rosi crawled out from under Will and rushed outside. "Where is General Pierce?" Rosi called out, barely hearing herself.

"Look!" Eustace pointed to the town.

Even at that distance, Rosi and the others could distinguish Pierce's large body as it flew at the head of a group of horsemen. The cavalry charged into a forming landing party of British and sent the invaders running. Pierce's infantry followed the horses.

The tower shook again.

Rosi looked out at the harbor. One of the ships had been damaged and was drifting away. The landing barges were being forced to the other side of the harbor. Rosi sighed with relief. She pointed out to Will that the potential landing areas were few and far between. The invaders could be bottlenecked and decimated.

Rosi put her arm around his neck and hugged him. "We'll win!" she cried.

The other men cheered, and kept the cannon firing.

Rosi was about to give Will a big kiss when she remembered something. She flew to the other side of the balcony and looked to the cliffs behind The Castle. "Oh, God!"

"What is it?" Will ran to her.

Rosi had never seen it before, but now that she did, it was clear as day. There was a narrow path running up the cliff at the far side of the house. "Secret ways in!" She remembered what she had heard Kirk saying to the naval officer. The path was covered with British soldiers and sailors. Already, quite a few of them were at the top and forming an attack line.

"Take them out!" Rosi screamed to her men, pointing.

Only a few could find places to fire, but they made each shot count. They were driven back, though, by a hail of return fire. More than one dropped and lay still.

"We can't stay here," Rosi decided.

"But those ships. We have to support Pierce," Eustace argued.

"If we stay here, we'll be trapped!" Already, Rosi could hear firing from the other side of The Castle. "One more shot!" Rosi called up to the gun crew. "Move it," she commanded the others.

The Second Platoon had fallen back to the stables by the time Rosi and the others reached the front door.

The British had formed a line and were firing with deadly accuracy. The overgrown front lawn was littered with bodies from both sides. Rosi fired her pistol at the British, and then ducked back into the foyer. If they stayed here much longer, Rosi realized, they would be lost.

"Is everyone here?" Rosi asked no one in particular.

"Yes," came a general cry.

Good enough, she thought. Rosi handed her pistol to Will, who started reloading it. "Spartacus!" Rosi yelled over to the man, whom she could see directing fire from behind the stables.

He waved.

"Cover us!" She shouted.

He nodded.

"Everyone fire at the line and run."

Spartacus and several men dodged out into the open and fired a volley at the British.

"Now!" Rosi screamed. She took off, hoping they would follow her. About half way across the lawn, she turned and fired without aiming. She did not care if she hit anyone, but she wanted the British to duck for cover. She was not the only one with the idea. Running was awkward with only one useful arm, but she made it to Spartacus, who grabbed her and threw her behind the building.

There were a few screams behind her, but most of the men made it.

"What now, captain?" Spartacus and Robin both asked.

Rosi tried to catch her breath. She stood up shakily. "Do we have any horses?"

Harry smiled and spoke up. "All of them."

"Will. I need you to do something."

"Anything."

"Take a horse. Go and find General Pierce and tell him we have been flanked. We will have to fall back to the trees. I don't know if we can even stay there." Even a cursory glance from behind cover showed that the enemy was streaming over the edge of the cliff. Rosi's small band of men was already vastly outnumbered.

"We have to get you to safety first."

"Do as I say."

"John." Will turned to him. "You get Rosi to safety."

"Yes, Will." John mounted one of the horses.

Rosi was furious. "Will, do as I say. I'm staying with the men.

Go! Now!"

"I'll go," he said. He grabbed her and tossed her like a sack of potatoes over the saddle in front of John. "Ride!" He slapped the horse's rump. The horse lunged forward, and John kicked him into a gallop.

The ride was horribly painful. Rosi cried out as the horse's movement jostled her arm and jolted her ribs. They were almost to the trees when Rosi heard the horse scream. It stumbled and Rosi was thrown clear, into the woods.

Rosi came to a stop, suddenly, when a tree rose out of nowhere and got in her way. It took her a few moments to catch her breath. She rose carefully. Everything hurt, but it did not seem as if anything was broken.

The horse stood about fifteen feet away. Its right haunch was matted and red.

"John?" Where was he? Rosi found him lying nearby. His neck was broken. His eyes were open and glazed over. "Oh, John." Rosi dropped to her knees and took his hand. "Oh, John."

Rosi stayed there, covered by the undergrowth while bullets and men flew all around her. Someone came up and stood next to her.

"What's this, then?" A hand roughly grabbed her and lifted her up. A tall man in a dirty red coat sneered at her. "We got us a find, mate," he said, looking to his companion.

The other man started to laugh, but his face exploded.

The first man turned in time to meet the butt of Spartacus' musket against his cheek. He went down.

"It's John," Rosi said sadly.

"Aye." Spartacus said. "Let's go."

Rosi looked out of the woods at The Castle. The British were coming steadily for the trees. They were swarming into the main building and the stables. Rosi's men and the remnants of the New Hampshire Fourth were routed.

"Who else?" Rosi asked.

"Don't know yet," Spartacus answered gently.

"What do we do now?"

"Robin's men will meet us down by the creek. We'll head

inland and hope to lose any pursuit. Is that what you want?"

"Yes." Rosi said.

"Come along then." He started to lead her off.

"What about Will? What about the others?"

"We can gather together the stragglers."

"We have to regroup," Rosi decided.

"We will," Spartacus assured her. "Then we can think about what to do. Come on, captain. They'll be here soon."

The British were only about fifty yards off.

Rosi allowed herself to be led off. Spartacus stopped only long enough to put the barrel of his musket to the wounded horse's head and pull the trigger. It fell without a cry.

"Sorry, miss. Had to be done."

They went further into the woods. The sound of battle faded in the distance, but not in the memory.

CHAPTER 14

ROSI and Spartacus missed Robin and his men at the creek. Robin and the others were chased off by a platoon of Royals Marines. Marines Rosi and Spartacus almost ran right into.

The two stopped at the last moment and watched the others being pursued by the soldiers to the south. Robin, at least, had kept his men together. Maybe he was the better man for the job.

They had not decided on a meeting place in case of defeat. Rosi had not planned on everything, though maybe it was a bad idea to go into battle expecting to lose. Then again, it was probably better to go into battle and win than to get beaten back in such a humiliating defeat.

It was her own house! And Kirk had known it better! This was not good.

"We have to head back to the farm. At least everyone will know how to get there. We can regroup and decide what to do then. Zilla will know." Rosi had tried to play captain. Look what that had done to everyone.

Rosi and Spartacus hid in some bushes for a few minutes while a company of British made their way by. Then they started on the journey back.

Rosi decided quickly that this would take a fair amount of time. She was battered and bruised. Her arm was bleeding. Just about every place else was bleeding. She could taste blood in her mouth. Her right eye was swollen shut. She must have banged it when she was thrown from the horse. They had hiked about fifteen minutes when Rosi had to stop. Spartacus did not complain when she called for a break. While Rosi sat breathing laboriously, he carefully reloaded his musket and her pistol. He was more dexterous with one hand than she was with two.

"Captain," he said after a few minutes. "Lie back. I need to check if any ribs are broken. Ye do not sound so good."

He was as gentle as he could be, but just about every inch of her body screamed out at his touch.

"No bones broken," he said. He went to her arm next.

The arm was a mess. What Zilla had been able to do was now undone. Rosi was bleeding freely and her fingers were clearly not pointed in the right direction.

"Will you pass out on me if I straighten your fingers?" Spartacus asked.

"I'll try not." Rosi was afraid. "What of the Redcoats? Will they hear?"

"Nay, lass. They be movin' away. But if I don't do somethin' about your hand soon, it will heal that way, and if I don't clean that wound now, you'll lose that arm." Spartacus used what little water they had to clean the wound. Harry showed up just as Spartacus tossed the skin away.

"Put yer head against his shoulder, captain," Spartacus ordered.

"What are you going to do?"

"Ye don't want to be knowing."

"Do what you have to do."

He gathered together some twigs and started a small fire. Then, he took his powder horn and began sprinkling gunpowder over her arm. Lifting up one of the burning twigs he looked at her. "In his chest."

She buried her face in Harry's chest and felt him put his arms around her. Rosi heard the fire start as Spartacus touched the flame to the powder. She smelled it. She could even feel what seemed like a thousand little feet running up and down her arm. She was surprised that it did not feel like it was burning her. It was actually a rather interesting sensation. The curious feeling did not last more than a few seconds before the pain began.

It was still light when Rosi opened her eyes. Or was it light again?

Spartacus smiled down at her. "Ye had a nice nap, captain."

"Spartacus?"

"Aye, captain?"

"If you have to do that again, just take the arm off."

Spartacus laughed. Several other laughs followed.

"Ye got some power behind yer screams, captain," Spartacus said, still laughing. "They was a beacon to many of our men."

"Yes," Harry agreed. "And some of theirs."

"They weren't no trouble, Harry, so don't you worry her none." Spartacus hoisted a full skin of water and put it to Rosi's lips. "I'm sorry, captain. Ye'll have to walk. I've done a lot of doctorin' since ye were sleepin'. Aren't no one can carry you."

"If I have to walk, Spartacus, I'll walk."

With Harry's help, Rosi struggled to her feet and promptly collapsed. Perhaps she would do this in stages.

"Are we in a hurry, Spartacus?"

"That's fer ye to decide, captain. But them soldiers'll be lookin' fer their mates before long."

"Then we'd better get going."

Harry helped Rosi up. He was just about the least knocked about person there. Spartacus, Rosi noticed, was limping. There was about ten men altogether. Each of them was splattered with blood. Most wore slings or had stained bandages tied around somewhere. At least half the muskets were being used as crutches.

As they moved further and further from the battlefield, and closer and closer to the farm, spirits rose. By late afternoon, the somber atmosphere was dissipating. The men were even able to laugh at the fear they had felt during the battle. Their blood had barely clotted and already they were telling tall tales of battlefield heroics.

Rosi wondered which were ultimately truer, the stories these men told now but would edit and polish to tell their children and grandchildren or the version Rosi had witnessed that morning. Had the valiant colonials barely been beaten by a sneaky enemy that had had the advantage of overwhelming numbers, or had a group of men playing at war and unprepared to actually fight in a real one, followed a girl into battle and gotten their butts kicked by men who were cleverer and better soldiers than they were?

Rosi supposed that the question could be said about the entire war. Did the glorious Armies of Freedom defeat the Forces of Tyranny, or had the British merely gotten tired of an expensive conflict that no one wanted to be involved with anyway and cut their losses by getting out before they lost too much?

When the sun went down, Rosi stopped the men to eat. Spartacus and a couple of the more able had shot some game, so there was plenty of food. The rest and the meal gave the men strength and spirit. Even she was feeling better and was able to make it some minutes without support.

Shortly after moonset, they came upon a dead horse. Even Rosi could tell that its leg had been broken and someone had put it down.

Half an hour later, they came upon a live horse, tied to a tree. Just beyond the tree were the clearing and the remains of the farm.

Rosi, Spartacus, Harry, and the others approached the still smoking remains slowly and cautiously.

Someone stepped out of what was once the farmhouse.

Rosi heard the muskets snap to the shoulders of the men around her. She hobbled in front of them.

"Stop! Don't shoot." Rosi turned to the figure. "Who are you? What are you doing here?"

"It's me," the figure said softly.

"Will? Someone, bring light!"

Someone brought one of the torches over. Rosi could see that it was indeed Will. His clothes were dusty and torn, but he looked otherwise unhurt.

"I was afraid you were—" Rosi began.

"No such luck. Eustace, Come on out here."

The young man came out from where Will had been hiding.

Rosi wanted to run over and hug both of them. Something about their faces made her stop.

"Are you hurt?"

"No," Will said. "Lost a horse a few hours back. Had to shoot him."

"We saw." Rosi looked around. "I'm sorry about the farm, Will."

He did not answer.

"I'm sure you and Zilla can build it up again. We'll all help." The men around made soft agreement noises. But there was something else to Will's face. Something darker. "Eustace. What is going on?"

Eustace shrugged and walked away.

"Will? Will, what's in the house?" Rosi started forward.

Will grabbed her by the arm. "Don't go in there," he said with a monotone.

Rosi shook her arm free and started forward.

"Don't go in there!" Will grabbed her and turned her away from the remains of the building.

"Let go of me, Will!"

"Don't go there. Go away! Go away!"

Rosi tried to jerk away, but only fell to the ground. Will followed her down and grabbed at her legs as she tried to crawl past him.

"Don't," he cried.

Rosi kicked him away with a yell and ran to the farmhouse.

It was black there. Black soot, no moon. But there were shapes. Rosi just could not make them out.

"Bring me a light!"

Harry held the torch. He looked to Will.

"Bring me the torch!" Rosi commanded. "Bring it now!"

The torch revealed enough. Two shapes. One taller and broader than the second. Both wore what had once been dresses.

"Oh, God," Rosi said to herself.

Harry said something as Rosi stood there trying to take in what she was seeing, but she did not hear it.

Angie!

Rosi stood up and staggered from the smoldering remains. Numbly, she reached out to Will, but he moved away from her with a glare. Her legs gave out and someone caught her and lowered her to the ground. She waved whoever it was away. All Rosi wanted to do was cry.

"Is that it?" Will asked, a few minutes later when Rosi's tears slowed down a little.

"What do you mean?"

"You're gonna cry and then that'll be it," Will said harshly.

"Will!"

"That's my ma there!"

"I'm sorry!"

"Sorry? Sorry?" Will was screaming. "Is sorry gonna bring back my ma?"

Spartacus stepped in. "Just hold it right there, boy."

"You stay out of this, old man. You just stay out of this. This is between me and her."

"I'm sorry about your mother, Will," Rosi said. "I'm sorry about Angie, too."

"Is that all?"

"What else is there?" Rosi asked.

"You tell me! My ma was fine. Now she's dead! If it wasn't for you—"

"Don't blame me for this."

"She didn't want to get involved. She tried to keep us both out of this."

Rosi went to Will and tried to hold him.

"Don't touch me! Don't you think you've done enough?" Will turned and started into the woods.

Rosi ran after him. "Stop, Will. Stop!" She caught up to him and grabbed his arm. "Just relax."

"If you hadn't come here, ma would still be alive. Don't you know that?" He tried to break away, but Rosi was able to trip him and bring him down.

"I didn't know!" Rosi tried to hold Will down, but he fought with her and was stronger.

"You did it. You did it. You might as well have put a gun to her head and pulled the trigger. My ma burned to death."

"So did my friend," Rosi cried.

"Good riddance to her," Will snarled.

Rosi slapped him. She had hoped it might snap him out of his rage but instead it sent him deeper in to it. Will slammed her against a tree and wrapped his hands around her neck.

"I should have left you by the cliffs where I found you."

Rosi tried to pull his hands away, but he was too strong.

"You and your friend," Will growled. "Come here and mess everything up. We were fine without you. No one was interested in us. No one wanted to kill us! Should have let you die. Should have shot you!"

The edges of Rosi's awareness were tingling and her lungs were screaming for air. She tried to dig her numbing fingers into his eyes. She tried to bite his arms. She tried anything, everything she could to dislodge him.

"You come here and all we try to do is help. Give me back my ma!"

Somehow, Rosi got her foot against Will's chest and pushed as hard as she could. Slowly, Will was lifted and thrown to one side. Rosi sucked in the air. Then she coughed and retched.

Will scrambled back at her. Desperately, Rosi turned and punched him in the face. Will lost his balance and tumbled behind the tree. Rosi collapsed, weeping and gasping for breath.

"Will!" Rosi called out after a while. "Will!"

"He i'n't here," said Spartacus, leaning over her.

"Where'd he go?"

"Don' know. He went."

Spartacus guided her back to the clearing. The others were sitting around quietly. Two shallow holes had been dug, and four of the men were carrying the bodies over.

"I can't do this, Spartacus," Rosi whispered.

"You got to," he said. "We're yer men. Ye lead us. Ye tell us what to do."

"I'm just a little girl. I want to go home. I want my Angie! I want my daddy!"

"Angie dead," Spartacus said matter of factly. "Zilla told me yer daddy dead. Now Zilla dead."

"I killed her," Rosi said.

"Zilla do what she wanted to do. No one made her take up with you. You didn't make no one burn the farm. You didn't shoot those women. I don' know much about yer daddy. I bet I know what'd he say t'ye. He'd tell ye to do yer best. He'd say there was a handful of men here who'd'a been killed without ye get them out of The Castle. Me, I'm jest a farmer. Not even a good one at that. But I know yer a fine girl. Fer as captaining goes, yer as good as any man I ever seen. I tell ye one thing, though. Now there's a war goin' on. Ye can cry some other time. Girl or boy, ye'll have plenty of time to cry once we do what we got to do."

Rosi could see that the men were looking at her. They were waiting for her to say or do something. Rosi took Spartacus' hand and walked forward.

"All rise," Rosi said softly. "Please take hands."

They did as she said.

Rosi raised her face and looked to the stars. "Angie and Zilla were my friends. I'm not sure why you chose to take them right now, but I hope that you helped them to go quickly. Look after them and tell them I love them. We all love them. A lot of men died today. Please...tell them...let them know that what we're fighting for means something. Their children's lives...their grandchildren's lives...our lives...will be better. Our lives are already better for having known them. My life is better. Please, guide us. Help us make the right decisions. Help us be the best we can be. Help us make this place, our lives, our families' lives, the best we can. Don't let our friends' have been wasted. Have mercy on us and on our souls."

The men stood silently for a minute. In their own time, each said "Amen," and moved away from the circle.

Rosi waited until most of them were gone before she took up a handful of dirt and sprinkled it over Angie and Zilla. "I'm sorry. I will make Kirk pay." She nodded to Spartacus, who started to shovel dirt on Angie and Zilla.

"We know who did this," Rosi said. A couple of men nodded. "I said: *We know who did this.*"

They all nodded in agreement.

"We know where they are!" Rosi went on.

"Yes."

"We're going back there. We're going to watch them! We're going to figure out how to beat them! We're going to make them pay for Angie. And Zilla. And John and all the others! We're going to scare them! We're going to hurt them!" The men were punctuating each statement with a loud "Yes!"

"We're going to kill them!" Rosi cried out.

"Yes!"

"And we're going to sent them straight to Hell!"

"Yes!"

The men cheered. Several clapped Rosi on the back, which almost made her pass out again. "Men! I'm not sure what our plan is. I'll figure one out. One thing I will tell you, we can't do it here. We're going to have to be careful and sneaky. The enemy is a clever worm. The enemy's a sneaky rodent. And he has an army to protect him. I don't need an army. I have you men! Trust me. You look after me, and I'll find us a way to out sneak that little good for nothing pile of horse—"

They cheered again, drowning her out. Rosi realized that they thought she was talking about the British. She did not care about the British right now. It was Kirk's fault. But if she had to beat the British to get to Kirk, then she would figure out a way. She searched her memory. She had to find a way into The Castle and New Richmond. She had to know what the British were up to.

In minutes, the men gathered together their things, hoisted Rosi, protesting, onto the horse, and started off.

They were going back to war.

CHAPTER 15

THEY reached the New Richmond area in midmorning. They could hear the British in the distance. Cleaning up pockets of resistance, Rosi assumed.

They saw quite a few colonial soldiers as well, but most of those were running. Few stopped even if only to tell Rosi what was going on. They had thrown away their weapons and were hightailing it away. Those who did stop and give out information told of a victorious British army that was systematically wiping out any remnants of opposition.

Rosi had no doubt that the British would be harsh masters.

"Don't go back there," was the refrain from most of the men they encountered.

Rosi urged her men forward. "New Richmond is where we have to be," she explained, wondering if she were telling the truth. "That's where the enemy is." *That's where Kirk is*, she told herself. By midmorning, they had picked up a few members of the company who had gotten separated from the main body. With them had been several members of the New Hampshire Fourth.

Four times they had run into British patrols. The first patrol, twenty men with five horses, had been too large. Rosi herself only had eighteen, not including herself. Even if she had more, Rosi could tell that this patrol was made of trained and disciplined soldiers and was led by an experienced officer. Her men were little more than a rag-tag group of armed individuals. The regulars who joined them were not much better.

Rosi had the foresight to send If-Christ-Had-Not-Died-For-Thee-Thou-Hast-Been-Damned Essex ahead as a scout. The man was quiet. Perhaps too quiet. The first time he had come back to report, Rosi had almost screamed at the sight of his remarkably ugly face. As it was, his report gave her enough time to evaluate their chances and move the men away from the path.

The British moved by quickly, but the time seemed like an eternity. Rosi wanted to act. Her men wanted to fight.

"The next one," Rosi promised with her eyes to as many of the men she could.

Rosi let her men attack the next British patrol. They got lucky. A group of seven men, led by a fairly young officer leading his horse rather than riding it, was stumbling along the path. They looked and sounded drunk. The officer looked and sounded just as drunk as the men. Just before they reached Rosi's concealed men, the young officer had tossed his reigns to one of the men and told them to take a rest. One of the older men produced a flask of something and began passing it around as the men sang a raunchy marching song. The officer wandered a few feet from the path and began unhooking his trousers.

"Hello," he said, smiling. "What have we here?" he was looking straight at Rosi, who had just stepped out from behind a tree. "Jeffy," he called out. "Get a rope! Pudding's here!" He turned back to Rosi. "Come along, lassie," he leered. "There's a bunch of us and we haven't got all day."

Rosi shrugged. She smiled brightly, showing off her well kept teeth. "You'll have to ask my pa," she sniggered, pointing to her right. Spartacus gave his best smile. It was not as brilliant as Rosi's and lacked a few teeth, but it was equally effective.

"Christ," the officer spat. He was reaching for his sword and opening his mouth to yell, when the side of his head exploded.

Spartacus dropped his musket and raised the second one he was carrying. Another British soldier fell. At this point, the rest of Rosi's men fired their weapons. Several charged at the patrol and began beating at the men with the butts of their weapons.

"They're already dead!" Rosi cried out. Her men were all good shots and no one thought about taking prisoners. *What would we do with prisoners?* Rosi wondered.

It was a very minor victory, but the men went crazy, beating the dead bodies, mutilating them. It took Rosi some time to get their attention. Finally, after yelling for some minutes, she fired her pistol into the air. That snapped several of the men, including

Spartacus, to their senses. They pulled the other men away and calmed them down. Eustace and Private Hollins, one of the regulars they had picked up, were fairly covered by blood. Spartacus and Essex grabbed them and frog marched them to a nearby stream to dunk their heads in the cold water.

By the time the four came back to the group, everyone could hear the approach of a larger force that had been drawn by the noise.

"Grab what you can," Rosi ordered a couple of men who were still standing by the bodies. "And come along."

When the group finally gathered together about half an hour later, all the men had been able to scavenge were three muskets and two horns of powder.

"We've got to be more careful," Rosi said. She refused them permission to attack the next two patrols, even though they were smaller than her group. One was even resting.

"Aren't we supposed to be killing them Redcoats?" Eustace complained later that morning when they stopped and divided up what little food they had. "Not standing by and watchin' them sleep." Several of the others nodded and grumbled in agreement.

"We're supposed to kill them, not get killed ourselves," Rosi explained. "We leave them be until we have a plan." She caught Spartacus' eye and looked beseechingly at him. He nodded. He would talk with Eustace.

Rosi needed the loyalty of all of her original men who remained. The other men, especially Private Hollins, were grumbling about taking orders from a girl. For the time being her men outnumbered the outsiders. That was the basis for her authority. She knew this was not the way an army should maintain discipline and the chain of command. She also knew that more often than not, this was how it really worked, not only in the military, but in business and even in government. It was somewhat depressing to think that the global society worked essentially the same as the average high school.

Rosi rubbed her temples. She had a bad headache and could really go for a massage or some aspirin. She was tired. She could barely stand. She was holding herself upright by leaning on a thick stick one of the men had given her to use as a walking staff. She dropped the staff and let herself sit down heavily and lean back against a tree. Someone shoved a large piece of dried beef and stale bread in her hand. "Get yerself some rest, Captain," Essex said with a well intentioned, but hideous smile.

Rosi patted his arm. She did her best not to look at his face, which might make her lose her appetite. "Take Spartacus and Eustace and keep a watch over that rise." They had passed a farm about half an hour earlier which had been teeming with Redcoats.

Rosi let herself doze a moment as she listened to the men exchange war stories. What amused her most was that the stories about this very day were already taking on epic proportions. The unfortunate and unsettling massacre of just a few hours ago had already become a vicious firefight. The patrol of four soldiers who had been sleeping under a tree while Rosi's men went more than a hundred yards out of their way to avoid them had become a large encampment that Rosi and her men had somehow sneaked straight through in a display of cunning and superhuman stealth.

Stay awake, Rosi ordered herself.

* * *

ROSI shook her head and sat up.

There was a strange silence. No one was talking. No one was laughing. Ben had been giving a credible impersonation of Rosi's pep talk at Zilla's farm to the roars of the others one moment. The next moment was silence.

Had Rosi nodded off? She poked her head around the tree. Her men were sitting where she had left them. Now they were frozen. Not a one moved.

Standing in the midst of them were three men, heavily armed, with weapons ready.

"Again! Who is in charge of your sorry bunch?" The leader of the three men demanded to know. Even though his volume was low, no doubt to avoid enemy ears, he was able to convey a bellow.

"Sergeant Zablonski," Hollins, one of Rosi's men, said.

"Who the hell are you?" The man was the shortest of the three, but looked the roughest.

"Hollins, sir. Private Hollins. Sergeant Welch's platoon."

"Where's your sergeant, boy?" Zablonski snapped.

"Got himself killed, Sergeant. Gut shot. Nothing I could do but watch him die. Then I ran into these boys. A few of us done."

Zablonski looked over the motley crew and smirked. "Think you'd'a been safer with the English. Who are these, soldiers?" He sneered the last word.

"We're the Carol Company," Ben shouted, leaping to his feet.

Zablonski knocked Ben to the ground. "The Carol Company. Hell, you ain't a company t'begin with, an' Beatitude Carol's near two hundred mile from here. Nah. You ain't in charge, boy," he spat at Ben, who scurried away. "Hollins! Which of these men gives the order?"

"I give the orders, Sergeant." Rosi stepped from behind the tree.

The three men stood there for a moment, nonplussed.

"Who's this wench, Hollins?" Zablonski asked.

"She's—"

"Quiet, Private," Rosi snapped. "I'm Captain Carol."

Zablonski looked at his friends and grinned. Tobacco juice ran down his chin. He did not bother to wipe it off. "That right?"

"That right?" He demanded.

"Yes, Sergeant," Rosi said. Zablonski moved closer to her. She had not noticed it happening, though it was not sudden or rushed. Simply, one moment he was one place, and the next moment he was another. It was an almost casual move that was even more threatening.

"I'm not talking to you, wench. Hollins! That so?"

"But, Sergeant," Rosi said, holding her ground, though her legs felt rubbery. "I was answering you. I am Captain Carol. Tell your men to lower their weapons."

Zablonski looked Rosi over for a second, and then he moved. Rosi saw it coming, but could not possibly have moved quick enough to avoid it. The butt of Zablonski's musket connected with her nose. She had been in the middle of flinching back, which is probably what saved her from serious injury. However, pain and lightning bolts of black blinded her for a moment. She found herself on the ground holding her nose to stop her blood from spraying out of it. She blinked her eyes. Tears were flowing freely. She hoped no one noticed.

Ben cried out, leapt to his feet, and rushed towards his Captain.

Zablonski grabbed him by the collar and lifted him off the ground. "You young pup!" The man yelled. He threw Ben at Rosi. The boy stumbled, tripped, and fell against her.

"I'm sorry, Captain," Ben wailed.

"It's okay," Rosi assured him. She took the dirty kerchief he offered her and pressed it against her nose.

The commotion by the tree distracted Zablonski's men, who had turned to look at Rosi. John Thatcher took the opportunity to shove Hollins roughly so that he bounced off one of the men and fell against Zablonski. Rosi's men snatched up their weapons and leveled them at the three.

Rosi was so proud. Squeezing the kerchief against her nose, she allowed Ben to lift her to her feet. She motioned for him to hand her the wooden staff.

"I am Captain Carol," Rosi said. "My command was recognized by General Pierce himself."

Zablonski grinned. "Aye. I recollect hearing about you. Playing at war with the officers. Yer general ain't around to help you now."

"These men are," Rosi pointed out.

"And these men are here to help me," Zablonski said.

A handful of men rose from concealment to one side of the confrontation.

Zablonski's laughter roared through the woods. "No need to kill these boys, men. They won't bother us. We gotta get back to the real war. Hollins, grab the girl and come along."

"Back off, Private," Rosi ordered.

Hollins appeared confused. He looked back at Zablonski.

"Grab the damn wench and come along," Zablonski yelled.

"First one to touch her gets a bullet in the head," a voice came from the trees behind Zablonski's men. "About a second after that, one will go through your eye."

It was Spartacus, Rosi realized. She almost cried with relief.

"Drop your weapons," Spartacus ordered.

"Why?" Zablonski snapped back.

"Or you will die." Spartacus. There was no anger in his voice. He would, Rosi knew, shoot these men down with the same lack of emotion he would castrate a pig with.

"Yer going to a lot of effort to help out this wench," Zablonski snarled.

"She's our captain."

"She ain't nothing of the sort. This is the army. I rank here. I'm in command."

Rosi walked closer to him. "No one can win this unless we all agree to lower our weapons."

Zablonski turned and looked at his men. One of them tried to warn him, but it was too late. The sergeant turned just in time to feel Rosi's staff smash into the bridge of his nose. He went down.

Before he had a chance to stand back up, Rosi dropped her knee onto his chest and shoved the barrel of her pistol into his mouth. "I think that you and I can discuss the chain of command without quite so much tension," Rosi said. She tried to sound as cool and collected as Spartacus had. She was sure everyone could tell she was terrified.

Zablonski appeared to consider his options. He nodded with his eyes and waved his men to lower their weapons.

Rosi stood up and wiped the end of her barrel on her sleeve before shoving it in her belt. "Spartacus," she said. "You're with me." She gestured for Zablonski to bring someone with him. *A witness*, she thought. A second, she feared.

Zablonski grinned. He knew what she was thinking, Rosi was sure. "Hollins," he barked.

"Sergeant." The young man snapped to attention. Nicely done, Rosi thought.

"You know these people," Zablonski said. "You come along

with me."

The Sergeant stepped to one side and bowed gallantly. Or was it sarcastically? "After you, Milady."

"If you can't say Captain, I will accept Miss. My name is Carol, not de Winter."

Zablonski cocked his head with a confused look on his face and glanced at Spartacus.

"We don't understand half what she says," Spartacus said with a shrug. "But she's a Carol and that's good enough for us."

As Rosi passed the rather hulking sergeant, she though she detected a snort somewhere in his raspy breathing. She had forgotten something. She stopped and pretended to adjust the rope that served as her belt. "Essex!" she snapped, not looking at him, but keeping an eye on Zablonski.

"Captain!"

Zablonski smirked. Rosi could see in the sergeant's eyes that Essex must have tried to snap to attention and failed miserably. She hoped he had not fallen down.

"Set a watch on the perimeter."

"On the what?"

Zablonski's grin grew wider.

Rosi turned and faced Essex. "Around the edges, just like we have been doing. We're going to stay here for a few hours, so put a fourth of the men on one watch and we'll switch every hour or two. Oh, and send two of our best trackers out to trap some food. Don't shoot anything. We don't want the British all over us."

Zablonski's grin remained, but now it changed into something slightly less menacing. He looked over to his men and nodded. "If you don't mind, Miss, I'll walk ahead. My eyesight's no better or worse than most, but my ears is good. I can hear a man pissing, er breathing, beggin' yer pardon, Miss, at a hundred paces if the wind be right and the stream be strong, if you know what I mean."

"Very well, Sergeant."

The four of them moved into the trees.

* * *

AFTER a few minutes, they stopped. They were in a small clearing, dominated by a large rather ominous looking tree at the far end.

Sergeant Zablonski nodded for Spartacus and Hollins to stop and let him and Rosi move a little forward. Zablonski waved for Rosi to sit on a large rock jutting out of the ground.

"I'm fine," Rosi lied. Her arm was screaming in pain and she felt like throwing up.

"Miss, you have been hurt. You look green. If you like, I'll sit on the ground if it's a question of face. But if you fall over, I suspect yer man will shoot me before he comes over to see what happened. Please, do sit down."

"Thank you, Sergeant. Do as you like." With relief, Rosi plopped down on the rock. She even took the flask Zablonski offered her. It was water. Rosi smiled and tossed it back when she was done.

The sergeant was the first to speak. "We got a problem here, miss. We got a war goin' on. A lot of good men were killed yesterday. This is not a tea party with yer dollies."

"I understand the seriousness of the situation," Rosi started.

"Then you understand that this is the place for men, not for little girls," Zablonski said.

"Men who were clever enough to lose the battle yesterday? Is that what you're saying?"

"You have a point, miss," Zablonski conceded with a scowl. "But it is a situation that men can fix."

"What do you propose?" Rosi asked. The sergeant seemed confused by the question, so Rosi repeated it.

"I propose, miss," he said after some thought. "To take my men south until I find General Pierce or someone else who will help us beat the British. We lost this battle. We will win the next one. Wherever that is."

"Here" Rosi said. "It has to be here."

Zablonski looked at the trees. "Here?"

"Not right in this spot, Sergeant." Rosi sighed. *Some people can be so literal.* "New Richmond."

"We lost that battle."

"I know!" *Jeeze!* "But we need to kick the Redcoats out."

"How?" Zablonski asked.

Rosi was not sure how. "Certainly not by running away."

Zablonski seemed to bristle at her choice of words. "It be foolishness t'stay."

"Then don't. You don't need to. Go south. You have enough men. You'll get there."

"But," he started. He seemed confused.

"Just go," Rosi repeated.

"Job's to kill the enemy," he finally said. He scratched his head.

Rosi thought she understood. Zablonski was a large rather hulking man. He clearly had a sort of native intelligence. He gave the appearance of someone who was good at his job. His job, however, was to follow orders given by a superior officer. If he took his handful of men south, he might find a larger body of men to join who had an officer to lead them. In that case, he would be fleeing an enemy that was, apparently, sitting there waiting to be fought. However, if he and his men stayed, they would be fighting the enemy, but they would not have a clear target or plan, as there was no officer. One of the other men, like Spartacus, might be able to come up with a short term plan, but Spartacus was, at best, simply a sergeant like Zablonski. Spartacus was a natural first among equals. He was smart, older than most of the men, and had a dignity which gave him a certain amount of clout. But he was not a leader. He was inclined to stop and ask the others what they thought and worry if he was making the right decision.

Zablonski was a natural sergeant. Rosi had seen enough movies to know that. In the real world, he would have been something of a bully. But, he would have been the leader of a small group of bullies. Rosi had seen this before, in her other life when her father was alive and before she moved to New Richmond. A small group of toughs who controlled a corner of a playground or a local hang out. No real danger as long as you gave lip service to their authority. Generally, they did not have enough gumption to be a real threat or danger, not enough initiative to even be a real street gang. Not enough leadership. Zablonski knew the enemy was nearby. He knew he was supposed to fight the enemy. He needed someone to tell him to do so.

Zablonski also had a fairly narrow view of the way things were supposed to be done. Rosi thought she knew how to deal with him. Flipping her hair and flashing her impossibly white and straight teeth might work with most men. It had worked with Pierce. Pierce, however, was a vain and pompous man who would have done just about anything for a pretty girl who stroked his arm and told him how clever he was. Zablonski was not like Pierce, or most other men. He might respond to overt flirtation, but not in a way Rosi wanted or could even handle. Zablonski needed to be bribed a different way. Zablonski might be a natural sergeant, but he was not a natural leader. However, he thought he was.

Rosi did not have any money. She had nothing that she could bribe the man with. Well, she did have one thing.

"Sergeant," Rosi began, carefully. "I need you."

"Miss?" He looked perplexed.

"I need you. My men need you. You see, we are staying. Right here. We are going to fight the British. Not today, of course. Not even tomorrow. But we are not going to wait long. I'm not exactly sure how, but I will figure it out. I will come up with a plan. That is why I am here. Frankly, if I thought I could walk away from them and leave them in your hands, I might. But these men are not soldiers. They simply want to get the British off their land, away from their homes. They made me their captain, partly because they don't want anyone else as their officer. If I quit, they might quit as well. I'm not quitting. But I need someone to help me get them ready. They aren't soldiers. You are. I need you to make them soldiers so that when I come up with a plan, they can fight and win. I need you to be my…Sergeant Major."

Zablonski thought for a moment, and then grinned. "Sergeant Major?"

"Of course, Sergeant...Major. You will be my chief advisor for planning, and you will train the men and command them in battle."

"And you'll be the officer."

"Yes, Sergeant Major. You'll be in charge. I'll take full responsibility. They work for you. You work for me."

Zablonski thought for a moment. "That'll do," he smiled, holding out his hand. Rosi took it and almost winced at the strength of his grip. "That'll do, until a real officer comes around."

"That's fine. Now, the first order of business is to find a safe place to hide, er, billet for the time being. Someplace warm."

"It's plenty warm, miss."

"Are you kidding? It's freezing."

"Billet's an officer's job, miss." Zablonski grinned and spat. He might have accepted her compromise, Rosi realized, but he was not going to make it too easy for her.

Rosi thought for a minute. She glanced around. It was perfect. She must have been too busy negotiating with Zablonski to pay close attention to her surroundings. "This place is perfect."

"This clearing?"

"Clearing?" This was no clearing. She and Zablonski must have wandered into an old abandoned village. The buildings were falling down, but they would give some shelter. The hill to one side would be a good vantage point. "Spartacus," Rosi called out to her sergeant, who stood leaning on a tree near the edge of the village. "See how far that old path goes." She turned back to Zablonski. "It's pretty overgrown, but has to lead somewhere. Possibly we can use it to flank...."

"Path, miss?" Zablonski said. "There's no path there."

Spartacus and Hollins came over. "There's no path, Captain," Spartacus said.

"Of course there is," Rosi protested. "It's right over there." She pointed. "By that building. The taller one."

"There's no building there," Spartacus said. "I'nt no building nowhere."

"Course there is." Rosi walked over to the building, which had once been at least two stories tall. It was surrounded by weeds. She kicked at a piece of wood. "See? It was once an inn or a pub. It has one of those old picture signs." She picked up the sign. "See? It's a woman being impaled by a—" she saw what the picture was and quickly dropped it. "Oh, my." She could feel herself blushing. "Anyway. The road is right—why are you looking at me like that?"

Zablonski and Spartacus looked at each other. They seemed confused. Hollins was openly smirking.

"What's going on, guys?" Rosi demanded.

"There's nothing here, Captain," Spartacus said. He was slipping to one side. Rosi could see Zablonski edging to the other.

"None of that!" Rosi dodged away. "We're right in the middle of a village."

"It's all right, Captain." Spartacus was walking slowly towards her.

"Y'must've hit yer head, miss." Zablonski was holding up both hands. "Easy."

"Look around," Rosi insisted. She had been through so much these last few days that she really did not need to go through this right now. "There are buildings all over the place. There's even something that looks like an old church on that hill."

Spartacus and Zablonski looked around and shook their heads. The sergeant major nodded to Spartacus and Hollins and the three began herding Rosi towards the large tree.

"Don't you see it?" Rosi was getting desperate.

She felt herself backed into the trunk of the tree. A chill ran down her back. Rosi reached up and grabbed a branch that waved in front of her face for support.

The branch felt strangely soft. Almost like....

Rosi looked up. She looked around. She saw....

* * *

SPARTACUS was not surprised when his young captain started talking about seeing things no one else could see. He rather expected it. Carols were funny people, he knew, even though he had never met one. Zablonski and Hollins were surprised, but Spartacus figured they could get through this once the captain calmed down a little.

Carols were odd. Women were odd. This particular Carol, she was very odd.

Spartacus felt like the situation had gotten a lot worse when the captain started screaming and dropped to her face on the ground by the old gnarly tree.

Movement from Zablonski caught his eye.

"I got this, Zablonski," Spartacus snarled.

He moved in cautiously and tried to grab the captain, who jerked out of the way. Spartacus had no choice but to lift her up into his two large arms. He was as careful as he could be, but he was sure it must hurt. He did not want to hurt the captain. She was just a girl.

The captain twisted and writhed in Spartacus' arms. He lost his balance and fell over, losing his grip. Screaming, the captain started crawling away. Spartacus grabbed her legs and held onto her. Then he saw the village, too. He was so surprised that he let go of the captain and sat there looking at it.

It was a village. He was in the middle of a village. There were buildings and houses. Sure, they were falling down, but they were there. The captain had seen what Rosi said she had seen.

When Spartacus turned to say something to Zablonski, he saw what was in the tree. He saw what had had such a profound effect on his captain.

"What is it, man?" Zablonski snarled.

"I—I—" Spartacus seemed unsure how to explain what he saw.

"Damn, you, man." Zablonski signaled Hollins. They both grabbed Spartacus. "I can't have you—"

Zablonski shuddered as if hit by a sudden frigid blast of wind.

Hollins dropped to his knees. "Jesus Christ." He had seen the village.

Zablonski was facing the tree. "Holy Mary Mother of God," he rasped, dropping to his knees and crossing himself.

"Spartacus!" he snapped. "Damn your eyes, man. Answer me!"

"Yes, sir," Spartacus forced out.

"I look like an officer to you?" Zablonski roared.

"N-n-no, sir, I mean, Sergeant M-m-major," the other man stammered.

"Get that girl out of here. Get over to that...over to there. That building. That one with the vines. With the chimney. Get her inside. Now, sergeant. Move it!"

Spartacus went over to the captain and started carrying her off.

"Hollins!"

"Sergeant Major!"

"You see that trail, there?"

"The small road? Yes, Sergeant Major!"

"You got a choice, boy! You can stay here and keep watch or go and get the others."

"I-I-I'll go and g-g-get the others."

"Good lad."

Zablonski crossed his arms and backed away from the tree. A tree from which dozens of bodies were hanging. Dead, burned bodies, clearly months old, if not longer. On the ground surrounding the tree were the remains of dozens more corpses, burnt and mutilated.

This village, which had not been here a minute ago, would be a fine place to hide and train, Zablonski thought. However, it needed to be cleaned up first.

And before they made any plans, he had to figure out this strange captain of his.

CHAPTER 16

WHEN Rosi awakened, she was in a bit of a haze. Spartacus had taken her to one of the buildings that still had something of a roof, given her a swig of something noxious tasting but quickly effective and left her there to sleep. It took her a minute to get her bearings straight and to shake the fog from her eyes. She was alone, which did not help. Then she remembered the bodies in the tree and on the ground.

"Spartacus!" Rosi called out. Someone had taken her boots off. She tried to pull them on, but could not. Her arm was certainly stronger than it had been earlier, but was not strong enough to pull. "Spartacus!" What was the other man's name? "Sergeant Major!"

Someone entered the room. It was a man Rosi did not recognize.

Rosi scurried back, reaching for her pistol, which was not in her belt. Keeping one eye on the man, who was stepping in closer, Rosi glanced around and saw her pistol lying against a nearby wall.

Rosi scooped up some gravel and dust in her hand and flung it at the man, who reacted with a yell. Then she dove to the wall, grabbed her pistol and brought it up, pulling back the hammer until it clicked.

"Who are you?" Rosi snapped. "Back away."

The man was swearing and rubbing dust from his eyes.

"I said, back away!" Rosi snarled. "Back up against that wall."

The man did and carefully raised his arms.

"Who are you?"

"Simmons," The man said. "I'm from—from—the Fourth. Ran into some of these—your men last night. Sorry to scare you, Miss, er, sir, er, Ma'am."

"Where's Spartacus?" Rosi asked.

"Dunno." The man glanced around the room. He was awfully nice to look at, but there was something....

"Where's—" *What is the name?* "Sergeant Major?"

"Zablonski?" Simmons asked.

"Yeah. Where is he?"

"Who?"

"Zablonski!"

Simmons looked around the small room. "He's not here."

"Yeah," Rosi said. "I guessed that. Do you know where he is?"

Simmons appeared to think about this. "Uh, n...n...." He seemed to consider his other options. "Mmm...I dunno?"

"Where did you see him last?" Rosi asked.

"Perhaps he was in the square?" Simmons answered.

Why are you asking me? "When was that?"

"Well, right before I came in here," Simmons said after a moment.

"So, he's in the square." Rosi concluded, happy that was established.

"Dunno."

"You just said that he was!"

"Coulda moved." Simmons explained.

"Could you go find him?"

"Yes." Simmons stood there and looked expectantly at Rosi.

Rosi sighed. "You related to my Uncle Richard?"

"I don't think so."

Zablonski came in, carrying a long musket. "What the—" he rasped. Then he saw Rosi kneeling there with a pistol pointed at Simmons.

"He's one of ours, Miss."

Cautiously, Rosi lowered the weapon and un-cocked it.

Zablonski turned to Simmons and shoved the musket in his hands. "Go on. Git outside and help the others. I'm sorry, Miss. We felt it best to have someone keep watch after what happened last night. We figured he couldn't do no harm."

So, I slept the whole day and night, Rosie thought to herself. "Good choice, Sergeant Major."

"He is a good looking boy, Miss."

"That he is, Sergeant Major," Rosi sighed. "He's also stuck."

Simmons was trying to leave the room but could not get his weapon through the door. Zablonski went and moved him along. "Sorry, Miss. Easy on the eyes, but dumber than guano, if you get my meaning. Probably shouldn't be in the army. He must be someone's cousin."

"Well, Sergeant Major," Rosi said. "There's cousins involved someplace. What happened last night?"

Zablonski considered her question for a moment. "Let's show you around."

As soon as they stepped outside, Zablonski bellowed for one of his men. A squat, rather bow legged man named Boats rushed into the center of the square and let loose with a piercing series of whistles. Men from around the village poured into the center and began forming into groups, or platoons, that looked vaguely military.

"We worked with them for almost two hours this morning," Zablonski explained. He turned to her and whispered. "Be impressed."

"I am, Sergeant Major," Rosi said. "I am."

It took a few minutes, but after some stumbling, tripping, a few chuckles and one bloody nose, the men formed four distinctly military looking units. Rosi noticed that most of the men were not from her original company and those that were had been spread out evenly in the four platoons.

"We picked a lot of men up the last day, Miss," Zablonski growled. The men were split up, he explained, so that there would be as many trained men in a platoon as possible. "Yer still captain, Miss. We agreed."

"No real officers come by?" Rosi asked, almost hoping at least one would.

"Only Lobsterbacks," Zablonski laughed. "Much prefer a girl to one of them." Which was about as good a joke as the gruff man could deliver.

Spartacus, Rosi was told, was out with several men keeping an eye on the road and for supplies. The British were apparently

planning on staying for a while. Quite a few wagons had come
and more were coming. A few simply would not make it to New
Richmond. "Best not ask questions, Miss," Zablonski said. "The
men can be a wee bit enthusiastic when foraging."

The soldiers had spent a fair amount of time cleaning up the
town. Zablonski understood that Captain Carol did not want to
linger too long before acting on her plan to remove the British
but he did need some time to put the men through something
resembling training.

The sergeant major was about to show Rosi around the small
village when he noticed her looking at the large tree that grew on
the west end of the square. She tried not to look at it, but failed.

"Seventy eight, Miss," Zablonski said.

"Seventy eight?"

"Bodies, Miss. Beggin' your pardon. Forty two in the tree.
Thirty six on the ground."

The thought of that many people hanging in the tree gave her
a chill that ran down her spine. "Why were they hanged? Does
anyone know? What is this village? Is anyone from here?"

"The thing about the village, Miss," Zablonski started. "Is no
one from the area has any idea that it be here. That is t'say that it
really isn't here."

This did not make any sense to Rosi, and she said so.

Zablonski sighed. "We was hoping it would to you. Spartacus
said that you seemed t'understand a lot and had some strange
notions."

Rosi shrugged her shoulders and nodded for him to continue.

"Where is this village, Miss?"

"I dunno. A couple miles from New Richmond," Rosi
guessed.

"Five or six, if you take the path," Zablonski nodded.

"And as the crow flies?"

"There's the thing, Miss. Where is this village?"

"New Hampshire. Massachusetts? I don't know how close we
are to the border." Rosi should have known that much. They
were pretty close. When Rosi moved to New Richmond, she had
come by train. The train's terminus had been in Massachusetts. A

car had driven her over the state line. *Smuggled her over*, she sometimes thought.

"That's not exactly what I mean to ask, Miss." Zablonski said. "How did we get here?"

"We walked through the woods. We're in a clearing in the woods. Is that what you meant?"

"Aye, lass, er, Miss. It is. But we aren't in the woods, Miss."

"Nonsense, Sergeant Major," Rosi laughed. "I came here with you, remember."

"We're on a hill, in a small valley, filled with pastures. There's the odd copse here and there, hedgerows. No forest."

"You're kidding me."

"Look for yerself, Miss."

Rosi did. It did appear as if the village was on a low hill surrounded by a stream or, rather, two branches of a stream. Beyond the stream were a few more structures—Rosi hesitated to call them buildings—and an expanse of overgrown fields and the occasional shack or hovel. Houses, they looked like to Rosi. Zablonski agreed.

"Their inhabitants have not come to investigate a company of soldiers occupying their village?" Rosi asked.

"Not as yet, Miss," Zablonski conceded. "It appears that there is no one living out there. As you can see, the buildings have been burnt."

Rosi looked more closely. Indeed, they looked burned out. "Have you sent someone to investigate?"

Zablonski appeared to think for a moment. "Not as such," he said finally.

"Then, damn it, man, send someone right away."

"Well." Rosi could see Zablonski searching for the right words. "Perhaps, if you would be so kind, Miss. You could investigate out there yourself."

Rosi was being challenged. She was being dared. Most of the men had drifted off, but several were still standing around and watching her conversation with Zablonski.

"Very well. Send one man along with me. We'll go to that shack out there. By the small pond." Rosi gave Zablonski what she thought was a challenging glare.

"That's fine, Miss." Zablonski turned. "Lenny!"

One of the men a few yards away, grabbed his weapons and rushed over to the two.

"Go with Miss, Captain Carol," the Sergeant Major roared. "Follow her to that house over there."

Rosi thought Zablonski put a strange emphasis on the word *follow*, but chose to ignore it. A walk through the rolling fields might be nice, and would get her away from that eerie tree. With a nod to her sergeant major, Rosi skipped down the hill and hopped across a narrow part of the stream....

* * *

...RIGHT into a tree. She was in the middle of the forest!

"What the—" Rosi spun around quickly and could not see the village. "Zablonski! Lenny! What the—"

"Hold right there," someone barked.

Rosi spun again and found the barrel of a musket pointing at her face. She shrieked and threw herself on the ground.

"Who is it?" yelled someone, presumably the one holding the gun.

Rosi looked up and saw a strange man pointing the gun at her. "Who are you?" he said nervously.

"It's the captain, you fool," Lenny said. He reached out and put his hand on the barrel of the musket. "She's okay."

"How do I know she's the captain?" the sentry asked.

"Because I just told you," Lenny said.

"How do I know you're not lying?"

Lenny groaned. "Because you've known me for twenty years, Shelley. Have I ever lied to you?"

The sentry, Shelley, appeared to consider this for a moment. "You lied to me two years ago when you told me you had not gotten me a birthday present and you really had."

"Don't you think that's a bit different?"

"It is still a lie," Shelley argued. "So, to answer your question, yes, you have lied to me. So, why should I trust you now?"

"Why would I lie about whether she is the captain?" Lenny

asked.

"She could be spy."

"Why would *I* lie about *that*?"

"You could be a spy as well," Shelley pointed out.

"How could I be a spy? You've known me my entire life."

"Perhaps you are more cunning than I thought," Shelley suggested.

Zablonski appeared from the stream. "What is with you two?" He reached out and knocked the musket away from Rosi's head.

"I was just guarding the village," Shelley pouted.

"Why don't you two go and get yourselves shot by the Redcoats," Zablonski roared. "Come along, Miss."

He helped her up and led her back into the clearing. Back into the village.

Looking back, Rosi saw the fields spreading out. She also thought she saw.... She squinted. It was almost as if she could see a hint of the forest, just to the edge of her vision.

Zablonski sighed. "It's a bit complicated, Miss."

"I'm not really doing anything else," Rosi said.

"Then let me show you around."

* * *

AT some point, it might have been a quaint little village. There was a cluster of small buildings built around a fairly sizeable square or common area. Not large enough to feed the local livestock for very long, Zablonski pointed out, sounding fairly knowledgeable, but enough to feed a fairly large stock for a short period of time.

The village was situated on a low hill that split a small stream in two, Zablonski reminded Rosi. He pointed to something just beyond the streams. A row of stakes, now hidden and overgrown by various weeds, circumvallated the village. *A palisade*, Rosi told herself. That, along with the stream, might well serve to protect the village for a short period of time, but only a short period of time.

To the west end of the village, where the streams rejoined

and moved through the pastures, which were stalked by a narrow rutted path that must be the local road, were the remains of a mill. The wheel was broken and lying across the stream. That was where Rosi had crossed over. She noticed that the flume was still operational and created something of a small waterfall.

"Pardon, Miss," Zablonski said. "Spartacus and I talked this morning. We figured that the men could use the water at the mill for the hour just before sunset. If you don't mind, we'll post a guard so that you don't accidentally surprise them."

"That's a very good idea," Rosi said. "Uhm. Sergeant Major?"

"First thing in the morning, Miss," Zablonski said, blushing slightly at the thought. "We'll have one of your staff keep an eye on things for you. That is...the men might get somewhat curious, as it were, Miss."

Rosi enjoyed Zablonski's discomfiture. "That's perfect, Sergeant Major," she said finally, after letting him stammer on for a few more seconds.

The mill itself was in pretty good shape. Most of its walls were standing and much of the roof was still there. The animals and supplies were being kept there. Harry Thatcher waved from the mill doors and then went back to work. Everyone looked so occupied. Rosi wondered if she were really necessary.

The handfuls of buildings around the commons were mostly destroyed. They had been knocked down and partially burned. Only a couple had partial roofs. At least they were a place to billet the men. Zablonski seemed hesitant when he talked about the men cleaning out the buildings.

Rosi recognized the standard adult way of not saying something that probably should be said. "What is it?"

"Nothing, Miss." He would not look her in the eyes.

"Sergeant Major!" Rosi snapped.

"The bodies in the tree," he said.

"Yes?"

"They were all men."

"So?" Then it dawned on her. "The women and children—"

"Inside the buildings. More'n sixty."

"You don't know the exact number?"

"No, Miss."

"What happened here?"

"Don't know, Miss."

"What can you tell me?"

"Well," he started. He seemed to hesitate, but went on. "Town was burnt. People was hung. Beggin' yer pardon, Miss, but they was cut up somethin' 'fore they was hung. Women and kids, too."

"Cut up?"

"Yes, Miss. Whoever done it must've really wanted them dead. Far as we can tell, they was all dead 'fore the place was burnt."

"Can you tell when?"

"Fields out there overgrown. Ain't been cared for this season. Few months. Not much longer."

"Explain," Rosi said. "How did you come to this conclusion?"

"Still meat on the bodies," Zablonski sighed. "Not much."

"What did you do with the bodies?"

"Took them over to the church," he gestured towards a stone ruin to the north. It was small, but had clearly been a church. "Was already a hole there. Put them in. Said some words. Best not to think about it."

Rosi considered going over to the church, but decided she would see it soon enough. "Any idea who did this?" she asked. "Or why?"

Zablonski mumbled something and started leading Rosi towards the far side of town.

"What was that?" Rosi asked.

He did not respond.

"Sergeant Major!" Rosi stopped walking and crossed her arms. She would pout if she had to.

"They also nailed the dogs and cats to the tree," he said, not looking at her.

"What does that mean?"

"Couple men left. Said it were witchcraft."

Rosi laughed. "Witchcraft? No one believes in that anymore."

"We're in a town that ain't here, Miss," Zablonski said, straightening his back. "It ain't just not here, it's far away. Boats, he was a sailor fer a while. He says the stars is all wrong. The sun is wrong. I don't know what he's talking about, but he does. You look out now and see all them fields. You look out at night and see the woods that're supposed to be there. That don't make no sense to no man here. Do you understand? Do you?"

She did. Rosi said nothing, wanting to consider her options, but her silence was enough.

"Those men as left said you was a Carol. I dunno what that means, but your boys do. You know things. You can do things. Hell, Miss, that arm of yers woulda killed most men. It's on the mend. No one heals that fast. Those men said we should get rid of you. That you was worse than the English. Yer boys wouldn't let them. Even in the night, when the fog came and the screaming started, yer boys stood by you. Almost a battle right here. Me and Spartacus put a stop to that. Those men left. Fled in the night."

"Why didn't you, Sergeant Major?" Rosi inquired.

"We made a deal, Miss. You keep yer end of the bargain, I keep mine." Zablonski seemed to think for a moment. "You a witch, Miss?"

"I don't know," Rosi answered. "But I do know things. I can do things."

"What?"

"I'm not all that sure. I do know that we need to kick the Redcoats out of here. That's for sure. I wish I could tell you why."

Zablonski considered her answer. "As long as that is what you are doin', Miss," he said, finally. "But try anythin'...witchy...then I'll string you up myself."

"Fair enough, Sergeant Major."

He turned and continued to the far side of the village. She followed. Just before the streams rejoined, there were two buildings larger than the others. They appeared to Rosi to have been commercial buildings. Several men were busy cleaning out one of them. One of them was Ben, who brightened when he saw his captain.

"Were smith," Ben said, rushing up to her.

"How do you know?"

"Still got anvil. Tools still lying around. Little work, could be useful." Ben grinned and led Rosi to the other building, opposite the smithy. "Were inn."

"Still have guests?" Rosi asked, smiling at her own joke.

"No, ma'am." He did not know she was joking. "Still has wine." Ben led Rosi down an old, rickety stair to a small cellar. There were the remains of several barrels down there. There were also two barrels that had not been destroyed by time or vagrants.

"Have you all been drinking this?" Rosi asked.

Ben's grin grew even wider.

"Sergeant Major!" Rosi called out.

The older man came running.

"I'll headquarter here. I want the trustworthiest men guarding this cellar. See if you can determine how much wine is here and if it's safe to drink. I want it rationed more carefully than water."

Several of the men grumbled. Zablonski stared them down.

* * *

THE old church to the north was just as much of a ruin as the rest of the village. Rosi only spent a couple of minutes there. The hole filled with bodies had a fresh layer of dirt on it. The church had been burned down. She glanced in it and noticed some odd carvings and drawings on the walls that might or might not have been made before it was burned down. A couple of the braver men, men Rosi did not know, had set up camp in the ruins and kept watch from there. She was told no one had seen any sign of life in the pastures beyond, other than birds and a few small animals. Foxes or badgers possibly.

The house on the other side of the village, opposite the church, was more interesting. Rosi surmised that this had been some sort of manor house. It was on a low rise beyond the stream, so was inaccessible.

It had also been burned, though not as completely as the other buildings. There was still something resembling a roof.

Most of the windows had been smashed. What Rosi found odd about the windows was that they had been made of glass. Rosi did not know that much about architecture, but she knew enough to guess that the village they were in was very old, perhaps even medieval. She was sure that few buildings in that time, let alone private houses, had glass windows. This raised the question of where the village was. Unless the history of the Americas she knew was completely wrong, there would not have been any European settlements in America before the sixteenth century, so they were probably nowhere near New Richmond. Of course, she could be completely wrong.

Whoever had lived there had taken some pains to fortify the place. Sergeant Major Zablonski pointed out that even at a distance, he could tell the building had been attacked. Whether successfully or not, no one could tell.

The windows had been boarded up, as had the door, though not very securely. Through the boards, Rosi could see that the main doors had been elaborately carved, though she was not close enough to see what the carvings were. She did notice that it appeared as if letters had been carved as well. She could not tell which letters, but they looked to be fancy 'I' or 'L' and maybe an 'M' or 'N'.

The men tended to avoid the area of the village across the stream from the manor house. That was where the screams had come from, Sergeant Major Zablonski explained to Rosi as they stood there looking at it.

"Screams?" Rosi asked.

"Yes, Miss," Zablonski said.

"You mentioned screams before," Rosi remembered. "And fog."

"Yes, Miss." He said nothing else.

* * *

THEY had spent much of the previous day rounding up as many men as they could find, Sergeant Major Zablonski explained. He decided the village was a good place to hold up and prepare the men because no one else could find it.

It seemed that the only way to find the village was to have been there and to have seen it. Several men had actually wandered into the clearing in the woods when the men in the village were occupied in the buildings. The only part of the village they saw was the great tree. They were surprised when Zablonski had appeared as if from nowhere and told them they were in a village. Once there was physical contact, then the ruins became clear.

The whole idea had spooked quite a few of the men, but there were a lot of British soldiers around. The possibility of staying in a haunted village was preferable to the probability of being hunted down and shot by marauding redcoats.

"Very sensible, Sergeant Major," Rosi said. "But surely you don't believe in ghosts."

"I've been many places in my life and seen a lot of things, Miss," he replied warily. "There be ghosts."

"But you stayed."

"I said there be ghosts, Miss. S'long as they leave me alone, I'll leave them be. 'Sides, there's nothing I ever saw, man nor beast, that wouldn't be stopped by a bullet to the head."

Rosi laughed. "You're a pragmatist, Sergeant Major."

He seemed slightly offended. "I'm a Christian as is all the other men."

Zablonski explained that as the sun began to go down the day before, they had noticed that the woods began to reappear. By sundown, the pastures were only a hint, like the woods were during the day. The village stayed, but everything else disappeared.

The men had lit small fires and gathered around them so that they could give all of the blankets they had to the men on watch. This plan seemed to satisfy everyone. Everything was quiet until around midnight.

Then they noticed the fog.

The fog started as a light mist drifting around the tree trunks, touching and digging its way into every hole, every nook. It stopped when it reached the stream like it had hit a wall. The mist kept pouring out of the woods and began to grow until it was a

fog higher than any of the men. It did not enter the town, but
seemed to be trying to. Gusts of the white cloud would rear up
and throw themselves against the barrier of the streams, only to
be beaten back.

Then came the shadows in the fog.

The men on higher ground saw them first, dark shapes that
seemed like smoke in the mist. Formless shapes that slithered
along the ground. One of the men would later say that these
shapes looked to be sniffing, trying to find a trail. Then the
indistinct shapes began to take form. Dragons sailed through and
stopped at the edge of the stream to the north.

"Dragons, Sergeant Major?" Rosi exclaimed. "Really."

"Dragons, Miss. Boats, he were t'sea as a lad and saw them in
the Indies. He knew what they looked like."

He continued to explain that the dragons stopped, and gave
birth to horned offspring who milled about, trying to find a way
through. These dragon spawn had hooks and long claws for
hands. They called out to each other in a language foreign and
evil. From the east, had come smaller figures that danced and
twisted in the breeze...that rode the fog and hid behind the
swirls.

When the impish figures and the dragon spawn saw each
other, they let out loud roars and fought. The shadows moved
and fought and danced and swung. Somewhere, in the distance,
they had heard yells and clashes of bone and steel. Black blood
ran and stained the fog. The blood gave birth to more figures,
and ran to and fro, trying to find a way out.

Then a breeze sprang up and seemed to cry out and search
for help. This breeze had carried the newborn spawn to the edge
of the village, where they tried to beat their way in. None of the
men was sure why, but each had the feeling that these newborn
were looking for their captain. They seemed to gather at a focal
point near her. En mass, they thrust themselves against the
invisible wall, pushing.

Spartacus took the first shot. His bullet raced through the fog
and was slapped away by one of the shapes. The other men then
began firing. The men from the heights began to shoot as well.

Desperately, they fired round after round at the fog. Round after round slashed through the fog, leaving little trails but having no other effect.

The men in the village huddled closer.

Arms of smoke began reaching through, trying to grab hold of something…anything.

Then the screaming started.

Something unholy was in the old manor house and wanted out. No one could understand what she was saying. But the female voice was filled with anger, hopelessness, fear, and rage.

That spooked the men even more than the fog had. The figures in the fog could not cross the streams. The voice could. The men watched and even tried to fight the fog creatures. But they ran to the buildings and hid while the screaming continued.

After a time, Zablonksi had no idea how long, the screaming stopped. By then, the fog was little more than a wisp.

Rosi felt a chill going down her spine. "Well," she said finally. "I'll see what happens tonight. I'm sure neither of them is something we need to worry about." She hoped she came across as convincing.

"If you say so, Miss," Zablonski said. It looked to Rosi as if he was trying hard to believe her.

Taking one last look across the stream at the manor house, Rosi let Zablonski lead her to the center of the village.

* * *

SERGEANT Major Zablonski spent the rest of the day training the men.

For two hours, they marched around the village square. For two hours they practiced shooting. Then they marched again. Then they shot again. The men grumbled at the idea of marching, but they got the hang of it. They were beginning to move as a group from one place to the other. There was a lot of tripping and cursing, but there was also a lot of laughing and ribbing.

The men resented shooting in ranks, though they enjoyed firing at the great tree. Rosi noticed that the musket balls did little damage to the tree. It was not as if she expected the men to cut it down, but they should have been able to do more than simply knock a few leaves off.

"Huntin' down redcoats like you was huntin' a hare in't going to work," Sergeant Major Zablonski bellowed at the men after quite a few of them, even regular militia men, simply gave up on firing practice.

"They die just as easy," one man yelled. "A bullet in the head and no more Brit."

"Aye," Zablonski agreed. "They die good. But they fire back, and they shoot in formation. Ain't going to win a war huntin' them down. Kill a few? Sure. Kill a lot? Sure. Kill enough? No. They can stick to the main roads. They can stay out of the forests. They have men. They have powder and shot. They have food. They have time. Every day we give them, they get stronger. To fight them, we will have to go to them. They have no reason to come to us. We have nothing they want. They will wait for us behind walls or in the field. They will have the advantage. If we move as a group, if we fire in ranks, we can even the odds a little."

"They'll still have more men. They will also have cavalry and cannon," the man argued.

The man's name was Bartlett and he had served in the Fourth Platoon under Boats. Bartlett was a distant cousin of Josiah Bartlett, who, Rosi knew, had signed the Declaration of Independence. Few of the men knew what that document was. None knew how important it was. This one at least knew what it was. He also knew that his cousin was an important man in New Hampshire. Rosi found out much later hat he had never met his illustrious relation, but he had told the others how well connected he was and was quite upset when he was not made a sergeant. His constant complaining made him unpopular. That he was one of the better shots in the company, could see better than most, and one of the few to own a rifle, only partially made up for his overall obnoxiousness.

"I'm goin' to teach you how to fight," Zablonski said calmly. Rosi could tell he was really anything but calm. "Yer officer will tell you where to fight."

Rosi nodded to the men. A few grumbled, but no one objected openly. Bartlett had clearly experienced Zablonski's calm before the storm act before and backed down.

Rosi watched the men practice firing for a while. She did not see any improvement, but Zablonski seemed satisfied.

"We'll most likely be overrun by sheer numbers," Zablonski said to her quietly a while later. "But they'll give a good account for themselves. The problem is that young Bartlett is right. Last night we heard that Cromwell has almost two hundred men in New Richmond. That's five companies against our one. That's half a regiment. They're commanded by Colonel Pride, a cold hearted swine if half of what I heard was true. They've sent for the other half, which is garrisoned in the Maine Territories. We captured a messenger."

"Well," Rosi said, relieved. "If we captured the messenger, then they certainly won't—"

"No one sends only one messenger, Miss." Zablonski squatted next to Rosi and began drawing rough diagrams in the dirt. "We have one company, Miss. Light infantry at best. The way real soldiers fight, Miss, is to form their armies into squares. That way they can protect their flanks and their rears. These squares can be large or small, but the larger the better. The more guns on any one side, the better. Squares protect themselves. They protect the others. Far as I can tell, that's the way wars have always been fought. If we had a wall of forty guns, then we might stand a chance against one company. But they have more than one company and they have cavalry. Even if we could meet them one company at a time, we might lose. If we won, then at some point we would have to face another company. Eventually, we would be whittled away. Give them time, then the rest of Pride's men will arrive. Perhaps even more. We have to beat them in one battle. And we have to do it soon. We need to find a place we can defend and somehow get them to attack us there. You find me the place. You get me the enemy. I'll figure out a way to defend it."

"I'll do my best," Rosi promised. Responsibility, Rosi decided, as she watched Sergeant Major Zablonski drilling her men, was one aspect of leadership she really did not like.

The long term strategy of fixing time was something Rosi would have to figure out on her own. Her men could not help her, even if they understood it. She wished Angie were around to help her. She squeezed her eyes shut for a minute to hold back her tears. *Not now*, she told herself. She was not sure how to do it. If she could get to Beatitude Carol, or even better, Uncle Richard, they would certainly have advice. They might even help.

Short term strategy was to somehow get the British out of New Richmond. How to do this was the trick. Rosi needed to find a place where the numbers and relative inexperience of her men would not be as big a liability. She had to find a place her company could defend. She also had to find a reason that would get the British to attack her there. Preferably, this would be a place where the British could not maneuver easily and would be unable to bring in their artillery.

* * *

ROSI spent the next hour or so wandering around the village trying to figure out where she was.

Boats had insisted that they were not in New Hampshire. The sun and the stars were all wrong. He had been a simple sailor and was not able to figure out their location.

At one point, Rosi went to the church, the high ground, and tried to shut out the noises from the men's drilling and work. She sent out her senses, as Uncle Richard had been teaching her. Almost immediately, she realized that the village was filled with doorways. But they were dark. They had been sealed. Not one or two of them, but dozens had been sealed.

Rosi had trouble describing the doorways to herself. She had tried just a few days ago to describe them to Angie and was sure she had come across as delusional. Rosi tended to feel the doorways in terms of temperature. Even then, she only felt them if she was moving at them in the right direction, at the right angle. They could only be entered if they were approached at that angle. If she was searching for the doorways, she could find them. She could see them at the edge of her vision. Like floaters.

When she tried to look directly at them, she could not see them unless she had gone through the doorway before. As far as describing them physically? They sort of reminded her of a spiral of intersecting three dimensional Mobius strips. Of course, that was only a guess. They seemed to rotate. She could never quite tell if they went clockwise or counterclockwise. It appeared as if they went both, at the same time. They spun not only in relationship to some outside point, her for example, but also internally. The spins were so fast that she could not see that they were spinning until she got closer. When she got closer, the spinning slowed down and stopped. That was how Guardians went through the doorways. That was why it was almost impossible for anyone else to go through.

Uncle Richard had explained that most people saw them from time to time, but since the shapes and spins were so irrational, most people simply waved them off as a shadow. A few people would investigate, but they could not see the doorways if they looked directly at them. A very few of those few would be able, somehow, to see and identify the doorways. Only those who were potential Guardians could slow the spinning down enough to use them intentionally.

The doorways did not have a color. Not in a traditional way. Their color was cold if the doorway led to the past. Doorways to the future looked warmer and kind of like those wet spots far ahead of you on the highway that were not there when you reached them.

There was a third kind of door that was neither warm nor cold, but looked the opposite of both. They spun the opposite of clockwise and counterclockwise. Uncle Richard simply changed the subject when Rosi had brought those up.

Rosi did not know much about how the doorways were sealed. Uncle Richard had explained that sometimes the tears became too dangerous or unstable. Then a Guardian could close it permanently. Sealing the tears was dangerous. Those doorways looked like they had been folded over on themselves and then tied up into knots. Instead of spinning, they quivered. It was as if they were struggling to undo themselves and return to spinning.

Once Rosi determined that the doorways were here in the village, it was easier for her to see them. Even out in the pastures beyond the streams, she could sense slight ripples in the air where they must be.

This village, wherever it was, was probably one of the other places Uncle Richard had told her about. Places where the doorways were clustered. Places like New Richmond. Uncle Richard had told her that wherever these places were, people had taken on the responsibility of guarding them. Some, like her family, were responsible. Some were self serving and corrupt. Great empires had been created by people who understood how to use the tears in time and space to their own advantage. Or at least thought they did. The early Caesars had known. What else would have driven Caligula mad? Nero had killed Claudius for the knowledge. By the end of the first century AD, the knowledge, or at least the ability to use the knowledge, had been lost, and Rome had begun its decline. All of these empires inevitably collapsed because those in the know became so corrupt that they were killed, or because the small groups who were aware of the source of their power died out before they could share their knowledge with new generations.

The Carols, the current Guardians, were only the last in a long line of families and peoples who had intermarried with the earlier Guardians. Certain families or genetic groups were born with an innate ability to sense the tears and could be taught how to travel back and forth without interfering too much and confusing things. However, it was important to keep the number of people who had the skill and knew about it small. It was difficult for the group to breed with outsiders. It would weaken the skill. Dilute it. Outsiders often looked on Guardians with fear and apprehension. New Richmonders, Rosi understood, knew the area was strange, perhaps haunted. Impossible things happened on a regular basis. The consensus was that the Carol family was somehow responsible for them. Locals might respect Uncle Richard, but they were also afraid of him.

As far as Rosi knew, Uncle Richard had no real friends in New Richmond. She herself had problems making friends with the townies. She was an Other. Everyone felt it. Even the men here in the village. They knew that she had been the first to see the village. They saw her wounds healing at a surprising, unnatural, rate. Imagine if they found out that she would live twice as long as any of them. Unless she was killed. It must have been a great deal more complicated for Guardians in distant times and places where people were even more insular and superstitious.

Rosi was the last of the Carols. Sure, there were distant relatives, but they were far removed from the gene pool. At best, they could sense the tears. They could not control them. Many of them, like her cousins in New York, simply rejected the legacy. Uncle Richard had made it clear that one of Rosi's jobs as Guardian would be to find someone to succeed, or to bear that person herself. At fifteen going on sixteen, she found the expectation that she would become a baby factory to fulfill her family's destiny vaguely abhorrent.

Rosi wondered, as she walked back into the village center, what had happened in this place. Had the then Guardian shut the doorways to protect the villagers or because of them? Or had there been so much corruption, that some other Guardian sealed them?

The men suddenly began cheering. As one, they rushed towards the north end of the village. Rosi followed them and saw Spartacus and his men coming into the town. They had picked up a few stragglers, and a wagon full of provisions, mostly food.

Rosi pushed her way through the crowd of men and threw her arms around Spartacus. "God, I'm so glad to see you," she laughed. She felt him stiffen in her arms. "What is it?"

When she stepped back, he snapped to attention. He learns fast, Rosi thought to herself. "What's wrong?"

"Nothing, Captain." His face was bright red.

The men were fidgeting. A couple grinned.

Rosi noticed Zablonski standing next to her. "What's wrong, sergeant major?" she asked.

Sergeant Major Zablonski sighed. "Perhaps, Miss, the officers should not be hugging their sergeants, don't you think?"

"Of course, sergeant major."

* * *

SO, Rosi thought. *Here we are.*

Rosi had cleverly brought her men to a haunted 'hidden' village. The men, instead of running away like any normal person would have done, had perversely decided to stay and follow her. To make matters worse, the number of men in her company kept increasing.

A few days ago, she and her men had left Zilla's farm to go on an adventure. Other than a few bruises, to Rosi it seemed was no more real than a video game. Perhaps in the back of her mind was the notion that if she was losing, she could simply restart. Eventually, she would figure out the game's strategy and figure out a way to beat it. While they marched to The Castle, her men had been high on testosterone. Stoned on it. Even if they could not see into the future, they had to have known that they were a small group of untrained farmers going up against soldiers from one of the best trained armies in the history of the world. Even Caesar, Alexander, and Patton had needed trained men.

Yesterday, they left Zilla's farm fueled by rage and driven by the desire for revenge. Buoyed by hatred, they sped back towards New Richmond with even less of a plan than they'd had the first time. Holding onto The Castle until relieved might not have been much of a plan, but it was one. Charging into a town held by an overwhelmingly larger force was not so much a plan as it was a remarkably stupid idea. Marching back with a machine gun or a few grenade launchers would be a plan. Better yet, a tank.

Rosi could exact revenge for the deaths of Zilla and Angie. Even for the others who had died fighting. Rosi could bring a storm of fire and destruction that would shake the British Empire to its very core. She could make the entire world grieve for her lost friends. Generations would grow knowing the pain Rosi felt right now. They would live in terror of her. She could grind them down and stop all wars and killing.

Even as she thought it, Rosi knew she would do no such thing. War was not a job for angry people. War was the province of rational men. Anger might win the occasional fight. Calm, reasoned thought won wars. That was the way it had always been. That was the way it always would be. That was the way it probably should be. Rosi felt that made the idea of war even more terrifying.

She had seen men yesterday use rage as a weapon. It was shocking what they had done to the small squad of soldiers. It was violent and frightening. Men could be beasts, animals to each other.

At The Castle, Rosi had seen death and destruction sent down on her people by reasonable and rational men. Death and destruction that had been planned, discussed, prepared for, and executed relatively calmly. The acts themselves might have been filled with anger and hate, but there was no emotion behind them.

It was a bloody chess game.

Their attack on the British squad had drained most of the anger from the men. The adrenaline of the encounter with Zablonski's men in the forest sapped away the rest. Now her men were simply men. Scared of a fight. Anxious to fight. Desperately in need of someone to tell them where to go and what to do. Rosi had already determined that it was useless to try and tell them why to fight. In the end, they would probably fight for each other. And for her. That was probably the way it had always been. Leaders had philosophy. Men had buddies and lovers and mothers and babies and a strong desire to not die.

They also had training. Rosi's men would certainly have been beaten had they fought an enemy anywhere close to the same size as the company now was. When she thought about it, had the squad they fought been prepared, the end might have been different. Why? Because the British were professional soldiers.

Rosi was hardly the only person in Revolutionary America to realize this. Washington had brought in Baron von Steuben for that very purpose. All other things being equal, trained soldiers will beat guerillas almost every time.

Rosi was faced with additional problems.

She could not wait indefinitely to retake New Richmond.

There was a whole war going on. New Richmond was simply a small part of it. She might be able to affect what happened here over the next few weeks. The further away from New Richmond, the less her ability to have any influence. Rosi figured that she had a week, maybe two, to bring about some sort of resolution before the damage to the historical war was irreparable.

Rosi knew what Kirk was after. She had to figure out how much he knew. She had to know how much he could do. She had to discern what he intended to do with this knowledge once he had it. If all he wanted to do was to get home, she could arrange that. She doubted that was all he wanted, though.

To do either required time.

So, now she had a plan. A week or two might not give her men time to become soldiers, but it would give them time to start. In that time, all types of things could happen. Beatitude could show up and take over. He would know what to do. Pierce could come back. He had fled the area rather ingloriously, she had heard, but he was still an important figure whose name and voice carried weight. More likely, though, Rosi was going to have to fight this battle without much outside help. She had to figure out a way to minimize the British advantage.

Rosi also needed to take the time to spy on Kirk and the British who were ensconced at The Castle. Fortunately, no one needed her while her men were being trained.

This strange village that existed in other time and place would be the perfect place to hide out and prepare. According to reports, there were a lot of British around. There was no place else Rosi's company could hide that would not be discovered. Here, at least, they were safe from the enemy.

As far as the eerie screaming and strange fog Zablonski spoke about went, at the very worst, the men would be scared off and go home. In an odd way, Rosi hoped most of them would.

In the center of the clearing near the tree, that until yesterday, had held so many bodies, Spartacus was handing out goods from the wagon he had stolen. Men were cheering as they grabbed packages and dove into them.

Rosi laughed as she started towards the men. She caught

Zablonski's eye and signaled him to come to her.

They would stay in this ghost town for a while. They would be safe. Beyond the streams was dangerous. The enemy filled the forest and ruled the roads. There was no way to tell if the foragers would have any luck in the coming days.

For now, Rosi thought as she approached the group of laughing, cheering, playing men, *I am going to be a leader and make myself extremely unpopular.*

About the Author

The Author and his son, Christopher

Edward Eaton has studied and taught at many schools in the States, China, Israel, Oman, and France. He holds a PhD is Theatre History and Literature and has worked extensively as a theatre director and fight choreographer. As a writer, he has been a newspaper columnist, a theatre critic, and has published and presented many scholarly papers. He is author of the young adult series *Rosi's Doors*, including: Rosi's Castle, Rosi's Time, and Rosi's Company. Other publications include the plays Orpheus and Eurydice and Elizabeth Bathory. In addition to his academic and creative pursuits, Ted is an avid SCUBA diver and skier. He currently lives and works in Boston, Massachusetts with his wife Silviya, a hospital administrator, and his son Christopher.

Rosi's Doors

Young Adult Fantasy Series
by Edward Eaton:

ROSI'S CASTLE
[Book I]

ROSI'S TIME
[Book II]

ROSI'S COMPANY
[Book III]

Published by
Dragonfly Publishing, Inc.
www.dragonflypubs.com

41377547R00148

Made in the USA
Middletown, DE
10 March 2017